PENGUIN POPULAR CLASSICS

LES MISÉRABLES

VICTOR HUGO

Translated by Norman Denny

D0231162

PENGUIN BOOKS

PENGUIN BOOKS

Published by the Penguin Group
Penguin Books Ltd, 27 Wrights Lane, London w8 5tz, England
Penguin Putnam Inc., 375 Hudson Street, New York, New York 10014, USA
Penguin Books Australia Ltd, Ringwood, Victoria, Australia
Penguin Books Canada Ltd, 10 Alcorn Avenue, Toronto, Ontario, Canada m4v 3b2
Penguin Books (NZ) Ltd, Private Bag 102902, NSMC, Auckland, New Zealand

Penguin Books Ltd, Registered Offices: Harmondsworth, Middlesex, England

Published in Penguin Popular Classics 1998
3

Translation copyright © The Folio Society Limited, 1976
This abridgement is taken from The Penguin Audiobook
Les Miserables copyright © 1996
All rights reserved

Set in 9.5/11 pt PostScript Monotype Plantin
Typeset by Rowland Phototypesetting Ltd, Bury St Edmunds, Suffolk
Printed in England by Cox & Wyman Ltd, Reading, Berks.

LES MISÉRABLES
BY VICTOR HUGO

VICTOR HUGO (1802–85). Poet, playwright and novelist, and one of the most prolific, versatile and acclaimed of the French Romantics. Hugo is chiefly remembered for his great novels *Les Miserables* and *Notre-Dame de Paris*.

Born the son of a colonel (later to become a general) in Napoleon's army, Victor Hugo travelled with his father to Italy and Spain before being educated in Paris. As a youth he was both Catholic and royalist (he received a reward from Louis XVIII for his *Odes* of 1822), but over the course of his life Hugo's social conscience developed and he became a democrat, while his Catholic faith weakened and he developed an interest in spiritualism and the occult.

Hugo wrote many volumes of verse, a number of dramatic works in both verse and prose, criticism and, perhaps most notably, several novels. A supporter of the 'new' writing of Romanticism, Hugo attacked the artistic orthodoxy of classical literature and came, after the publication of *Orientals* (1829) and its manifesto of a preface, to be regarded as the leader of the movement. His first great novel was *Notre-Dame de Paris* (1831), a sombre, pessimistic work. Hugo's later novels were characterized by his alert social conscience, the first and most famous of these being *Les Miserables* (1862).

In 1833 he began a relationship with Juliette Drouet, which lasted until her death in 1883, his wife Adèle and the poet Charles Sainte-Beuve having destroyed his domestic happiness with their affair. His family life was further blighted by the death of his daughter Leopoldine and her husband in 1843, following which some of his energies were channelled into an active political life. This led eventually to his exile from France to the Channel Islands during the period 1851–70 after an attempt to organize resistance to Napoleon III (*Napoleon le petit*). He had been elected to the Assembly in 1848, was again chosen as a deputy in

1870 and went on to become a senator of the Third Republic.

Hugo lived out the last years of his life as a great public figure, and on his death he was mourned as a hero, his body laying in state under the Arc de Triomphe before burial in the Pantheon.

Les Miserables is both a vivid illustration of France at the beginning of the nineteenth century and a thrilling story of massive scope and compassion.

ONE

In the year 1815 Monseigneur Charles-François-Bienvenu Myriel was the Bishop of Digne. He was then about seventy-five, having held the bishopric since 1806.

M. Myriel had come to Digne accompanied by his sister, Mademoiselle Baptistine, an unmarried woman ten years younger than himself. Their only servant was Madame Magloire, a woman of the same age as Mlle Baptistine, who assumed the twofold office of a personal maid to Mademoiselle and housekeeper to Monseigneur. The bishop's palace in Digne was next door to the hospital. It was a large and handsome stone mansion built at the beginning of the previous century. Everything was on the grand scale – the apartments, the broad courtyard flanked by arcades and the gardens planted with splendid trees. The hospital was a narrow, two-storeyed house with a small garden. The bishop called at the hospital on the third day after his arrival. Having concluded his visit, he asked the director to accompany him to the palace.

'Monsieur le Directeur,' he said, 'there has been a mistake. You have twenty-six persons in five or six small rooms, while in this house there are three of us and room for sixty. We must change places. Let me have the house that suits me, and this one will be yours.' On the following day the twenty-six paupers were moved into the palace and the bishop took up residence in the hospital.

M. Myriel had no private means; his family had been ruined by the revolution. His sister's annuity of five hundred francs had sufficed for their personal needs during his curacy. As bishop he received a stipend of fifteen thousand francs. On the day of his removal to the hospital he laid down how this money was to be used for the relief of the poor. He kept only a thousand francs for himself which, with his sister's annuity, made a total of fifteen hundred francs a year. Upon this sum the two old women and the old man lived. Nothing would cause him to change his daily life or accept any trifle beyond his daily needs. But we may confess that of his former possessions he still retained a set of six silver knives and forks and a large silver soup-ladle which rejoiced the heart of Mme Magloire when they lay splendidly gleaming on the white tablecloth and, since we are depicting the Bishop of Digne as he was, we must add that he had more than once remarked, 'I should find it hard to give up eating with silver.'

To this treasure must be added two massive silver candlesticks which he had inherited from a great-aunt. They held wax candles and stood as a rule on the bishop's mantelpiece. But, when there was a guest, Mme Magloire lit the candles and placed them on the dining-table. In the bishop's room, at the head of the bed, was a small cupboard in which she locked the silver cutlery and ladle every night; but it must be added that the key was never removed. No door in the house could be locked. The dining-room door, which gave directly on to the cathedral close, had originally been as heavily equipped with locks and bolts as the door of a prison. The bishop had had all these removed so that by day or night the door was only latched and anyone could enter at any time. His view of the matter is conveyed by three lines which he wrote in the margin of a Bible: 'This is the distinction: the doctor's door must never be shut; the priest's door must always be open.'

It being customary for bishops to preface their pastoral letters and orders with the full list of their baptismal names, the people of the region, from instinctive affection, elected to call him by the name which, for them, had the most meaning, Monseigneur Bienvenu.

At the beginning of October 1815 the bishop, after returning from his customary walk through the town, had stayed late in his own room. At eight o'clock that evening he was still at work, when Mme Magloire entered as usual to get the silver cutlery out of the cupboard by the bed. A few minutes

2

later the bishop, suspecting that the table was laid and that his sister might be waiting, closed his book and went into the dining-room. Mme Magloire had just finished laying the table and was chatting with Mlle Baptistine. At the moment when the bishop entered, Mme Magloire was talking with some vehemence to her mistress about a matter which constantly occupied her mind, namely, the fastening of the front door. It seemed that while she had been out shopping for the evening meal she had heard rumours. There was talk of a stranger in the town, a vagabond of forbidding aspect who must still be lurking in the streets. The man was a gypsy, a ne'er-do-well, a dangerous beggar. He had tried to get a lodging with Jacquin Labarre, who had turned him away. A man with a knapsack and a terrible look on his face.

'Monseigneur, something dreadful will happen tonight, everyone says so. What I say is that this house is not safe and that, if Monseigneur permits, I should go round to Paulin Musebois, the locksmith, and ask him to put back the bolts on the front door. I say the door should be bolted, even if it's only for tonight.'

At this moment there was a heavy knock on the door.

'Come in,' said the bishop.

The door opened. A man entered. He was a man in the prime of life, of medium height, broad-shouldered and robust, who might have been in his late forties. A cap with a low, leather peak half hid his face. He stepped across the threshold and then stood motionless with the door still open behind him. His knapsack hung from his shoulder and a large, knotted stick was in his hand. The firelight falling on his face disclosed an expression of exhaustion, desperation and brutish defiance. He was an ugly and terrifying spectacle. The bishop was calmly regarding the stranger. He opened his mouth to speak, but before he could do so the man, leaning on his stick with both hands and gazing round at the three elderly people, said in a harsh voice: 'Look. My name is Jean Valjean. I'm a convict on parole. I've walked from Toulon in four days and today I have covered a dozen leagues [about thirty miles]. When I reached this place I went to an inn and they turned me out because of my yellow ticket-of-leave which I had shown at the *Mairie* as I'm obliged to do. I tried another inn and they told me to clear out. Nobody wants me anywhere. I crawled into a dog-kennel and the dog bit me and drove me out just as if he were a man and knew who I was. I lay down on a bench in the square outside and a good woman pointed to your door and told me to knock on it. So I've knocked. Will you let me stay?'

'Madame Magloire,' said the bishop, 'will you please lay another place.'

The man moved nearer to the light of the table-lamp, seeming not to understand.

'Weren't you listening? I'm a convict. I've served in the galleys.' He pulled a sheet of yellow paper out of his pocket and unfolded it. 'This is my ticket-of-leave. That's why everybody turns me away. Do you want to read it? I can read. There were classes in prison for anyone who wanted to learn. You can see what it says – "Jean Valjean, released convict, served nineteen years, five years for robbery with violence, fourteen years for four attempts to escape – a very dangerous man." So there you are. Everybody kicks me out. Will you take me in?'

'Madame Magloire,' said the bishop, 'you must put clean sheets on the bed in the alcove.' Mme Magloire went off without a word. The bishop turned to the man. 'Sit down and warm yourself, Monsieur. Supper will very soon be ready, and the bed can be made up while you're having a meal.'

And now the man had really understood. His face, which had been so hard and sombre, was suddenly and remarkably transformed by an expression of amazement, incredulity and pleasure.

'You really mean it? You'll let me stay? I'll pay whatever you ask. You're a good man. You are an innkeeper, aren't you?'

'I'm a priest,' said the bishop, 'and this is where I live.'

'A priest! But a good priest. I suppose you're a cure. Once I saw a bishop – a Monseigneur, as they say. He said mass at an altar in the prison yard and he had a sort of pointed hat on his head, gold, it glittered in the sun at midday.'

Mme Magloire came back into the room with the additional cutlery.

'Put them as near as possible to the fire, Mme Magloire,' the bishop said. He turned to his guest. 'The night wind is raw in the Alps. You must be cold, Monsieur.' Each time he uttered the word 'Monsieur' in his mild, companionable voice the man's face lighted up. The courtesy, to the ex-convict, was like fresh water to a shipwrecked man. Ignominy thirsts for respect.

'This lamp doesn't give much light,' the bishop said.

Perceiving what he had in mind, Mme Magloire fetched the two silver candlesticks from his bedroom mantelpiece, lit them and set them on the table.

'Monsieur le cure,' said the man, 'you are very good. You don't despise me. You have taken me in and lighted your candles for me. But I have not concealed from you where I come from and what I am.'

The bishop, seated at his side, laid a hand gently on his arm. 'You need have told me nothing. Why should I ask your name? In any case I knew it before you told me.'

The man looked up with startled eyes. 'You know my name?'

'Of course,' said the bishop. 'Your name is brother.'

The bishop was regarding him. 'You have suffered a great deal.'

'Well, yes – the red smock, the ball-and-chain, a plank to sleep on, heat, cold and hard labour, the galleys and the lash. Chained even when you're sick in bed. Nineteen years of it. I'm forty-six. And now a yellow ticket. That's the story.'

Mme Magloire had meanwhile dished up the meal, which consisted of a broth of water, oil, bread and salt with some scraps of bacon and mutton, figs, a fresh cheese and a large loaf of rye bread. She had taken it upon herself to supplement the bishop's table-wine with a bottle of old wine from Mauves.

The bishop had recovered the cheerful expression of a man who is hospitable by nature. 'Supper is served,' he said gaily. The man at first paid no attention to anyone. He ate as though he was starving. But after the broth he said:

'Monsieur le cure, all this is too good for me, but let me tell you that the wagoners, who would not let me share their meal, eat better than you.'

'Their work is more tiring than mine.'

'No,' said the man. 'They have more money. I can see that you are poor. Perhaps you are not even a cure. Are you a cure? If God were just you would be that at least.'

Near the end of the meal, Valjean was looking very tired. Turning to him the bishop said, 'I'm sure you're ready for bed.' Having bidden his sister good-night Monseigneur Bienvenu picked up one of the two silver candlesticks and handed the other to his guest, saying, 'I will show you to your room, Monsieur.' The man followed him.

The arrangement of the rooms was such that to reach the oratory with its alcove, or to leave it, one had to go through the bishop's bedroom. They did so while Mme Magloire was in the act of replacing the silver in the cupboard by the bed, this being invariably the last thing she did before retiring.

The bishop showed his guest into the alcove, where the bed was newly made. The man put the candle on a small table.

'Sleep well,' said the bishop. 'Before you leave tomorrow you must have a bowl of warm milk from our cows.'

'Thank you, Monsieur l'abbe,' the man said.

Jean Valjean came from a very poor peasant family in Brie. When he was old enough he had gone to work as a tree-pruner at Faverolles. He had lost both his parents when he was still very young. His only living relative was a widowed sister older than himself who had seven children, boys and girls. She had housed and fed him while her husband was still alive, but the husband had died when the oldest child was eight and the youngest only one. Jean Valjean, who was then just twenty-four, had stepped into the breach and supported the sister who had cared for him. They were a sad little group, engulfed in poverty and always on the verge of destitution. And then came a particularly hard winter. Jean was out of work and there was no food in the house. Literally no bread – and seven children!

One Sunday night when Maubert Isabeau, the baker in Faverolles, was getting ready for bed, he heard a sound of shattered glass from his barred shop-window. He reached the spot in time to see an arm thrust through a hole in the pane. The hand grasped a loaf and the thief made off at a run. Isabeau chased and caught him. He had thrown away the loaf, but his arm was bleeding. The thief was Jean Valjean.

Valjean was tried in the local court for housebreaking and robbery. He possessed a shotgun that he used for other than legitimate purposes – he was something of a poacher – and this told against him.

Jean Valjean was found guilty. The Penal Code was explicit. There are terrible occasions in our civilization, those when the Law decrees the wrecking of a human life. It is a fateful moment when society draws back its skirts and consigns a sentient being to irrevocable abandonment. He was taken to Toulon, where he arrived, still chained by the neck, after a journey of twenty-seven days in a cart. Here he was clad in the red smock and everything that had been his life was blotted out, even to his name. He was no longer Jean Valjean, but No. 24601. He was released in October 1815, after being imprisoned in 1796 for having broken a window-pane and stolen a loaf of bread.

Jean Valjean had gone to imprisonment weeping and trembling; he emerged impassive. He had gone despairing; he emerged grim-faced. Under the lash and in chains, on fatigue and in the solitary cell, he withdrew into his own conscience and reflected.

He admitted that he was not an innocent man un-justly punished but, admitting the offence, had not the punishment been ferocious and outrageous? Did not the penalty, aggravated by his attempts to escape, become in the end a sort of assault by the stronger on the weaker, a crime committed by society against the individual and repeated daily for nineteen years?

He asked these questions and, having answered them, passed judgement on society.

He condemned it to his hatred. Hatred was his only weapon, and he resolved to sharpen it in prison and carry it with him when he left.

A detail which we must not fail to mention is that in physical strength Jean Valjean far surpassed any other inmate of the prison. On fatigue duties, or hauling an anchor chain, he was worth four men. He could lift and carry enormous weights and on occasion did duty for the appliance known as a 'jack'. His dexterity was even greater than his strength. There are prisoners, obsessed with the thought of escape, who make a positive cult of the physical sciences, daily performing a mysterious ritual of exercises. The climbing of a sheer surface was to Valjean a pastime. Given the angle of a wall and applying the thrust of his back and legs, he could climb three storeys as though by magic; he had even reached the prison roof.

He spoke seldom and never smiled. His impulses were governed by resentment, bitterness and a profound sense of injury which might vent itself even upon good and innocent people, if any such came his way. Year by year, slowly but inexorably, his spirit had withered. Dry of heart and dry-eyed. During his nineteen years' imprisonment he had not shed a tear.

Valjean awoke as the cathedral clock was striking two.

He was in a state of great mental perturbation. Many thoughts occurred to him, but there was one in particular that constantly returned, overshadowing the rest. It was the thought of the silver on the bishop's table.

Those silver knives and forks obsessed him. There they were, only a few yards away. They were solid pieces and would fetch at least two hundred francs. The ugly thought came and went and, at the same time, unaccountably, with the obstinate irrelevance of a distracted meditation, he was thinking of something entirely different. One of his fellow-prisoners had been a man named Brevet who kept his trousers up with a single brace. The check design of that brace repeatedly occurred to him.

He got to his feet and stood listening. The house was quite silent. He picked up his knapsack and got something out of it. It was a short iron bar, sharpened to a point at one end. By daylight it could have been seen to be an ordinary miner's spike.

Grasping it in his right hand and holding his breath, Valjean moved stealthily towards the door of the bishop's bedroom. He found it ajar. Valjean moved on into the bedroom and cautiously forward, hearing from the far side of the room the quiet, steady breathing of the bishop. For nearly half an hour the sky had been darkened by cloud. At the moment when Valjean stopped by the bed the clouds were torn asunder and moonlight, flooding through the tall window, fell upon the bishop's face. He was sleeping peacefully. His face wore a look of serenity, hope and beatitude. Motionless in the shadow, gripping the spike in his hand, Jean Valjean stood gazing in a kind of terror at the old man. All that clearly emerged from his attitude and expression was that he was in a state of strange indecision, seemingly adrift between the two extremes of death on the one hand and salvation on the other – ready to shatter that skull or to kiss that hand.

Valjean suddenly moved to the cupboard. The first thing he saw when he opened the door was the basket of silver. He grabbed it, crossed the room with long strides, re-entered the oratory, picked up his stick, opened the window, climbed over the sill, emptied the silver into his knapsack, threw away the basket and, scrambling like a great cat over the wall, took to his heels.

At sunrise Monseigneur Bienvenu was in his garden. Mme Magloire came running out to him in great agitation.

'Monseigneur, Monseigneur, do you know where the silver basket is?'

'Yes,' said the bishop.

'Thank the Lord! I couldn't think what had happened to it.'

The bishop had just retrieved the basket from one of the flowerbeds. He handed it to her saying, 'Here you are.'

'But it's empty!' she exclaimed. 'Where's the silver?'

'So, it's the silver you are worrying about?' said the bishop. 'I can't tell you where that is.'

'Heaven save us, it has been stolen! That man who came last night!'

With the zeal of an elderly watchdog Mme Magloire ran into the oratory, peered into the alcove and came running back to her master, who was now bending sadly over a cochlearia that had been damaged by the basket when it fell.

'Monseigneur, the man's gone! The silver has been stolen!'

The bishop after a moment's pause turned his grave eyes on her and said gently:

'In the first place, was it really ours?'

Mme Magloire stood dumbfounded. After a further silence the bishop went on:

'I think I was wrong to keep it so long. It belonged to the poor. And what was that man if not one of them?'

'Saints alive!' exclaimed Mme Magloire. 'It's not on my account or Mademoiselle's. But Monseigneur – what will Monseigneur eat with now?'

He looked at her in seeming astonishment, 'There is always pewter.'

'Pewter smells.'

'Well, then, wooden forks and spoons.'

A few minutes later he was breakfasting at the table where Jean Valjean had sat the night before and remarking cheerfully to his sister and Mme Magloire that no spoon or fork, even wooden ones, was needed for dipping bread into a bowl of milk.

As the brother and sister were in the act of rising from

the table a knock sounded on the door and the bishop called, 'Come in!'

The door opened to disclose a dramatic group. Three men were holding a fourth by the arms and neck. The three were gendarmes; the fourth was Jean Valjean.

A sergeant of gendarmes entered the room and saluted. 'Monseigneur,' he began.

At this Valjean raised his head in stupefaction.

'Monseigneur . . .' he repeated. 'He isn't the cure?'

'Silence,' said one of the gendarmes. 'This is his lordship the Bishop.'

Monseigneur Bienvenu was meanwhile coming towards them as rapidly as his age allowed.

'So, here you are!' he cried to Valjean, 'I'm delighted to see you. Have you forgotten that I gave you the candlesticks as well? They're worth a good two hundred francs. Did you forget to take them?'

'Monseigneur,' said the sergeant, 'do I understand that this man was telling the truth? When we saw him he seemed to be on the run. We found this silver in his knapsack and –'

'And he told you,' said the bishop smiling, 'that it had been given to him by an old priest with whom he stopped the night. I can see how it was. You felt bound to bring him here, but you were mistaken.'

'You mean,' said the sergeant, 'that we can let him go?'

'Certainly.'

The gendarmes released Valjean.

'But this time,' said the bishop, 'you must not forget your candlesticks.'

He fetched them from the mantelpiece and handed them to Valjean.

'And now,' said the bishop, 'go in peace.' He turned to the gendarmes. 'Thank you, gentlemen.'

The gendarmes withdrew. Valjean stayed motionless as though he were on the verge of collapse. The bishop came up to him and said in a low voice:

'Do not forget, do not ever forget that you have promised me to use the money to make yourself an honest man.'

Valjean, who did not recall having made any promise, was silent. The bishop had spoken the words slowly and deliberately. He concluded with solemn emphasis:

'Jean Valjean, my brother, you no longer belong to what is evil but to what is good. I have bought your soul to save it from black thoughts and the spirit of petition, and I give it to God.'

Jean Valjean left the town as though he were still on the run. He was overwhelmed by new sensations. He had moments of strange tenderness which he resisted with all the hardness of heart which twenty years had brought him. He perceived with dismay that the kind of dreadful calm instilled in him by injustice and misfortune had begun to crumble. What was to take its place?

Thus he spent the day in a state of growing turmoil; and in the evening, when the sun had sunk so low that every pebble cast a shadow, he was seated on the ground by a thicket, in an expanse of russet plain that was totally deserted. A footpath crossed the plain a few yards away from the place where he sat.

Into his sombre meditations a lively sound intruded. A boy of about ten was coming along the footpath, singing as he came. He carried a *vielle*, a kind of small hurdy-gurdy, slung over his shoulder, and a box with his belongings on his back; one of those gay and harmless child vagrants, generally chimney-sweeps, who go from village to village with knees showing through the holes in their trousers. Now and then he paused, still singing, to play at 'bones' with the coins he was carrying, tossing them in the air and catching them on the back of his hand. They probably represented his entire fortune, and one was a piece of forty sous.

He stopped at the thicket to play his game without having noticed Jean Valjean. Thus far he had caught all the coins, but this time he'd dropped the forty-sou piece, which rolled in the direction of Valjean, who promptly set his foot on it.

The boy had seen where it went. Without appearing in any way disconcerted, he went up to him.

'Monsieur,' said the boy with a childish trustfulness that is a mingling of innocence and ignorance, 'may I have my coin?'

'What's your name?' asked Valjean.

'Petit-Gervais, Monsieur.'

'Clear out,' said Valjean.

'Please, Monsieur,' said the child, 'may I have my money back?'

Valjean seemed not to hear him. The boy seized hold of his collar and shook him, while at the same time he tried to shift the heavy, iron-studded shoe covering his coin.

'I want my money, my forty-sou piece.'

He began to cry, and Jean Valjean, who was still seated, raised his head. His eyes were troubled. He stared with a sort of amazement at the child, then reached for his stick and cried in a terrifying voice, 'Are you still there? Damn you, clear out!'

The boy looked at him and was suddenly frightened. He turned and ran. Out of breath, he eventually came to a stop, and amid the tumult of his thoughts, Valjean heard the sound of his distant sobbing. A minute later he had vanished from sight.

The sun had set. The shadows were closing about Jean Valjean. He remained standing in the same place, not having moved since the boy had run off. Suddenly, his eye caught the glitter of the forty-sou piece, half buried by his foot in the earth.

It affected him like an electric shock. 'What's that?' he muttered under his breath. After some moments' pause he moved convulsively forward, snatched up the coin and then stood gazing to every point of the compass.

There was nothing to be seen. Night was falling, the plain was cold and empty and a purple mist was rising to obscure the twilight. He uttered an exclamation and began to walk rapidly in the direction taken by the boy. He shouted at the top of his voice:

'Petit-Gervais! Petit-Gervais!'

He waited, but there was no reply.

He went on walking and then broke into a run, stopping now and then to cry out amid the solitude in a voice that was at once terrifying and despairing, 'Petit Gervais! Petit Gervais!' If the boy had heard, he would certainly have hidden; but by now he was probably far away.

Valjean ran for a long time, calling as he went. Finally, at a place where three paths intersected, he stood still. Gazing into the distance he called for the last time, 'Petit-Gervais! Petit-Gervais!' and his voice sank without echo into the mist. His legs suddenly buckled under him as if struck down with all the weight of his guilty conscience. He sank exhausted on to a piece of rock with his hands clutching his hair and his head between his knees, and he exclaimed, 'Vile wretch that I am!'

His heart overflowed and he wept, for the first time in nineteen years.

How long did he stay weeping? What did he then do and where did he go? We do not know. But it is said on that same night the stage-driver from Grenoble, passing through the cathedral square in Digne at three in the morning, saw in the shadows the figure of a man kneeling in an attitude of prayer outside the door of Monseigneur Bienvenu.

1817 was the year which Louis XVIII, with a royal aplomb not lacking in arrogance, called the twenty-second of his reign. And in that year of 1817 four young gentlemen of Paris played 'a merry prank'.

The four Parisians came, one from Toulouse, one from Limoges, the third from Cahors and the fourth from Montauban; but they were students, and to say 'student' is to say 'Parisian'. To study in Paris is to belong to Paris.

They were unremarkable young men, average representatives of their kind, named Felix Tholomyes, from Toulouse, Listolier from Cahors, Fameuil from Limoges and Blachevelle from Montauban.

Each, of course, had his mistress. Blachevelle loved Favourite, so-called because she had been in England; Listolier adored Dahlia who had chosen a flower for her *nom de guerre*; Fameuil idolized Zephine, short for Josephine; and Tholomyes had Fantine, called 'la Blonde' because of her golden hair.

Favourite, Dahlia, Zephine and Fantine were enchanting girls, scented and glowing, still with the flavour of the working class, since they had not altogether abandoned the use of their needles. Distracted by love affairs but with a last trace of the serenity of toil in their expressions. It must be said that the three older ones were more experienced, more heedless and more versed in the ways of the world than Fantine la Blonde, who was encountering her first illusion.

Favourite, Zephine and Dahlia were philosophical, whereas Fantine was virtuous. Fantine's was her first and only love, and she was wholly faithful.

She had been born at Montreuil-sur-mer, but nothing was known of her parents. She was called Fantine because she had never been called anything else. At fifteen she had gone to Paris 'to seek her fortune'. She was beautiful and had stayed pure as long as she could – a beautiful blonde with fine teeth. Gold and pearls were her dowry, but the gold was on her head and the pearls were in her mouth.

She worked in order to live, and presently fell in love also in order to live, for the heart, too, has its hunger. She fell in love with Tholomyes.

Tholomyes, being the liveliest, was the guiding spirit of the small group formed by Blachevelle, Listolier, Fameuil and himself.

One day Tholomyes took the other three aside and said, with an oracular flourish:

'For nearly a year Fantine, Dahlia, Zephine and Favourite have been asking us for a surprise and we have solemnly promised to give them one. They keep on about it. I think the time has come. Let us now consider.'

Tholomyes then lowered his voice and what he said was so mirth-provoking that it drew a great burst of laughter from all four and caused Blachevelle to exclaim:

'That's a stupendous idea!'

The rest of the conference was lost in the smoke of an

adjacent alehouse, but its outcome was a pleasure party which took place on the following Sunday. The four young men and the four girls were at the Cabaret Bombarda, whose sign hung on the Rue de Rivoli at the corner of the Passage Delorme.

A big ugly room with an alcove containing a bed at one end (the place was so full on a Sunday that they had to put up with this); two windows through which the embankment and the river could be seen through the elms; the radiant glow of August beyond the windows; two tables, one piled high with bouquets and male and female hats, and the other, at which the four pairs were seated, loaded with plates and dishes, bottles and glasses. Such was the scene at about half past four that afternoon, with the sun beginning to set and the appetites to diminish.

Fameuil and Dahlia were humming, Zephine was laughing and Fantine was smiling. Listolier was blowing a wooden trumpet he had bought at Saint-Cloud, but Favourite confronted Tholomyes with a resolute expression.

'Well,' she said, 'and what about the surprise?'

'Quite so,' said Tholomyes. 'The time has come. Gentlemen, it is time for us to surprise our ladies. Ladies, we must ask you to wait here for a few minutes.'

'It begins with a kiss,' said Blachevelle.

'On the forehead,' said Tholomyes.

Each solemnly kissed his mistress on the forehead; then the four young men moved in single file to the door, each with a finger to his lips.

Favourite clapped her hands as they went out.

'It's fun already,' she exclaimed.

'Don't be too long! We shall be waiting,' murmured Fantine.

The girls, left to themselves, leaned in pairs on the two window-sills and chattered as they gazed down into the street. They saw the young men come out arm-in-arm and turn to wave gaily before disappearing in the dusty Sunday hubbub of the Champs-Elysees.

Their attention was presently caught by a stir of activity

at the water's edge. It was the hour of departure for mails and diligences, when nearly all the stage-coaches of the south and west passed by way of the Champs-Elysees, generally following the river embankment and leaving the town by the Passy gate. Great yellow- and black-painted vehicles with jingling harness drove by at short intervals, grinding the cobblestones to dust and thundering past the crowd in a shower of sparks.

One of these conveyances, of which they had only a glimpse through the thick cluster of elms, stopped for a moment and then drove on at a gallop. This surprised Fantine.

'Surely that's unusual,' she said. 'I thought the stage-coaches never stopped.'

Favourite made a gesture.

'Fantine is wonderful,' she said. 'She's amazed by the most ordinary things. It happens every day, my love.'

Some time passed in chatter of this kind and presently a thought struck Favourite.

'Well!' she said. 'What about this surprise?'

'They're being very slow,' sighed Fantine.

As she finished sighing the waiter who had served their meal entered. He had something that looked like a letter in his hand.

'What's that?' asked Favourite.

'It was left behind by the gentlemen, to be handed to the ladies.'

'Then why didn't you bring it to us at once?'

Favourite snatched it from him and found that it was indeed a sealed letter.

'There's no address, but this is what is written outside: "Here is the Surprise."'

She hurriedly broke the seal, unfolded the sheet and read aloud (she was the one who could read):

Beloved mistresses!

Be it known to you that we have parents. The word is one that means little to you, but in the simple and honourable definition of the Code Civil it means fathers and mothers. They want us back. Being dutiful, we obey. When you read these lines five fiery horses will be taking us home to our papas and mammas. The Toulouse coach is rescuing us from the primrose path which is yourselves, sweet loves. Our country requires that, like everyone else, we should become fathers of families, rural guards and Councillors of State. Honour us for our self-sacrifice. Weep for us a little and speedily replace us. If this letter rends your hearts, treat it in a like fashion. Adieu.

For nearly two years we have made you happy. Do not bear us ill-will.

Signed: Blachevelle
               Fameuil
               Listolier
               Felix Tholomyes
Postscriptum: the dinner is paid for.

The four girls gazed at one another.

Favourite was the first to break the silence.

'All the same,' she said, 'it's a good joke.'

'It's very funny,' said Zephine.

'I am sure it was Blachevelle's idea,' said Favourite. 'It makes me quite in love with him. No sooner lost than loved. That's how things are.'

'No,' said Dahlia. 'It was Tholomyes's idea. It's typical.'

'In that case,' said Favourite, 'down with Blachevelle and long live Tholomyes!'

'Long live Tholomyes!' cried Dahlia and Zephine and burst out laughing.

Fantine joined in the laughter; but when, an hour later, she was back in her room she wept bitterly. It was her first love, as we have said. She had given herself to Tholomyes as to a husband, and the poor girl had a child.

During the first quarter of this century, in the village of Montfermeil not far from Paris, there existed a small tavern which has since disappeared. It was kept by a couple called Thenardier and was situated in the Ruelle de Boulange.

Nailed to the wall over the door was a board with a painted design depicting a soldier carrying another on his back, the latter clad in the starred and braided uniform of a general. Across the bottom ran the inscription: 'The Sergeant of Waterloo.'

Nothing is more commonplace than a cart or wagon outside a tavern, but the vehicle, or remains of a vehicle, which was to be seen outside the Sergeant of Waterloo on a certain spring evening in 1818 must surely have attracted notice by its massive proportions. From the axle a looped chain hung close to the ground, and seated on it as though it were a swing, forming a pretty group, were two little girls, the elder, aged about two-and-a-half, holding the younger, aged eighteen months, in her arms.

The two children, who looked well cared-for, were clearly delighted with it. One was russet-haired, the other dark. The innocent faces shone with excitement. The mother, a woman of no very attractive appearance but likeable at that moment, was seated a few yards away in the doorway of the tavern, swinging the children by pulling on a length of string. Her preoccupation with them caused her to ignore what was going on in the street. But suddenly a voice spoke from close beside her.

'You have two very pretty children, Madame.'

The mother looked round. A young woman was standing near her. She too had a child which she held in her arms. She also had with her a large travelling-bag.

The child was the most enchanting creature imaginable, a little girl of between two and three, the prettiness of whose attire matched that of the innkeeper's children. She was apple-cheeked, pink and healthy. Nothing could be seen of her closed eyes except that they were large with very long lashes. She was sleeping in her mother's arms with the perfect confidence of age.

The mother who seemed poor and unhappy, had the look of a town worker reverting to her peasant state.

It was Fantine, but scarcely to be recognized, although a closer examination would have shown that she still retained her beauty. But now a line of sadness, like the beginning of cynicism, ran down her right cheek.

Ten months had elapsed since the 'merry prank', and it is not hard to imagine what had happened in that time.

After heedlessness had come the reckoning. Being abandoned by the father of her child – and such partings, alas, are irrevocable – she was thrown entirely on her own resources. She resolved to return to her native town, Montreuil-sur-mer, where someone who knew her might give her work. It meant that she would have to conceal the evidence of her wrong-doing, and confusedly she foresaw another separation, even more heartrending than the first.

She had renounced all personal adornment, wearing the plainest clothes and reserving her silks and laces for her daughter. The girl had nothing in the world except her child, the child, nothing except her mother. Fantine had breast-fed her, and this had weakened her chest, causing her to cough a little.

Passing the Thenardiers' tavern, she had seen the two children on their improvised swing. Such was her delight she could not refrain from murmuring:

'You have two pretty children.'

The fiercest animals are disarmed by a tribute to their young. The mother thanked her and invited her to sit on the bench by the door while she herself remained seated on the step.

'My name is Thenardier,' she said. 'My husband and I keep this inn.'

This Madame Thenardier was robust, big-boned and red-headed, a typical soldier's woman with the roughness characteristic of her kind. She was still young, not more than thirty. Had she been standing upright, instead of sitting crouched in the doorway, her height and general look of a fair-ground wrestler might have alarmed the stranger and so shaken her confidence as to prevent the events to be related from taking place. Destinies may be decided by the fact that a person is seated and not standing.

Fantine told her story, altering it slightly. She was a working woman whose husband had died, and since she could not find work in Paris she was on her way to look for it in her own part of the country.

As she spoke she gave her daughter a most loving kiss, waking her up. The child opened wide eyes as blue as her mother's and wriggled free with the irresistible vigour of a child who wants to be on the move. Seeing the other children on their swing she stopped short and put out her tongue in a token of delight. Mme Thenardier lifted the little girls off the swing and said:

'Now you can all play together.'

Friendly relations are soon established at that age. In a matter of minutes the three were busily digging holes in the ground, to their great satisfaction. The newcomer had a self-assured gaiety which reflected her mother's devotion.

The two women went on talking.

'What's your little girl's name?'

'Cosette.'

'How old is she?'

'Nearly three.'

'It's wonderful how quickly children get to know each other,' said Mme Thenardier. 'Look at them. They might all be sisters.'

This, no doubt, was the encouragement the other mother had been hoping for. Taking Mme Thenardier's hand, she turned to her and said:

'Will you look after my daughter for me?'

The Thenardier woman started slightly, expressing neither acceptance nor refusal. Fantine went on:

'I can't take her with me where I am going. I have to find work, and it's not easy if you have a child. As you say, they would be like sisters. And besides, I shall soon come to fetch her. Will you look after her for me? I could pay six francs a month.'

At this point a man's voice called from inside the house:

'Not less than seven and six months in advance.'

'Very well.'

'And another fifteen francs for extras,' called the man.

'Total, fifty-seven francs,' said the Thenardier woman.

'You shall have them,' said Cosette's mother. 'I've got eighty francs. I shall still have enough to get me to my own part of the country if I go on foot, and I'll find work and when I've saved a little money, I'll come back for her.'

The man's voice asked: 'Has she enough clothes?'

'That's my husband,' said Mme Thenardier.

'I guessed as much. Certainly she has enough clothes. She has a beautiful wardrobe. They're all in my bag.'

'You'll have to let us have them,' said the man's voice.

'Well, naturally. Did you think I'd leave my daughter to go naked?'

The man's face appeared in the doorway. 'All right,' he said.

And so the bargain was concluded. Fantine paid the money, left her daughter and the clothes, and set off expecting soon to return. It had happened quietly enough, but such partings are loaded with despair. A neighbour who saw her leave the town said later to Mme Thenardier:

'I've just seen a girl in the street sobbing as though her heart would break.'

The man Thenardier said to his wife: 'Well, that takes care of the bill that falls due tomorrow. I was fifty short. Do you realize I might have been summoned? That was a neat trap you set, you and the kids between you.'

'And not even meaning to,' said the lady.

A modest bag, but to the cat even the smallest mouse is better than none.

Who were these Thenardiers?

They belonged to that indeterminate layer of society, sandwiched between the middle and the lower classes, which combines the worst qualities of both, having neither the generosity of the worker nor the respectable honesty of the bourgeois.

There was a seed of cruelty in the woman and of

22

blackguardism in the man, and both were highly susceptible to the encroachments of evil.

Thenardier, so he said, had been a soldier, a sergeant who, by his own account, had fought bravely in the 1815 campaign. His tavern-sign bore witness to his feats of arms. He had painted it himself, being a jack-of-all-trades who did everything badly.

It was the period when historical novels with classical settings, high-minded in tone but increasingly vulgar in content, were indulging the romantic tastes of Paris concierges and penetrating further afield. Mme Thenardier had just sufficient intelligence to read books of this kind. One cannot be unaffected by that sort of thing. One of its results was that her elder daughter was named Eponine. The younger, having narrowly escaped being called Gulnare, was christened Azelma.

Mere lack of scruple does not ensure prosperity. The tavern was doing badly.

Thanks to their visitor's fifty-seven francs, Thenardier was able to honour his signature and escape a summons, but a month later they were again short of money. Mme Thenardier took Cosette's wardrobe to Paris and pawned it for sixty francs. When this was spent the couple came to regard her as a charity child and to treat her accordingly. Since she no longer had any clothes of her own she was dressed in the Thenardier children's discarded garments – that is to say, in rags.

When the first six months expired, Fantine sent them the agreed monthly sum of seven francs. By the end of the year Thenardier wrote demanding twelve, and Fantine, being persuaded that her child was happy and 'doing fine', meekly paid up.

Thus two years passed.

Meanwhile Thenardier, having discovered that the child was probably illegitimate, had raised the price to fifteen francs. 'She'd better not argue,' he said to his wife, 'or I'll dump the brat on her and give the show away.' Fantine paid the fifteen francs.

The years went by, the child grew and so did her state of wretchedness. By the time she was five she became the household drudge.

At the age of five this may seem inconceivable, but alas it is true. Social oppression may begin at any age.

Ill-treatment had made her sullen and misery had made her ugly. Only the beauty of her eyes remained, and this was the more distressing because, being large, they mirrored a greater measure of unhappiness. It was heartrending to see her, a child not yet six, shivering in scanty, tattered garments, busy before daybreak on a winter's morning sweeping the pavement outside the house with a broom far too big for her small, chapped hands.

She was known locally as *l'Alouette*, the Lark. The village people, with instinctive symbolism, had thought it a suitable name for the apprehensive, trembling little creature; scarcely more than a bird, who was always first up in that house and out of doors before dawn. But this was a lark that never sang.

After leaving Cosette with the Thenardiers, Fantine had journeyed on to Montreuil-sur-mer. It was ten years since she had left the district, and in that time things had greatly changed. While she had been sinking into the depths of poverty, her native town had grown prosperous.

The traditional local industry of Montreuil-sur-mer was the manufacture of imitation English jet beads and the 'black glass' of Germany. Because of the cost of raw materials the industry had never been prosperous and its workers had been underpaid, but this situation had recently been transformed. Towards the end of 1815 a newcomer to the town had had the idea of substituting shellac for resin, and had also devised a simpler and less expensive form of clasp for such things as bracelets. These trifling changes amounted to a revolution. In less than three years the innovator had grown rich, which is good, and had spread prosperity around him, which is better.

He was a stranger to the district. Nothing was known of

24

his origins and little about how he started in life. But it seems that on the December evening when he unobtrusively entered the town, with a pack on his back and a thorn stick in his hand, a serious fire had broken out in the Town Hall. Plunging into the flames he had, at the risk of his life, rescued two children whose father, as it turned out, was the Captain of Gendarmerie, so no one had asked to see his identity papers. He went by the name of Pere Madeleine.

Pere Madeleine's profits were so great that in the second year he was able to build a new factory consisting of two large workshops, one for men and the other for women. The needy had only to apply, and they could be sure of finding employment and a living wage. Unemployment and extreme poverty were forgotten.

Through the stir of activity of which he was cause and centre, Pere Madeleine had made a fortune for himself; but, strangely in a man of business, this did not seem to be his principal concern. He seemed to give far more thought to others than to himself. In 1820 he was known to have a credit of some 635,000 francs at the banking-house of Lafitte; but, in addition to setting aside this sum, he had spent more than a million on the town and the poor.

The district owed him a great deal and the poor owed him everything. He was so invaluable that he had to be honoured and so kindly that he had to be loved. His workpeople in particular adored him, and he accepted their adoration with a kind of grave melancholy. When it became known that he was extremely rich the 'society' of the town took notice of him, addressing him as Monsieur Madeleine; but his work-people and the children still called him Pere Madeleine, and it was this that drew from him his warmest smile.

By 1820, five years after his arrival in Montreuil-sur-mer, the services he had rendered were so outstanding, and public opinion so unanimous, that the king appointed him mayor of the town. He refused; but, faced by the prefect's rejection of his refusal, the insistence of local dignitaries and the supplications of the people in the streets, he finally gave way.

This was the third stage of his rise in the world. 'Le pere Madeleine' had become Monsieur Madeleine, and Monsieur Madeleine had become *Monsieur le Maire*.

It happened often that Monsieur Madeleine, walking amiably through the streets and receiving the affectionate greetings of his fellow-citizens, was observed by a tall man in a grey tail-coat, carrying a heavy stick and wearing a low-brimmed hat.

He was one of those people who, even glimpsed, make an immediate impression; there was an intensity about him that was almost a threat. His name was Javert and he belonged to the police.

In Montreuil-sur-mer he performed the distasteful but necessary duties of police-inspector. He had not witnessed Madeleine's beginnings. When he took up his present post, the manufacturer's fortune was already made. His mental attitude was compounded of two very simple principles – respect for authority and hatred of revolt against it. Theft, murder and every other crime were to him all forms of revolt. His judgements were absolute, admitting no exceptions.

Javert had an eye constantly fixed on Monsieur Madeleine, an eye filled with suspicion and puzzlement. Madeleine bore his heavy scrutiny without appearing to notice it, treating him, as he treated everyone, with an easy good-humour. Javert was plainly disconcerted by Monsieur Madeleine's ease and tranquillity of manner, but an occasion arose when his own strange demeanour attracted the notice of Monsieur Madeleine.

Passing one morning through one of the unpaved alleys of the town Madeleine heard sounds of disturbance and saw a group of people gathered not far away. He found, on going up to them, that an old man known as Pere Fauchelevent had been trapped beneath his cart after the horse had fallen. The manner of the fall was such that the whole weight of the heavily loaded cart was on his chest. Javert, who was already on the spot, had sent for a jack.

The crowd drew back respectfully as Monsieur Madeleine approached. He at once asked if a jack was available and was told that someone had gone for one to the nearest smithy, but that it would take a quarter of an hour to bring it. It had rained hard the day before; the ground was very soft and the cart was sinking deeper into the mud, pressing more heavily on the old man's chest. In a matter of minutes his ribs might give way.

'This can't wait a quarter of an hour,' said Madeleine, turning to the men standing around. 'Look, there's still room for a man to crawl under the cart and lift it on his back. In half a minute the old man could be pulled out. Is there anyone here with the muscle and heart? I'm offering five louis d'ors.'

No one moved.

'Ten,' said Madeleine.

The bystanders avoided his gaze.

'Come!' said Madeleine. 'Twenty.'

'It's not that we don't want to,' a voice said.

Monsieur Madeleine turned and recognized Javert. He had not noticed him before.

'It's a question of strength,' Javert went on. 'You need to be tremendously strong to lift a load like that on your back.' With his eyes fixed upon Madeleine he said slowly: 'I have only known one man, Monsieur Madeleine, capable of doing what you ask.' Madeleine started. Still with his eyes upon him, Javert added casually: 'He was a convict – in Toulon prison.'

Madeleine turned pale.

Meanwhile the cart was sinking and Pere Fauchelevent was gasping and crying:

'My ribs are breaking! For God's sake, do something!'

Madeleine looked about him. 'Is there no one prepared to save this man's life for twenty louis d'ors?'

No one moved. Javert repeated: 'I have known only one man capable of doing the work of a jack. The man I mentioned.'

'It's crushing me,' the old man cried.

Madeleine hesitated for another instant, met the vulture gaze of Javert, and smiled sadly. Without a word he went on his knees and before anyone could speak was under the cart.

There was a moment of hideous uncertainty and silence. Madeleine, almost flat on his stomach beneath the terrifying weight, was seen to make two fruitless efforts to bring his elbows and knees together. The onlookers stood breathless. The cartwheels were still sinking and it was already almost impossible for Madeleine to extricate himself.

Then suddenly the cart with its load was seen to rise slowly upwards, its wheels half emerging from the quagmire. Crying in a stifled voice, 'Hurry up! Help me!' Madeleine made his supreme effort.

There was a sudden rush. The gallantry of a single man had lent strength and courage to all. The cart was lifted by ten pairs of arms and old Fauchelevent was saved.

Madeleine got to his feet. The old man clasped him round the knees invoking the name of God. His own expression was an indescribable mingling of distress and triumph, and he gazed calmly back at Javert, who was still fixedly regarding him.

Fauchelevent had broken a knee-cap in his fall. Monsieur Madeleine had him taken to the infirmary, served by two Sisters of Mercy, which he had set up in his factory for the benefit of his workers. Fauchelevent recovered, but with a permanently stiff knee. Acting on the advice of the sisters and the cure, Madeleine got him a job as gardener in a convent in the Saint-Antoine quarter of Paris.

Shortly after this Monsieur Madeleine was elected mayor and when for the first time Javert saw him wearing the robes which vested him with full authority over the town, a tremor went through him like that of a hound which scents a wolf in sheep's clothing. Thereafter he avoided him wherever possible, and when his duties obliged him to have direct dealings with the mayor, he addressed him in terms of the utmost formality.

When Fantine returned to Montreuil-sur-mer, no one remembered her, but fortunately the doors of Pere

Madeleine's factory were open. She found employment in the women's workshop. Not being able to claim she was married, she was careful to say nothing about her daughter. At first she was meticulous in her payments to the Thenardiers. Since she could only sign her name she had to resort to a public letter-writer. She sent frequent letters and the fact was noted. It was whispered in the women's workshop that she 'gave herself airs'. No one is more avidly curious about other people's doings than those persons whom they do not concern.

It was discovered that she sent at least two letters a month, always to the same address, paying the postage in advance. The name of her correspondent was also discovered, Monsieur Thenardier, innkeeper at Montfermeil. The letter-writer, an elderly man who could not keep his mouth shut when his stomach was filled, was plied with wine in an alehouse, and so it became known that Fantine had a child. 'So that's the kind of woman she is!' A townswoman made the journey to Montfermeil, talked to Thenardier and on her return reported as follows: 'Now I know everything, I've seen the child.'

This was the month when Thenardier, having already raised the price from seven francs to twelve, raised it again to fifteen.

Fantine's case was hopeless. She could not leave the district because she owed money for rent and furniture, a sum of about one hundred and fifty francs. She went and begged the workshop supervisor for money, who gave it to her but forthwith dismissed her. She lacked the courage to plead her cause and did not venture to approach the mayor although she was advised to do so.

As for Monsieur Madeleine, he knew nothing whatever about the matter. The best of men are often obliged to delegate their authority; and it was with the full assurance that she was acting rightly that the supervisor had tried the case of Fantine, given judgement and pronounced sentence.

Fantine did piecework, stitching of shirts for the soldiers of the garrison, which brought her in twelve sous a day. Her child cost ten sous. Excess of work exhausted her, and the small, dry cough from which she suffered grew worse. But in the mornings, combing with a broken comb the hair that flowed like silk over her shoulders, she still had moments of happy vanity.

Fantine had been dismissed at the end of the winter. She survived the summer, but then came the next winter, shorter days and shorter working hours.

She could not earn enough and her debts grew. The Thenardiers wrote to say that Cosette was obliged to go almost naked in the cold and that at least ten francs were needed to buy her a woollen dress. Receiving this letter, Fantine carried it crumpled in her hand throughout the day, and in the evening went to the barber at the corner of the street and withdrew her comb, letting her fair hair fall to her waist.

'Such beautiful hair!'

'What will you give me for it?'

'Ten francs?'

'Then cut it off.'

She bought a woollen dress and sent it to the Thenardiers, who were furious. The money was what they wanted. They gave the dress to their daughter Eponine, and the little lark, Cosette, went on shivering.

'My daughter's not cold any more,' thought Fantine, 'I have dressed her in my hair.' She wore small mob-caps to hide her shorn head and still looked pretty.

But a dark change was taking place within her. Now that she could no longer do up her hair she conceived a hatred of all mankind. She had long shared the universal veneration for Pere Madeleine, but now, by dint of telling herself that he had dismissed her and was the cause of all her troubles, she, came to hate him more than any man. And then Thenardier wrote to say that if she did not send one hundred francs forthwith he would be obliged to turn Cosette out into the street to fend for herself amid the rigours of the season.

A hundred francs! In what calling was it possible to earn

a hundred sous a day? There was only one. She became a prostitute.

In every small town, and this was particularly so in Montreuil-sur-mer, there is a class of young men who squander an income of fifteen hundred francs in the provinces much as their peers in Paris squander an income of two hundred thousand. They belong to the great species of nonentities who own a little land, a little silliness, and a little wit; who would look like clods in a fashionable salon but think themselves gentlemen in a tavern.

Some eight or ten months after the events just recorded, on a snowy evening at the beginning of January 1824, one of these elegant idlers was exercising his wit at the expense of a woman in a low-cut evening-gown with flowers in her hair who was prowling to and fro outside the officers' cafe. The name of the gentleman was Monsieur Bamatabois. The woman, a sad garish ghost coming and going through the snow, paid no attention to him, but continued her silent patrol, which every few minutes brought her within range of his sarcasms. Finding that he was producing no effect, the gentleman got to his feet, crept up behind her, scooped up a handful of snow and thrust it down her back between her bare shoulders. The woman uttered a cry and, turning, sprang at him like a tigress, ripping his face with her finger-nails and screaming at him in language that might have shocked an army sergeant. The woman was Fantine.

A circle of laughing, hooting, applauding spectators formed around this whirlwind composed of two creatures, the man seeking to defend himself with his hat knocked off, the woman hitting, kicking and screaming.

Suddenly a tall man broke through the circle, seized the woman by her mud-stained satin corsage and said:

'You come along with me.' The woman looked round and was abruptly silent. From being livid with fury she became pale and trembling with alarm. She had recognized Javert.

Monsieur Bamatabois took advantage of the interruption to hurry away.

Thrusting aside the onlookers, Javert made rapidly for the police post on the far side of the square, dragging the unhappy woman with him. She made no resistance. Neither spoke a word.

The police post was a low room heated by a stove with a barred, glass-panelled door opening on to the street. Fantine crouched down in a corner of the room, huddled like a frightened animal. The duty-sergeant placed a lighted candle on the table. Javert seated himself at it, and getting a sheet of officially stamped paper out of his pocket began to write.

Under present laws women of this class are wholly at the mercy of the police. Javert was quite impassive. This was one of those cases where he must use his formidable discretionary powers without resort to any higher authority, but with all the scruples dictated by his own rigid conscience. What he had witnessed was undeniably a crime. A prostitute had assaulted a citizen. He, Javert, had seen it with his own eyes. He wrote on in silence.

When he had finished writing, he signed the document, folded it and, handing it to the duty-sergeant, said: 'Have this woman taken to the gaol under guard.' He then turned to Fantine and said: 'You're getting six months.'

She uttered a cry of despair. 'Six months. Six months in prison, earning seven sous a day! What about Cosette? What about my daughter? And I still owe more than a hundred francs to the Thenardiers, Monsieur l'inspecteur – did you know that?'

Without getting to her feet she dragged herself across the floor, shuffling hastily on her knees with her hands clasped.

'Have pity on me, Monsieur Javert. Let me off just this once – I'm not really a bad woman. It isn't idleness or greed that made me what I am. It was all the fault of that vile monster, the mayor. He dismissed me because of the things that some of the women said. Wasn't that abominable, to turn away an honest working-girl?' She crouched there, her face wet with tears while the words poured out in a low heartrending flow, broken by that small, dry cough.

Javert turned his back on her and two policemen took her by the arms.

A few minutes previously a man had entered unobserved. Closing the door behind him he had remained with his back to it listening to Fantine's despairing plea. Now, while the men were trying to drag her to her feet, he emerged from the shadows and said:

'One moment if you please.'

Javert looked round and saw that it was Monsieur Madeleine. Removing his hat, he bowed stiffly.

'I beg your pardon, Monsieur le maire.'

The words had a remarkable effect on Fantine. Rising instantly from the floor, she thrust aside the two men and she planted herself fiery-eyed in front of Madeleine.

'So, you're the mayor are you?'

She laughed and spat in his face.

Monsieur Madeleine wiped his cheek and said:

'Inspector Javert, this woman is to go free.'

Javert with lowered eyes but in a firm voice was heard to make the unprecedented reply:

'Monsieur le maire, that cannot be allowed.'

'Why not?' asked Monsieur Madeleine.

'The woman insulted a respectable citizen.'

'Listen to me, Inspector Javert,' Madeleine said in a calm, conciliatory voice. 'I know you to be an honourable man and I am very ready to explain my actions to you. This is the truth of the matter. I was crossing the square when you took the woman away. There were still people about and I asked what had happened. I heard the whole story. The respectable citizen was at fault, and by the letter of the law it was he who should have been arrested.'

Javert persisted: 'But she has insulted you too, the mayor of this town.'

'That is my affair,' said Madeleine. 'An insult to me

may be said to be my property. I can do what I like with it.'

'If you'll forgive me, Monsieur le maire, the insult was not to yourself but to justice.'

'Conscience is the highest justice, Inspector Javert. I heard what the woman said. I know what I'm doing.'

'As for me, Monsieur le maire, I have to do my duty. Duty requires me to send her to prison for six months.'

Monsieur Madeleine said gently: 'You must be quite clear about this. She will not serve a single day in prison.'

The peremptory words emboldened Javert to look at Madeleine full in the face. He said, still in a tone of profound respect:

'It distresses me deeply to take issue with Monsieur le maire, but this is a matter of police regulations and comes within my province. I am holding the woman Fantine.'

At this Monsieur Madeleine folded his arms and said:

'The regulations you refer to are those affecting the Municipal Police. Under Articles Nine, Eleven, Fifteen and Sixty-six of the Criminal Code I have authority over them. I order you to release this woman.'

'But Monsieur le maire –'

'Kindly leave the post,' said Monsieur Madeleine.

Javert received this body-blow standing as rigidly as a Russian soldier. Bowing to the mayor, he turned and left. Fantine stared at him in stupefaction as he did so.

She too had undergone a strange upheaval, feeling with every word that Monsieur Madeleine spoke the knot of hatred dissolve within her, while a new feeling took its place, heartwarming and inexpressible, a sense of deliverance, trust and love.

She fell on her knees before Monsieur Madeleine and before he could prevent it had taken his hand and pressed it to her lips.

Then she fainted.

Monsieur Madeleine had Fantine taken to the factory infirmary where she was placed in the charge of the nursing sisters. She now had a raging fever and for part of the night was delirious. Eventually, however, she fell asleep.

Madeleine spent the night and morning ascertaining the facts and now he knew the whole tragic story of Fantine. He wrote at once to Thenardier. Fantine owed the couple a hundred and twenty francs. He sent them three hundred, instructing them to use the balance of this sum to bring the child immediately to Montreuil-sur-mer where her mother lay ill.

Thenardier was amazed. 'By God,' he said, 'we aren't going to let the brat go, she's turned into a goldmine. I can guess what has happened. Some rich joker has taken a fancy to the mother.'

Fantine, meanwhile, remained in the infirmary; she was not recovering. Indeed, as the weeks passed her condition grew worse. The doctor examined her.

'Well?' asked Monsieur Madeleine.

'Hasn't she got a child she wants to see?'

'Yes, a small daughter.'

'You'd better get her here as soon as possible.'

Madeleine was dismayed, but when Fantine asked what the doctor had said he forced himself to smile.

'He says we must get your daughter here as soon as possible, and then you'll get well.'

'He's right,' she said.

But the Thenardiers held on to Cosette, adducing a hundred dishonest reasons.

'I shall have to send someone to fetch her,' said Madeleine. 'If necessary, I'll go myself.'

He wrote the following letter at Fantine's dictation and then got her to sign it:

Monsieur Thenardier,

You will hand Cosette over to the bearer.

Everything owing will be paid.

I send you my regards,

Fantine.

But at this point a most serious thing happened. Do what we may to shape the mysterious stuff of which our lives are composed, the dark threads of our destiny will always re-emerge.

On a morning when Monsieur Madeleine was busy in his office, disposing of urgent business in case he should find it necessary to go to Montfermeil, he was informed that Inspector Javert wished to speak to him. The name affected him disagreeably. Since their encounter in the police post he had not seen Javert, who had been more careful than ever to avoid him.

'Show him in,' he said, and Javert entered.

Monsieur Madeleine stayed seated at his desk, pen in hand, intent on the report he was reading of certain minor infringements of the law. He received Javert with deliberate coldness, being unable to forget Fantine. At length the mayor put down his pen and half turned towards him.

'Well, Javert, what is it?'

'Monsieur le maire, a serious breach of discipline has been committed.'

'What breach?'

'An inferior member of the public service has shown the utmost disrespect for a magistrate. I have come, as in duty bound, to inform you of the fact.'

'Who is the offender?' asked Madeleine.

'Myself,' said Javert.

'You?'

'Yes.'

'And who is this magistrate who has been disrespectfully treated?'

'You are, Monsieur le maire.'

Monsieur Madeleine started up in his chair. Javert proceeded inexorably.

'I have come to ask you to recommend to the authorities that I should be dismissed.'

'But what in the world are you talking about?' cried Madeleine. 'In what way have you treated me with disrespect?'

'I will explain, Monsieur le maire. I was so furious after our dispute six weeks ago over that woman that I denounced you.'

'You denounced me?'

'To the Prefecture of Police in Paris.'

Monsieur Madeleine, who was not much more given to laughter than Javert himself, now laughed heartily.

'As a mayor who had encroached on the function of the police?'

'As an ex-convict.'

Madeleine's expression abruptly changed. Javert, who was staring at the floor, continued:

'That is what I believed. I had had the idea for a long time. A certain facial resemblance, the great physical strength you displayed in the Fauchelevent episode and your slight limp . . . all trifles. Nevertheless I suspected you of being a man called Jean Valjean.'

'What name did you say?'

'Jean Valjean. He was a convict I saw twenty years ago, when I was a prison-warder at Toulon. It seems that after being released that this Valjean committed a robbery at the house of a bishop and then robbed a small boy on the public highway. There has been no trace of him for eight years. Well, I believed . . . Anyway that is what I did. In my resentment, I denounced you to the Paris Prefecture.'

Monsieur Madeleine had returned to the documents on his desk. He asked in an entirely casual voice:

'And what did they say?'

'They said I was mad, since the real Jean Valjean has been found.'

The sheet of paper fell from Madeleine's hand. He looked hard at Javert and murmured expressionlessly:

'Indeed?'

'The facts are these,' said Javert. 'There was a man named Champmathieu living near the village of Ailly-le-Haut-Cloche. He was more or less destitute. Well, last autumn he was arrested for stealing cider apples. The evidence was clear enough. So he was taken into custody. Up to that point it was no great matter, but one of the prisoners at Arras was an old lag called Brevet who had been made a trusty for good conduct. The moment he set eyes on

Champmathieu he exclaimed, "But I know this man – we were in prison together in Toulon twenty years ago. His name's Jean Valjean." Champmathieu of course denied it, but the matter had to be followed up. Further inquiries were made in Toulon and here they found two other convicts who had known him. They were brought to Arras and at once confirmed Brevet's statement that the so-called Champmathieu was Jean Valjean. The confrontation took place almost on the day when I posted my letter of denunciation to Paris. They wrote back saying that I was out of my wits and that Jean Valjean was in custody in Arras. I need not tell you the shock this gave me. I obtained permission to go to Arras to see this Champmathieu for myself . . .'

'And?'

'Truth is truth, Monsieur le maire,' said Javert with the same sombre, implacable expression. 'I am forced to admit that that man is Jean Valjean. I, too, recognized him.'

Madeleine asked in a very low voice:

'You're sure?'

'Oh yes – I'm sure. He's to be tried at Arras Assizes and I have been subpoena'ed as a witness.'

Monsieur Madeleine had returned to the papers on his desk and was again poring over them and making notes with the air of a man with many things on his mind. He looked up at the inspector.

'Thank you, Javert. The details do not greatly interest me, and in any case we have business to attend to. You say you have to go to Arras. I take it that will not be for a week or so?'

'Sooner than that, Monsieur le maire. The case comes up tomorrow. I am catching the coach tonight.'

Monsieur Madeleine started slightly.

'How long will it take?'

'Certainly not more than a day. Sentence will be passed tomorrow evening at the latest, but I don't intend to wait for it, since there's no doubt what it will be. I shall leave directly I've given my evidence.'

'Good,' said Madeleine.

He made a gesture of dismissal, but Javert did not move.

'Forgive me, Monsieur le maire, I have to remind you that I must be dismissed from the service.'

Monsieur Madeleine rose to his feet.

'Javert, you are an honourable man and I respect you highly. You are exaggerating your offence, which in any case is a matter that only concerns myself. You deserve to go up in the world, Javert, not down. I want you to stay in your present post.'

Javert confronted the mayor with a clear-eyed gaze in which there was the glint of a narrow conscience as rigid as it was upright. He said quietly:

'I shall continue to perform my duties, Monsieur le maire, until I have been replaced.'

He went out; Monsieur Madeleine stood thoughtfully listening to the firm, decided footsteps as they died away down the corridor.

During the afternoon following his interview with Javert, Monsieur Madeleine paid his customary visit to Fantine. Before doing so he asked to see Sister Simplice, one of the two nursing sisters of the order of St Lazarus who did duty in his infirmary, the other being Sister Perpetua.

Monsieur Madeleine took Sister Simplice aside and recommended Fantine to her care in a tone so earnest that later she was to remember it. Then he went in to see Fantine.

On this day she had a high fever. Directly she saw him she asked:

'And Cosette?'

He anwered, smiling, 'Very soon.'

His manner towards her was normal except that he stayed an hour instead of his usual half hour, much to her delight. Then he returned to the *mairie* where his clerk saw him carefully studying a road-map of France that hung in his office. He pencilled some figures on a sheet of paper. From the *mairie*, Madeleine crossed the town to call upon a Fleming named Scaufflaire, who hired out horses and carriages.

'Master Scaufflaire, I want a horse that can do twenty leagues in a day.'

'Twenty leagues! Harnessed to a chaise? And how much rest will it get at the end of it?'

'It will have to come back the next day.'

'The same distance?'

'Yes.'

'Love us and save us! A whole twenty leagues?'

Madeleine produced the scrap of paper on which he had jotted down the figures 5, 6 and 8½.

'Nineteen and a half to be exact. Call it twenty.'

'Well, Monsieur le maire,' said the Fleming, 'I've got what you want, a small white horse, a wonderful animal, goes like the wind. And he'll last the course. He'll do it at a steady trot in under eight hours. I take it that the chaise is for yourself, Monsieur le maire, and that you know how to drive?'

'Yes.'

'The charge will be thirty francs a day, including rest days. I won't take a penny less, and you will pay for the animal's feed.'

Monsieur Madeleine got three napoleons out of his purse and laid them on the table.

'There's two days in advance.'

'One last thing,' said Monsieur Scaufflaire, 'a chaise would be too heavy for this trip. I must ask Monsieur le maire to use my tilbury.'

'Very well. Please be sure to have the horse and tilbury round at my house punctually at half past four,' said Madeleine, and went out, leaving the Fleming 'flabbergasted', as he later said.

Scaufflaire called his wife and told her the story. Where the devil was the mayor going? They talked it over. 'He must be going to Paris,' the lady said. 'I don't think so,' said her husband. Madeleine had left behind the scrap of paper on which he had scribbled his figures. Scaufflaire studied it carefully. 'Five – six – eight and a half – they must be post stages.' He looked at his wife, 'I've got it!' . . .

'Where?' . . . 'It's five leagues from here to Hesdin, six from Hesdin to Saint-Pol, and eight and a half from Saint-Pol to Arras. He's going to Arras.'

Of course, you will have realized that Monsieur Madeleine was indeed Jean Valjean.

Following his encounter with the boy Petit-Gervais, he was a changed man, enacting in his life what the bishop had sought to make of him. It was more than a transformation; it was a transfiguration.

He contrived to vanish, sold the bishop's silver, keeping only the candlesticks as a reminder, and worked his way from town to town across France, until eventually he came to Montreuil-sur-mer. Here he established himself in the manner we have described, with a conscience darkened by his past but in the knowledge that the second half of his life was a repudiation of the first, settled down to live peaceably with only two objects in mind – to conceal his true identity and find his way back to God.

When the name he had sought to bury was so unexpectedly uttered he had been completely stunned. His first thought, as he listened to Javert, was to give himself up, get the man Champmathieu out of prison and take his place. But then he said to himself, 'Steady – steady!' Repressing that first generous impulse, he recoiled from the heroic act.

During the rest of the day he remained in that state of inward turmoil and outward serenity, taking only what may be termed 'safety precautions'. He had a vague notion that he should go to Arras, without being at all decided about it, telling himself that since he was exempt from all suspicion it could do no harm for him to go and see what happened; and so he hired the horse and tilbury, in case he should need it.

He dined with a good appetite; but back in his bedroom he began to think.

He asked himself where he stood. He confessed to himself that to let things take their course was quite simply outrageous. To acquiesce in this blunder, to endorse it by his silence, in short, to do nothing, was in fact to do *everything*.

He would be robbing a man of his life, his peace, his place in the sun, morally murdering him by condemning him to the living death that is called a convict prison. He felt the presence of the bishop and knew that henceforth, Monsieur Madeleine the mayor would seem to him abominable, whereas Jean Valjean the felon would be admirable and pure.

'Well then,' he said, 'let us decide upon it. Let us do our duty and save this man.'

Without knowing it, he spoke the words aloud.

He perceived that this was the second turning-point in his spiritual life and in his destiny: the bishop had been the first, and the man Champmathieu marked the second. This was the uttermost crisis, the final trial of his fortitude.

Then suddenly he thought of Fantine. The abrupt recollection, coming as it were out of the blue, seemed to shed an entirely new light on his predicament.

He began now to consider the consequences of his departure from the scene. The town and the whole region would suffer. He had come to a place that was moribund and made it prosperous, brought life to a desert. With his going that life would start to ebb, without him the place would sink and die. And did he owe nothing to Fantine, for whose sufferings he was in some degree responsible? He had promised to retrieve her child. If he failed in this, she too would surely die, and the Lord knew what would become of the child. All this would follow if he gave himself up.

But at that moment it seemed to him that he heard a voice speaking within him.

'Jean Valjean! An old man who understands nothing of what has happened, whose only crime may be that your name is now inflicted upon him, is to be sentenced in your place. And you will remain an upright citizen, the respected and honoured Monsieur le maire.'

For a moment, and in utter despair, he envisaged the consequences of giving himself up, all he would be losing and what he would be getting in its place: the chain gang, the convict smock, the plank bed. Whichever way he turned, he faced the same alternatives – to cling to his paradise and become a devil, or become a saint by going back to hell. In God's name, what was he to do?

Without being aware of it, the mayor of Montreuil-sur-mer had acquired a degree of celebrity. The name of Madeleine was everywhere held in high esteem, and towns such as Arras and Douai envied the fortunate small town of Montreuil-sur-mer.

The Councillor of the King's Court at Douai, who was presiding over the assize court at Arras, was familiar with his name. When the usher, discreetly bending over his chair, handed him a slip of paper saying, 'The gentleman would like to be present at the hearing,' he at once nodded.

A minute or two later, Madeleine was standing in the court-room. No one paid any attention to him. All eyes were directed to a single point, a wooden bench with a small door behind it, set against one wall. The bench was lighted by candles and on it a man was seated, flanked by two gendarmes.

This was the man.

Madeleine thought with a shudder, 'Oh, God, am I to become that again?'

Room had been made for Madeleine when he entered. The presiding judge had looked round, and realizing that this must be the mayor of Montreuil-sur-mer, had bowed his head in greeting. He had entered at the moment when it was time for the case to be concluded. Ordering the accused to rise, the presiding judge put the formal question to him: 'Have you anything to add in your defence?'

The man stood twisting a grimy cap in his hands. Turning to face the judge he opened his mouth and began:

'You're wicked, that's what you are. I'm one of those that don't eat every day. I was on my way on foot from Ailly where there were floods and the countryside swamped, and there was this branch with apples lying on the ground and I picked it up not meaning any harm. You keep talking about Jean Valjean. My name's Champmathieu. I think my mother and father were tramps, but I don't know for sure. When I was a kid they called me little Champmathieu and now I'm old Champmathieu. That's my baptismal name and you can make what you like of it. You make me tired with all your questions. Why does everyone have to pick on me?'

The prosecutor now addressed the presiding judge.

'Monsieur le president, in view of the denials on the part of the accused, I request the Court's permission to recall the witnesses Brevet, Cochepaille, and Chenildieu and Inspector Javert, so that they may reaffirm their testimony identifying the prisoner with the convict Jean Valjean.'

'I must remind you,' said the presiding judge, 'that Inspector Javert is no longer in Court. He has returned to his duties in Montreuil-sur-mer.'

He gave the order and a minute later the prisoner Brevet was brought back into court escorted by a gendarme.

'Brevet, look hard at the man in the dock and tell the Court if in all conscience you still recognize him as your former prison-mate, Jean Valjean.'

Brevet did as required and then said:

'Yes, Monsieur le president, I do. That is Jean Valjean, who came to Toulon in 1796 and went out in 1815.'

'You can sit down,' said the judge. 'The accused will remain standing.'

Chenildieu was then brought in. When the judge asked if he still recognized the accused he burst into laughter.

'How could I help recognizing him? We did five years on the same chain.'

Then came Cochepaille. The judge put the same question to him and he answered promptly:

'It's Jean Valjean all right. We used to call him "Jean-the-crow-bar" on account of he was so strong.'

Each of the three affirmations, so clearly uttered in good faith, had drawn from the spectators a murmur of increasing volume and hostility towards the accused.

'The ushers will call for silence,' said the presiding judge, 'I am about to pronounce sentence.'

But at this moment there was a movement behind the bench and a voice cried:

'Brevet, Chenildieu and Cochepaille! I want you to look at me.'

All eyes turned in the direction of this voice, which was so grief-stricken, so terrible, that it chilled the hearts of all who heard it.

A man who had been seated among the privileged spectators behind the judges had risen to his feet. He strode to the centre of the court-room. The presiding judge, the prosecutor and twenty others recognized him and exclaimed with one voice:

'Monsieur Madeleine!'

The profound sensation caused by his sudden appearance was followed by a bewildered silence. But the pause was only brief. Before the judge or prosecutor could speak or any gendarme or usher make a movement, the man who was still known to everyone as Monsieur Madeleine advanced towards the three witnesses.

'Do you not recognize me?' he asked.

They shook their heads, staring at him in astonishment. Monsieur Madeleine turned to face the Court and said quietly:

'Gentlemen of the jury, I am the man you are looking for. I am Jean Valjean.'

No one breathed. The first stir of amazement was followed by a deathly stillness.

'This man must be released. I am that wretched convict. What I now tell you is the truth, and it is sufficient for me that God is my witness. I did the best I could. I sought to reinstate myself in the ranks of honest men. But it seems that it is not to be. But it is true that I robbed the Bishop of Digne, and the boy Petit-Gervais. You are right in supposing that Jean Valjean was a very evil wretch, although perhaps the fault was not wholly his. It is not for a man so lowly to seek to advise society, but the degradation from which I sought to escape is none the less an evil thing. It is gaol that makes the gaolbird, and this is something that you must bear in mind. Before going to prison I was a peasant with very little intelligence. It was prison that changed me. I grew malignant, but goodness and compassion saved me after brutality had come near to destroying me. But I see the advocate-general shake his head. You do not believe me, you think me mad. It is a pity Javert is not here, for he would recognize me. These men say that they do not, but we shall see.'

The gentleness and melancholy of his voice was such as no words can convey. He turned to the three convicts.

'I recognize you, Brevet. Do you remember –' he paused for an instant, ' – do you remember the braces you used to wear, with a check pattern?'

Brevet gave a start of surprise and stared at him wide-eyed. He went on:

'And you, Chenildieu. You have a bad scar on your right shoulder. You held it against a hot stove, trying to burn away the letters TFP which were branded on it, but they are still visible. Is that not so?'

'It's the truth,' said Chenildieu.

He turned to Cochepaille.

'At the bend of your left arm, Cochepaille, there's a date in blue lettering tattooed with gunpowder. It is the date of the Emperor's landing at Cannes – 1 March 1815. Pull up your sleeve.'

Cochepaille did so, and a gendarme held a lantern so that its light fell on his bare arm. The date was there.

Madeleine then turned to face the court with a smile that still wrings the hearts of those who remember it, a smile of triumph and utter despair.

'Now do you believe that I am Jean Valjean? I will trouble the Court no further. If I am not to be arrested at once I will leave. I have things to attend to. The Court knows who I am and where I am going, and can send for me when it chooses.'

He turned towards the door. No voice was raised, no arm outstretched to stay him. They stood aside to let him pass. He was invested at that moment with a hint of the divine which causes crowds to fall back in homage. He walked slowly. No one could say afterwards who had opened the door for him, but certainly it was open when he reached it. He turned and said to the prosecutor:

'Monsieur, I am at your disposal.'

He went out and the door closed behind him as unobtrusively as it had opened.

It took the jury a very short time to acquit the man Champmathieu of the charge against him, and being at once released he went off in a state of total stupefaction, thinking all men mad and understanding nothing of what had transpired.

Day was beginning to break. Fantine, after a restless night, but one filled with happy anticipation, had at length fallen asleep, and Sister Simplice had taken advantage of the fact to leave her bedside in order to prepare a new draught of quinine. She was bent over the array of bottles in the dispensary, obliged to peer closely at them in the misty dawn light, when suddenly she turned and uttered an exclamation. Monsieur Madeleine had silently entered the room.

He said in a low voice: 'How is she?'

'She seems better at the moment, but we've been very worried about her.'

Sister Simplice went on to tell him that Fantine had seemed to be sinking the day before but had recovered when she came to believe that he had gone to Montfermeil to fetch her child. She did not venture to question the mayor, but she saw from his expression that this was not the case.

The light was growing and his face was more plainly visible. The sister looked at him and suddenly she exclaimed:

'Merciful Heaven! Monsieur le maire, what has happened to you? Your hair is quite white.'

'White? So!' he said, but absently, as though he were thinking of other things. The sister's heart was chilled with apprehension of events unknown to her.

He asked: 'May I see her?'

'Is Monsieur le maire not going to have her child brought here?' the sister asked, scarcely daring to put the question.

'Of course. But it will take two or three days.'

'If she does not see you until then she will imagine that you are still away. We can persuade her to be patient. And when the child is here she will naturally suppose that you have brought her. We shall not have to tell a lie.'

Again Monsieur Madeleine paused for thought, but then he said in his calm, firm voice:

'No, sister, I must see her now. I may perhaps have very little time.'

The sister seemed not to notice the word 'perhaps', which lent an enigmatic quality to his reply. She lowered her eyes and said respectfully:

'In that case, although she is resting, Monsieur le maire may go in.'

For some time Monsieur Madeleine stayed motionless at the bedside, looking from the sick woman to the crucifix above her head. Presently she opened her eyes, looked up at him, and said tranquilly, with a smile:

'And Cosette?'

The question had been asked in a tone of such absolute trust that he was at a loss.

He looked up at the crucifix.

'But where is Cosette? Why did you not sit her on my bed, ready for when I woke up?'

He murmured something in reply and afterwards could not remember what he had said. Fortunately the doctor had been summoned and now came to his rescue.

'You must keep calm, my child. Your little girl is here.'

Fantine's eyes shone with a brilliance that lighted all her face.

'Oh,' she cried, 'won't someone bring her in?'

'Not yet. Not for the present. You're still feverish and the excitement would be bad for you. First you must get well.'

Monsieur Madeleine had seated himself on a chair by the bed. She turned towards him, making a palpable effort to appear calm, but she could not restrain herself from pouring out a flood of questions.

'Monsieur le maire, it was so wonderfully kind of you to go for her. At least you can tell me how she is? Have the Thenardiers taken good care of her? Ah! I so long to see her. Did you think her pretty, Monsieur le maire?'

He took her hand.

'Cosette is beautiful. She's well and you will soon see her. But now you must rest.'

Monsieur Madeleine was still holding her hand while he gazed anxiously at her. There were things he had intended to say, but now he hesitated. The doctor had left and only Sister Simplice remained with them.

The silence that ensued was suddenly broken by a cry from Fantine.

She was staring with wide, startled eyes at some terrifying sight that, it seemed, had just appeared at the far end of the room.

'What is it, Fantine?' he asked. 'What's the matter?'

She did not answer, but still staring, touched him on the arm while with her other hand she pointed behind him.

He turned and saw Javert.

Javert, as we know, had returned to Montreuil-sur-mer immediately after testifying. He was just getting up when a warrant for Monsieur Madeleine's arrest reached him. The messenger, himself an experienced police officer, gave him a terse account of what had taken place after he left Arras. Javert's instructions were as follows:

'Inspector Javert will take into bodily custody Sieur Madeleine, mayor of Montreuil-sur-mer, who, at today's hearing, was formally identified as the released convict, Jean Valjean.'

In the moment when the eyes of the two men met, Javert, without having made the least gesture, became hideous. He had the face of a fiend who has found the victim he thought he had lost.

*

49

Fantine had not set eyes on Javert since the day when the mayor had rescued her from him. Her sick mind understood nothing, but she did not doubt that he had come on her account. The sight of him was like a foretaste of death and she hid her face in her hands and cried:

'Monsieur Madeleine, save me!'

Jean Valjean had risen to his feet. He said in the calmest of voices:

'Don't be afraid. He hasn't come for you.' And to Javert he said: 'I know what you're here for.'

Javert advanced into the room and barked: 'Well, are you coming?'

Fantine looked in bewilderment about her. Only the sister and the mayor were present. Whom else could he be addressing in that peremptory tone except herself? And, trembling, she witnessed something unbelievable. She saw the policeman Javert seize the mayor by the collar, and the mayor meekly submit. It was as though her whole world had collapsed.

'Monsieur le maire!' she cried.

Javert uttered a hideous laugh baring all his teeth. 'He isn't mayor any longer.'

Jean Valjean made no attempt to loosen the hand gripping his coat collar.

'Javert –'

'Inspector, if you don't mind.'

Jean Valjean turned towards him and said rapidly in a very low voice:

'Inspector, give me three days! Three days to fetch the unfortunate woman's child. I'll pay anything you like. You can come with me if you want to.'

'I didn't think you were so stupid,' said Javert. 'Three days to clear out! To fetch the woman's child, you say. That's rich.'

Fantine began to tremble. 'To fetch my child? But isn't she here? Sister, answer me – where is Cosette? I want to see her. Monsieur Madeleine, I want to see her, Monsieur Madeleine –'

Javert stamped his foot. 'And now she's started! You hold your tongue, you slut! It's a fine state of affairs when gaolbirds become magistrates and whores are nursed like countesses. But we're going to put a stop to all that.' He turned to regard Fantine. 'I tell you there's no Monsieur Madeleine here, no mayor either. There's no one but a criminal, a convict called Jean Valjean. That's the man I'm holding.'

Fantine sat upright. Her eyes travelled from Valjean to Javert and then to the nun. She seemed about to speak, but only a whimper issued from her lips. And suddenly she fell back against the pillow. Her head struck the head of the bed and then sank limply against her shoulder.

She was dead.

Jean Valjean seized the hand gripping his collar and detached it as effortlessly as if it had been that of a child. He said to Javert:

'You have killed that woman.'

'That'll do,' Javert cried furiously. 'The escort's waiting below. March, or I'll put the handcuffs on you.'

In a corner of the room was a dilapidated iron bedstead. Valjean went across to it and in an instant had broken up the rusty frame. Then with one of the crossbars in his hand he stood confronting Javert, who retreated towards the door.

Armed with his metal cudgel, Valjean walked slowly to Fantine's bed and said in a voice that was scarcely audible:

'I would advise you not to interfere with me at this moment.'

One thing is certain; Javert trembled.

Taking Fantine's head in both his hands, Valjean set it on the pillow like a mother with her child. Then he closed her eyes. One hand was hanging down beside the bed. He knelt and gently lifted it and touched it with his lips.

Then he rose and turned back to Javert. 'I am at your service,' he said.

Javert consigned Jean Valjean to the town lock-up.

The arrest of Monsieur Madeleine created a sensation in

Montreuil-sur-mer. It is sad to have to record that at the mention of the word 'felon' nearly everyone deserted him. In a matter of hours all the good he had done was forgotten and he was simply 'the ex-convict'.

Only three or four persons in the whole town remained faithful to his memory, among them the old concierge who had served him.

On the evening of that day the devoted creature was seated in her porter's lodge, still bewildered and sadly pondering.

At this moment the window of her pigeon-hole was opened, and a hand reached for the key and lit the taper at her own lighted candle. She stared open mouthed, stifling the cry that rose to her lips. The hand and coat-sleeve were unmistakably those of Monsieur Madeleine.

For a moment she could not speak, but then she cried:

'God forgive me, Monsieur le maire, I thought you were –'

She could not finish the sentence and he did so for her.

'You thought I was in prison. So I was. I broke a window-bar, and here I am. I'm going up to my room. Will you please fetch Sister Simplice?'

The old woman hurried off. He had uttered no word of warning, knowing that she would never betray him.

Climbing the stairs leading to his room, he left the taper on the topmost tread, cautiously opened his door, groped his way across the room and closed the shutters. Then he went back for the taper.

He got an old shirt out of a drawer and tore it into strips in which he wrapped the two silver candlesticks.

There was a soft knock on the door and Sister Simplice entered.

She was pale and red-eyed and the candle she carried was shaking in her hand. The emotions of that day had turned the nun again into a woman. She had wept and she was trembling.

Jean Valjean had written a note. He handed it to her unfolded and said, 'I should be grateful, sister, if you would give this to the cure. You can read it.'

She read: 'I would ask Monsieur le cure to take charge

of the money I am leaving here. He is to use it to pay the costs of my trial and the funeral expenses of the woman who died today. The rest is for the poor.'

The sister tried to speak, but then they heard sounds from below, the tramping of feet and mingled with them the voice of the servant loudly protesting:

'I swear to you by God, Monsieur, that I have been here all the day and all this evening and that I have seen no one enter.'

A man said: 'But there is a light in his room.'

They recognized the voice of Javert.

The room was arranged so that the door, when it was fully opened, masked one corner. Jean Valjean blew out his light and slipped into this hiding place. Sister Simplice went on her knees at the table.

The door opened and Javert entered.

Seeing the sister, Javert's first impulse was to withdraw. But on the other hand he had a duty to perform which also admitted of no denial. So on second thoughts he stayed, resolved to hazard at least one question.

And there knelt Sister Simplice, who in all her life had never told a lie. Javert knew this and held her in a special veneration because of it.

'Sister,' he asked, 'are you the only person in this room?'

There ensued a terrible instant during which the trembling servant thought that she would faint. The sister looked up.

'Yes,' she said.

'Forgive me,' said Javert, 'if I ask you one thing more. Have you seen anyone this evening, a man? He has escaped from the prison – the man called Jean Valjean. Have you seen him?'

'No,' replied the sister.

'I apologize,' said Javert, and bowing deeply he withdrew.

Her denial was to Javert so conclusive that he did not even notice the fact that a taper, recently blown out, still stood smoking on the table.

An hour later a man on foot might have been seen amid

the trees and mists, heading rapidly away from Montreuil-sur-mer in the direction of Paris. It was Jean Valjean. The testimony of two or three carters whom he passed on the road subsequently established that he was carrying a bundle and wearing a smock.

The cure thought it well to retain, for the benefit of the poor, as much as possible of the money left behind by Jean Valjean. Perhaps he was right. After all, what were the persons directly concerned? – a criminal and a woman of the town. So he limited the funeral to the barest essentials, consigning Fantine to a pauper's grave in the free corner of the cemetery. Mercifully, God knows where to look for our souls. Her mortal remains were laid to rest, in company with other unconsidered bones, in a public grave resembling her own bed.

TWO

The battle of Waterloo is an enigma as incomprehensible to the winners as to the losers. It was a battle of the first importance won by a commander of the second rank. There exists a highly respectable school of liberal thought which does not deplore Waterloo. We are not of that number. To us Waterloo is the date of the confounding of liberty and with it a European system collapsed. The Napoleonic Empire dissolved in a darkness resembling the last days of Rome, and chaos loomed as in the time of the barbarians. Our story now requires us to return to the battlefield.

The 18th of June 1815 was a night of full moon. With the firing of the last shot, the plain of Mont-Saint-Jean became deserted. The English moved into the French encampments, and Wellington sat down in the village of Waterloo to write his report to Lord Bathurst. War has tragic splendours, but it also has its especial squalors, among which is the prompt stripping of the bodies of the dead. The day following a battle always dawns on naked corpses.

The number of pillagers following in the wake of an army varied according to the severity of the commander. Wellington had very few.

Nevertheless, the bodies of the dead were robbed during that night of 18–19 June. Wellington was uncompromising: any person caught in the act was to be shot forthwith. The looters preyed on one end of the battlefield while they were being executed at the other.

The moon shed a sinister light on the plain.

At about midnight a man prowled near the sunken lane of Ohain. From the look of him he was one such as we have described, drawn to the scene by the smell of the dead. An eye capable of penetrating the darkness might have discerned not far away from him a small sutler's cart in which what seemed to be a female figure was seated on a pile of boxes and bundles. There was perhaps some connection between the cart and the prowler.

The night was wonderfully calm, without a cloud in the sky. A breath that was almost a sigh stirred the hedgerows, and a tremor ran over the grass like the passing of souls.

Our night prowler stopped suddenly. A few yards away a hand protruded from the tangled mass of men and horses. The moonlight drew a gleam from something shining on one finger, a gold ring. The man bent down and for a moment crouched, and when he rose the ring was no longer there.

He did not rise to a standing position but stayed kneeling with his hands on the ground, in the posture of the jackal he resembled, while he looked cautiously about him. Finally, deciding that all was well, he got to his feet.

As he did so he started, feeling something tug him from behind. Swinging round, he saw that it was the hand that he had robbed, which now clutched the hem of his cape.

An honest man would have been appalled, but this one laughed.

'Only the dead,' he said. 'Better a ghost than a gendarme.'

The hand relaxed its grip and fell back, having exhausted its strength.

'Is he alive after all?' the prowler wondered. 'Better see.'

Bending down again, he contrived to extricate the now unconscious body and drag it clear of its fellows. It was that of a cuirassier, an officer of fairly high rank. By a fortunate chance, other bodies had formed an arch above him which had prevented him from being crushed.

The officer opened his eyes. 'Thank you,' he said weakly.

The prowler did not answer but looked up sharply, hearing a distant sound of footsteps, probably those of a patrol.

'Someone's coming!' said the prowler, starting to move away. The officer painfully raised his arm and held him back.

'You have saved my life. Who are you?'

The prowler muttered hurriedly:

'I was in the French army like you. I've got to leave you.

They'll shoot me if they catch me. I've saved your life. You must look after yourself now.'

'What's your rank?'

'Sergeant.'

'And your name?'

'Thenardier.'

'I shall not forget that name,' the officer said. 'And you must remember mine. My name is Pontmercy.'

Jean Valjean had been re-captured.

Before being arrested he contrived to withdraw from the banking house of M. Lafitte the sum of over half a million francs which he had placed there on deposit and which he had acquired quite legitimately in the course of his trade.

On his return to prison Jean Valjean was given a new number. He became No. 9430.

We may add, before dismissing the subject, that with the departure of Monsieur Madeleine, prosperity also departed from Montreuil-sur-mer. Everything he had foreseen during his night of feverish indecision came to pass. Madeleine had inspired and directed everything, and without him organization became slovenly, orders fell away. This led to lower wages, unemployment and bankruptcy. And nothing was left over for the poor. It all vanished after the assize court verdict which transformed Madeleine into Jean Valjean for the benefit of the penal system.

Towards the end of October of that year of 1823 the ship-of-the-line *Orion*, which was at that time attached to the Mediterranean squadron, put into Toulon dockyard for repairs after a spell of heavy weather.

The presence of a ship of the line in a sea port is something that always attracts a crowd of onlookers. She was a big ship, and the crowd loves bigness.

One morning the crowd of onlookers witnessed an accident.

The crew were taking the sails off her. The man loosening the starboard peak of the main-topsail suddenly lost his balance. A cry of alarm rose from the watching crowd as they saw him reel and slip, clutching the foot rope as he fell, first with one hand and then with both; and there he hung, with the sea a hideous distance below him.

Suddenly a man was seen climbing the rigging with the agility of a wildcat. He wore a red smock, which meant that he was a convict, and a green cap, which meant that he was serving a life sentence. As he reached the topsail-yard a gust of wind carried his cap away revealing a head of white hair; he was not a young man.

It was learned later that the man was one of a labour gang brought in from the prison. At the first alarm he had asked permission to try and save the luckless seaman. When this was granted he had broken the chain welded to the manacles around his ankles with a single blow of the hammer, and then, snatching up a coil of rope, had started up the shrouds.

The convict at length drew level with the seaman, only just in time, for in another minute he must have relaxed his grip. Hanging on with one hand, the convict used the other to lash the bight of the rope securely round the man's waist. Having done so he climbed back on to the yard and hauled the seaman up after him. He held him there for a moment to allow him to recover. Then, taking him in his arms, he walked with him along the yard to the masthead, whence he lowered him down to the cross trees, where another member of the crew took charge of him.

And now the crowd burst into applause, and a cry of frenzied acclamation arose – 'That man must be set free!'

The man, meanwhile, was making it a point of duty to return promptly to his labours. In order to do so the more rapidly he slid down the rigging and ran along one of the lower yards, while all eyes were fixed upon him. And then, for one terrible moment, he was seen to hesitate and stagger, overtaken, perhaps, by the giddiness of exhaustion. A great cry went up from the crowd as he was seen to fall into the sea.

Four men at once put out in a boat to rescue him, while the crowd cheered. But he did not come to the surface. He had vanished into the sea making scarcely a ripple, as though he had plunged into a vat of oil. The boat's crew sounded and dived in vain. The search continued until nightfall, but they did not even find his body.

Next day the local news-sheet contained the following item:

17 November 1823. Yesterday a convict working aboard the *Orion* fell into the sea and was drowned after rescuing a member of the crew. The body has not been recovered. It is assumed that it was caught in the piles under the Arsenal jetty. The man's prison registration-number was 9430 and his name was Jean Valjean.

Montfermeil is situated between Livry and Chelles, on the southern slopes of the high plateau separating the river Ourcq from the Marne. In 1823 life there was inexpensive and comfortable. The only problem, due to the height of the plateau on which it stood, was that of water.

Water had to be brought from a small spring about a quarter of an hour's walk from the village. The larger houses, the aristocracy and the Thenardier tavern all contributed a trifling daily sum towards the payment of a water-carrier. But he worked only until seven o'clock in the evening in summer and five o'clock in winter. After that, when darkness had fallen and the ground floor shutters were closed, anyone who had run short must fetch water for himself or go without.

This was the nightmare of the little girl, already known to us as Cosette. It will be recalled that Cosette was useful to the Thenardiers as an unpaid servant, and it was she who was sent to fetch water when it was needed. Being terrified of going to the spring after dark, she took great care to see that the house was always well supplied.

On Christmas Eve 1823 a group of men, carters and carriers, sat drinking in the low-ceilinged general room of the Thenardier tavern. Mme Thenardier was attending to the joint which was roasting over a clear fire while her husband drank and talked politics with the customers. Cosette was in her usual place, seated on the cross-bar under the kitchen table near the hearth. Clad in rags, her bare feet in wooden clogs, she was knitting woollen stockings for the Thenardier children by the light of the fire. A kitten was playing under the chairs and two fresh childish voices could be heard laughing and chattering in the next room, those of Eponine and Azelma.

Occasionally, the cry of a younger child, coming from somewhere in the house, made itself heard amid the hubbub of the tavern. This was the son born to Mme Thenardier during a previous winter – 'No knowing why,' she said. 'The cold weather no doubt' – and whose age was now a little over three. His mother had nursed him but did not love him, and he was left to go on screaming in the dark.

Four new travellers had arrived and Cosette was prey to gloomy misgivings. She was thinking as she sat under the table that the night was very dark, and that the jugs and pitchers in the bedrooms of the new arrivals had had to be filled, so that there was no more water in the house.

Then a travelling huckster came into the general room and said angrily:

'My horse hasn't been watered.'

'Indeed, it has,' said Mme Thenardier.

'I tell you he hasn't, mistress,' the man said.

Cosette scrambled out from under the table.

'But he has, monsieur. I took him water myself, a whole bucketful, and I talked to him.'

This was not true. Cosette was lying.

'I tell you he hasn't, my girl. I know it for sure. When he's thirsty he snorts in a particular way.'

Cosette stuck to her guns, speaking in a voice so stifled with terror as to be scarcely audible.

'All the same, he has.'

'Look,' said the man angrily, 'there's not much to watering a horse, is there? Why not just do it?'

'Well, that's right,' said Mme Thenardier. 'If the horse hasn't been watered it ought to be.'

'But, madame,' said Cosette faintly, 'there's no water left.'

Mme Thenardier's answer was to fling open the street door.

'Then go and get some,' she said.

Disconsolately Cosette fetched an empty bucket from a corner of the hearth. It was larger than herself, large enough for her to have sat in it.

Cosette went out and the door closed behind her.

A row of open-air stalls extended from the church as far as the Thenardiers' tavern. All were brightly lit to attract the custom of the village people who would presently be going to midnight mass. The last of the stalls, exactly opposite the tavern door, dealt in bric-a-brac, and in the front, against a background of white drapery, the stallkeeper had set a large doll nearly two feet high, clad in a dress of pink crepe, with real hair and enamel eyes. This marvel had been on display all day, to the ravishment of passers-by under the age of ten, without any Montfermeil mother having been rich enough to buy it for her child. Eponine and Azelma had spent hours gazing at it, and even Cosette had dared to glance at it now and then.

But now when she came out of the inn, tired and wretched though she was, she could not restrain herself from crossing the narrow street to examine that prodigious doll. She stood entranced, not having seen it so close before.

So enthralled was she that she quite forgot her errand until a harsh voice called her abruptly back to earth. 'Why, you slut, haven't you started yet? Just you wait – I'm coming after you.'

Mme Thenardier had happened to look out into the street. Cosette snatched up her bucket and ran, pausing only for a moment to get her breath, and not ceasing to run until she had entered the wood.

By now she was on the verge of tears, surrounded by the night-time stirrings of the trees, as unable to think as she was to see. The night closed in upon her, all the immensity of darkness bearing down upon the tiny creature that she was.

The spring was only a few minutes' walk from the edge of the wood and Cosette was familiar with the path, having followed it often in daylight. So, being guided by habit, she did not lose her way. Looking to neither left nor right, for fear of seeing something in the undergrowth, she finally came to it.

Without pausing to rest, she dropped her bucket into the water. Her state of nervous tension was such that she seemed to possess twice her normal strength. She pulled up the bucket, nearly full, and set it down on the grass.

She was still afraid, with only one thought in her mind – to run as fast as her legs would carry her out of the wood, back to the world of houses and lighted windows. She looked down at the bucket. Such was the dread of her mistress that she dared not go without it. She seized the handle with both hands and found that it was all she could do to lift it.

She struggled with it for a dozen paces, but it was too full and too heavy and she was forced to put it down again. Then she went on with the weight of the bucket dragging on her thin arms and the metal handle biting into her small chilled hands, pausing frequently to rest; and each time she put the bucket down a little of the water slopped on to her bare legs. And this was happening to a child of eight in the woods at night, in winter, far from any human gaze. Only God was there to see and perhaps her mother, alas, for there are things that rouse the dead in their graves.

She was nearly at the end of her strength, and still she had not got out of the wood. Coming to an old chestnut tree, she made a last pause, then bravely started again; but such was her despair that now she could not prevent herself from crying aloud – 'Oh, God help me! Please, dear God!'

And suddenly she found that the bucket no longer weighed anything. A hand that seemed enormous had reached down and grasped the handle. Looking up, she saw a burly, erect form beside her in the darkness. The man had come up behind her without her hearing him, and he had taken the bucket from her without speaking a word.

There are instincts which respond to all the chance meetings in life. The little girl was not afraid.

The man spoke to her in a low, deep voice.

'Child, this is a very heavy thing for you to be carrying.'
She looked up and answered:

'Yes, monsieur.'

'Let me have it.'

Then he asked: 'How old are you?'

'I'm eight, monsieur.'

'How far have you to go?'

'About a quarter of an hour from here.'

The man was silent for a moment, then he said sharply:

'But haven't you a mother?'

'I don't know,' the child replied. 'I don't think so.' And
after a pause she added: 'I don't think I've ever had one.'

The man stopped walking. He put down the bucket and
bending forward with his hands on the little girl's shoulders
tried to make out her features.

'What's your name?'

'Cosette.'

At this the man started violently. For a moment he continued to stare at her; then, taking his hands off her shoulders
he picked up the bucket and they walked on. Presently he
asked:

'Who sent you out to fetch water at this time of night?'

'Madame Thenardier.'

The man's next words were spoken in a voice that he
tried to make casual, but in which there was an odd tremor.

'What does she do, this Madame Thenardier?'

'She's my mistress. She keeps the inn.'

'An inn? Well, that's where I'll stop the night.'

The man was now walking fast but she had no difficulty
in keeping pace with him. She no longer felt tired. Now and
then she glanced up at him with an expression of wonderful
trust and assurance.

They had reached the village and Cosette led the way
through the streets. As they approached the tavern she
touched the man timidly on the arm.

'Please, monsieur, may I have the bucket?'

'But why?'

'If madame sees someone carrying it for me she will beat me.'

He gave her the bucket.

Cosette could not refrain from glancing at the splendid doll, which was still on display on the bric-a-brac stall. Then she knocked and the door was opened. Mme Thenardier appeared carrying a candle.

'So there you are. You've been long enough.'

'Madame,' said Cosette trembling, 'here is a gentleman who wants a room for the night.'

Mme Thenardier's glare was promptly replaced by the grimace of hospitality that is proper to innkeepers. She looked calculatingly at the stranger.

'This gentleman?'

'Yes, madame,' the man said and raised a hand to his hat.

Well-to-do travellers are not ordinarily so polite. The gesture and her rapid inspection of the stranger's clothes and his bundle wiped the smile from Mme Thenardier's face. She said coolly:

'Well, come in, my good fellow.'

The 'good fellow' did so. Mme Thenardier looked him over, taking especial note of his threadbare ochre yellow coat and slightly dented hat. Her husband was still seated with the customers. The man, meanwhile, had deposited his stick and bundle on a bench and seated himself at a table where Cosette hurried to place a bottle of wine and a glass. The customer who had demanded water went to see to his horse. Cosette got back under the table with her knitting. After taking a sip of wine the man proceeded to study her with interest.

Cosette was plain. She was thin and pale, and so small that although she was eight years old she looked no more than six. Her clothes were a collection of rags – torn garments of cotton, with no wool anywhere. Her bare legs were rough and red. Everything about her, her general attitude and bearing, her every movement expressed a single impulse – fear.

The man in the yellow coat continued to observe Cosette.

At this moment the door opened and Eponine and Azelma entered.

They were two very pretty little girls, one with glossy chestnut curls and the other with long dark plaits down her back. They were warmly clad but with the maternal skill which ensured that the thickness of the materials did not detract from their elegance. Their mother greeted them in a tone of mock-reproach, overflowing with indulgence. 'So there you are, and high time too!'

They went and sat in the chimney-corner, cooing over a doll which they shared between them. Cosette looked up now and then from her knitting and mournfully regarded them.

Eponine and Azelma, for their part, showed no interest in Cosette, being now absorbed in a highly important matter. They had caught hold of the kitten, letting their doll fall to the floor, and Eponine, the elder, was now dressing it in an assortment of red and blue rags. While Eponine and Azelma were dressing the kitten, Cosette noticed the Thenardier children's doll lying on the floor. It was only a yard or two away from the kitchen table and nobody was watching her. With a last cautious look round, she crawled out on hands and knees, seized the doll and a moment later was again under the table, but with her back now turned to the fire, and crouching to conceal the fact that she had the doll hidden in her arms.

Cosette's rapture lasted only a few minutes. With all her precautions she had failed to notice that one of the doll's legs was sticking out so as to be visible from behind her. Azelma suddenly caught sight of a pink foot shining in the firelight. She nudged her sister and, without letting go of the kitten, Eponine ran across to her mother and tugged at her skirt.

'Look,' said Eponine, and pointed to Cosette, who, lost in the ecstasy of possession, was oblivious of all else.

Mme Thenardier's face assumed that particular expression, a mingling of the vile and commonplace, which causes women of her kind to be known as harridans.

In a voice hoarse with fury she cried:

'Cosette!'

Cosette swung round, trembling as though the earth were shaking under her feet.

'Cosette!' repeated Mme Thenardier.

Cosette laid the doll down with a gentle movement in which there was something like love as well as despair. And then she did something that not all the cruel events of the day had forced her to do. She burst into a flood of tears.

The stranger, meanwhile, had got to his feet.

'What's the matter?' he asked Mme Thenardier.

'The brat has had the impudence to take my children's doll!'

'But what of it?' the stranger said. 'Why shouldn't she play with the doll?'

'She handled it,' pursued Mme Thenardier. 'She touched it with her filthy hands!'

Cosette sobbed more loudly than ever.

'Stop that noise!' the woman shouted.

The stranger turned abruptly towards the street door, opened it, and went out. Madame Thenardier took advantage of his sudden disappearance to administer a kick under the table which drew a cry from Cosette.

In a very short time the stranger was back, and now he was carrying the fabulous doll which during that day had been coveted by every child in the village. He set it upright in front of Cosette and said:

'Here – it's for you.'

Cosette looked up, and then she slowly shrank back, withdrawing as far as she could under the table to huddle, silent and motionless, against the wall, scarcely daring to breathe. Mme Thenardier, Eponine and Azelma were standing like statues. The drinkers themselves had paused. A silence had fallen on the room.

Mme Thenardier, thunderstruck, was again reduced to conjecture. What *was* this man? Was he a pauper or a millionaire?

Over her husband's face passed a look of strained intensity. Glancing from the doll to the traveller, he seemed to sniff the man as he might have sniffed a hoard of treasure. But this lasted only an instant. He drew near to his wife and murmured:

'That thing cost at least thirty francs. Don't be a fool. Crawl to him.'

Cosette crept out of her retreat.

'The gentleman has given you a doll, dear child,' said Mme Thenardier. 'It's yours. You must play with it.'

'Is it true, monsieur? Is it really mine?'

The stranger nodded to Cosette.

'I shall call her Catherine,' she said.

At that moment there was no one on earth whom Mme Thenardier detested more than she did this stranger. She hurriedly sent her daughters off to bed and then went so far as to ask the 'yellow man' for permission to send Cosette to bed as well, observing in motherly accents that the child had had a tiring day. Cosette departed with Catherine in her arms.

Mme Thenardier then crossed the room to where her husband was seated, and there relieved her feelings by pouring out a flood of words that were the more venomous because they had to be spoken in an undertone. The stranger meanwhile had returned to his attitude of meditation.

Several hours went by. The midnight mass had been celebrated, the revelry was ended and the revellers departed; but the stranger remained where he was.

Thenardier went up to the man and ventured to ask:

'Is monsieur not going to retire?'

He had chosen the word with care. 'Retire' sounded more respectful than 'go to bed'. The phrase had the especial virtue that it would be reflected in tomorrow's bill. A room where one merely goes to bed costs twenty sous, but a room where one retires may cost twenty francs.

'Of course,' said the stranger. 'You're quite right.'

'If monsieur will allow me,' said Thenardier, smiling, 'I will lead the way.'

A good two hours before daylight the next morning, Thenardier, seated pen in hand at a table in the general room, was composing the stranger's bill by the light of a candle, while his wife was looking over his shoulder.

'Twenty-three francs!' exclaimed the lady in a tone of rapture not unmingled with apprehension. 'It's fair. But it's a great deal. Do you think he'll pay?'

'He'll pay,' said her husband with his small, cold laugh. The laugh was the expression of perfect assurance and authority. She did not pursue the matter. She began to tidy the room while he paced up and down. After a silence he said:

'I owe a good fifteen hundred francs.'

He dropped on to the settle in the corner of the hearth and sat brooding with his feet in the warm ashes.

'While I think of it,' the woman said, 'I'm turning Cosette out today. The sight of that doll makes me sick.'

Thenardier was lighting his pipe. He said between puffs, 'Give the man his bill.' Then he got up and went out.

He had scarcely done so when the stranger entered, and instantly Thenardier reappeared behind him, standing in the half-open doorway visible only to his wife.

The stranger was carrying his stick and bundle.

'Up so early!' said Mme Thenardier. 'Is monsieur leaving us already?'

'Yes,' said the stranger in a preoccupied manner, 'I'm leaving. How much do I owe you?'

Without answering, Mme Thenardier handed him the folded slip of paper. He glanced at it, but his thoughts were evidently elsewhere.

'Tell me, madame, are you doing well here in Montfermeil?'

'Fairly well,' said Mme Thenardier, for the moment astounded that the sight of the bill had not produced an immediate explosion. But then she resumed in a voice of extreme pathos: 'Times are very hard, monsieur. We have so many expenses. There's that child, for instance – you've no idea how much she costs.'

'What child?'

'Why, the one you saw last night, Cosette. "The lark", as the people round here call her. These peasants with their nicknames. She's more like a bat than a lark. I have my own daughters to consider. I can't keep other people's children as well.'

The stranger hesitated and then said in a voice which he strove to make casual but which trembled slightly:

'Suppose I were to take her off your hands?'

The woman's red, coarse face was illumined with a sudden, atrocious radiance.

'Why monsieur, my dear monsieur, take her! Take her away, care for her, cosset her, pamper her and may you be blessed by the Holy Virgin and all the saints in Paradise!'

'Well then, I will. Call her in here.'

'Cosette!' cried Mme Thenardier.

'In the meantime,' said the stranger, 'I might as well pay what I owe you. How much is it?'

He looked at the slip of paper and started slightly. 'Twenty-three francs!' Looking hard at his hostess, he repeated the amount in a tone that was half one of amazement and half a question.

But Mme Thenardier had had time to steel herself for the ordeal. She answered calmly:

'Certainly, monsieur – twenty-three francs.'

The stranger placed five five-franc pieces on the table.

'Well, go and fetch the child,' he said.

But at this moment Thenardier came right into the room saying:

'Monsieur owes twenty-six francs.'

'What!' exclaimed his wife.

'Twenty for the room,' said Thenardier coldly, 'and six for his supper. As for the child, that is something that I must discuss with the gentleman. Kindly leave us, my dear.'

Mme Thenardier had one of those flashes of enlightenment that are the reward of natural talent. Perceiving that the leading actor had now entered the stage she said nothing and withdrew.

When they were alone Thenardier invited the stranger to be seated but himself remained standing.

'You must forgive me, monsieur, but one does not hand over one's child to a passer-by. Am I not right? You have the look of an honest man. But I need to be certain as I am sure you will understand. I do not even know your name. I must at least ask to see a scrap of paper, a passport or something.'

The stranger, without ceasing to regard him with eyes that seemed to pierce to his heart, said in a firm, incisive voice:

'Monsieur Thenardier, one does not need a passport to travel five leagues from Paris. If I take Cosette with me that will conclude the matter. You will not be told my name or my dwelling or where she will be. I mean to break every connection with her present life. Do you agree to that – yes or no?'

Thenardier realized that he had to do with a man of great moral strength. He understood it instantly. Throughout the previous evening he had had his eye on the stranger. Even before he had shown that he was interested in Cosette, Thenardier had guessed it. Was he perhaps her grandfather? But if one has a rightful claim one produces it. Evidently the man had no claim on Cosette. Thenardier, guessing there was a secret that the stranger had reason for concealing, had felt he was in a strong position. The plain and forthright answer, showing the man of mystery to be so uncompromisingly mysterious, had taken the wind out of his sails. He felt that this was the moment for the straightforward approach.

'Monsieur,' he said, 'I need fifteen hundred francs.'

The stranger got an old black leather wallet out of an inside pocket, extracted three bank notes and laid them on the table. He then pressed his large thumb on them and said:

'Fetch Cosette.'

When Cosette appeared in the downstairs room the stranger undid his bundle. It contained a woollen dress, an apron, a camisole, a petticoat, a shawl, woollen stockings, a pair of shoes – all the clothing needed for an eight-year-old girl. Every article was black.

'Take these, child,' the stranger said, 'and get dressed as quickly as you can.'

Day was breaking when the people of Montfermeil, engaged in opening their shutters, saw a poorly clad man go along the Rue de Paris hand-in-hand with a little girl dressed in mourning who was carrying a large doll.

Cosette was going away, she did not know with whom or whither. All she knew was that she was leaving the Thenardiers' house for good.

She walked gravely, gazing up at the man beside her. She had a queer feeling, as though she had drawn close to God.

Mme Thenardier, as her habit was, had left matters to her husband, expecting great things. After the stranger and Cosette had left he allowed a quarter of an hour to elapse before taking her aside and showing her the fifteen hundred francs.

'Is that all?' she said.

It was the first time in their association that she had ventured to criticize any of her lord's acts. The blow went home.

'You're right, and I'm an idiot. Where's my hat?'

He folded the three banknotes, put them in his pocket and hurried out of the house, discoursing to himself as he went.

'The man must be a millionaire, yellow coat and all. He handed over twenty-five francs and then fifteen hundred, all without a murmur. He'd have paid fifteen thousand! But I'll catch up with him.'

That bundle of clothes bought in readiness for the child, that was extraordinary. There was more than one secret here, and a man of sense does not let go of a mystery when he has caught sight of one.

When he reached the old aqueduct of the Abbaye de Chelle, Thenardier saw above a bush a hat which had already given him much food for thought and, although the child was too small to be seen, he could see the head of her doll.

He suddenly confronted them.

'I beg your pardon, monsieur,' he said breathlessly, 'I am returning your fifteen hundred francs.'

The man looked up.

'What does this mean?'

'It means, monsieur,' Thenardier said in a respectful tone, 'that I am taking Cosette back.'

Cosette shuddered and pressed herself against the man.

'I've been thinking. The child is not mine. She was entrusted to my care by her mother and I can only return her to her mother. You will say, "But her mother is dead." In that case I can only hand the child over to a person bringing me a document signed by the mother saying that I am to hand the child over to that person.'

Without speaking the man put a hand in his pocket and Thenardier witnessed the reappearance of the wallet stuffed with bank notes. 'Stick to your guns, lad,' he thought. 'You're going to be bribed.'

The stranger opened the wallet, but instead of bringing out the sheaf of notes which Thenardier was looking for, he produced nothing but a sheet of paper which he handed to him.

'You were right to ask for this. Please, read it.'

Thenardier read:

25 March 1823 Montreuil-sur-mer

Monsieur Thernadier,

You will hand Cosette over to the bearer. Everything owing will be paid.

I send you my regards,

Fantine

'You recognize the signature?' the stranger said.

It was unmistakably Fantine's handwriting. Thenardier had no reply. He was filled with a violent, twofold resentment, at losing the handsome bribe he had been hoping for, and at having been defeated.

'You can keep the letter as your quittance,' the stranger said.

Brazen audacity had served Thenardier once already.

'Mr Don't-know-your-name,' he said, casting civility aside, 'either you pay me another thousand crowns or I take Cosette back.'

The stranger said calmly: 'Come here, Cosette.'

He reached out his left hand to the child and with his right picked up the stick which was lying beside him on the grass. Thenardier became aware of the formidable nature of this cudgel, and also of the loneliness of the spot. Without another word the stranger turned and, clasping Cosette by the hand, led her away into the wood, leaving the innkeeper, motionless and thunderstruck, to stare at his slightly bowed and massive shoulders and the size of his fists.

But he still did not give up. 'At least I'll find out where they're going,' he thought.

The time of year, robbing the trees of their foliage, made it easy for Thenardier to keep them in sight while following at a safe distance. Nevertheless the man suddenly turned and saw him. His gaze was so formidable that Thenardier decided it would be unwise to follow him further. He turned back.

Jean Valjean had not died when he had fallen, or rather flung himself, into the sea, from the *Orion.* He had swum under water to a moored vessel to which a boat was tied, and had hidden in the boat until nightfall. After dark he had taken to the sea again and swum along the coast to a place a short distance from Cap Brun. Here, since he did not lack money, he was able to buy clothes. There was a small drinking-place nearby which specialized in supplying the needs of escaped convicts. Thereafter Valjean had travelled a dark and circuitous road. Eventually he reached Paris and thence had gone to Montfermeil.

His first act on reaching Paris had been to buy a complete set of mourning clothes for an eight-year-old girl, after which he had rented a lodging. On the occasion of his first escape from arrest he had paid a mysterious visit to Montfermeil, or to its environs, and the police had certain theories. But he was still believed to be dead, and this was his greatest safeguard. Reading the report in a newspaper he had felt reassured and almost at peace, as though he had really died.

On the evening of the day when he rescued Cosette from the Thenardiers they returned together to Paris, entering the city after dark by the Monceaux barrier. Here he took a cab to the Esplanade de l'Observatoire and then, with the little girl's hand in his, walked through deserted alleyways to the Boulevard de l'Hopital.

Here stood an ancient building which seemed at first sight to be no bigger than a cottage but was in fact as vast as a cathedral. The postmen called the tenement No. 50–52 Boulevard de l'Hopital; but it was known in the neighbourhood as the house of Gorbeau.

Jean Valjean came to a stop outside the Gorbeau tenement. Like a bird of prey he had sought out the remotest spot he could find for the building of his nest.

At daybreak the next morning Jean Valjean stood at Cosette's bedside waiting for her to awake.

Something quite new was taking place within him.

Valjean had never loved anything. He had been alone in the world, never a father, a lover, husband, or friend. The feeling he had once had for his sister and her children had become so remote as to have vanished almost entirely. But when he had seen Cosette, snatched her up and borne her out of captivity, everything in him that was passionate and capable of affection had been aroused and had flowed out to the child.

Valjean had been careful in his choice of a refuge, and he seemed to have found one which afforded them absolute security. The lower part of No. 50–52, which was used as a storehouse by market-gardeners, had no communication with the single upper storey. The upper storey consisted of a number of rooms and a few attics. Of these only one was occupied, by an old woman who did Valjean's housework. The rest were empty.

It was this old woman, who went by the title of 'chief tenant', who had let the room to him on Christmas Eve.

He had told her that he was a gentleman of private means, ruined by the failure of the Spanish loan, and that he proposed to live there with his granddaughter.

Weeks passed, and the two lived happily in their drab dwelling. Children sing at daybreak as naturally as the birds, and Cosette laughed, chattered and sang throughout the day. At moments she grew serious and reflected on the black dress she wore. She was clad no longer in rags but in mourning, emerging from misery into life.

She called Valjean 'father', never any other name. He was content now that this child loved him. He saw a radiant future enchantingly lighted by Cosette. None of us is wholly free from egotism. There were moments when it pleased him to think that she would never be pretty.

As a precaution, Jean Valjean never left the house during the day. He walked for an hour or two every evening, sometimes alone but often with Cosette.

He still wore his yellow coat, black breeches and battered hat. The people of the neighbourhood supposed him to be very poor, and now and then, when he was out walking, a good-natured housewife would stop and offer him a sou. He accepted it, bowing, but it also sometimes happened that, encountering some poor wretch begging for charity, he would look cautiously about him, furtively thrust a coin into his hand, often silver, and then hurriedly walk on. This was unwise. He became known in the neighbourhood as 'the beggar who gives alms'.

The 'chief tenant', a soured old creature consumed with envious curiosity concerning her neighbours, took a great interest in Jean Valjean without his realizing it. One day she caught sight of Valjean entering one of the empty rooms on the corridor in what seemed to her a suspicious manner. She crept after him and watched through a chink in the door, which he had closed. She saw him reach into his pocket and take out a case containing scissors and thread. He then unstitched a part of the lining of his tail-coat and brought out a yellowed piece of paper which he unfolded. The old woman saw to her amazement that it was a thousand-franc note. She fled in great alarm and the thousand-franc note, embroidered and multiplied, became the subject of many excited conversations among the housewives in the Boulevard de l'Hopital.

There, was a beggar with a pitch near the church of Saint-Medard on whom Jean Valjean bestowed alms. Sometimes he talked to him. But there were those who said that the beggar was a police informer. He was a one-time beadle, aged seventy-five, who constantly intoned prayers.

On a certain evening Valjean went that way unaccompanied by Cosette. The beggar was in his usual place apparently praying. Valjean stopped and thrust the customary gift into his hand. As he did so the beggar looked up and gazed searchingly at him, then quickly bowed his head. It had happened in an instant, but Valjean seemed to have caught a glimpse not of the vacant, devotional countenance of the beggar, but of quite another face that was already known to him. He stepped back, frozen with alarm, and stared at the beggar who, with his head now hidden beneath a tattered covering, looked precisely as usual.

'I'm mad,' thought Valjean. 'The thing's impossible.' Nevertheless he returned home in a state of profound disquiet, scarcely daring to admit, even to himself, that the face he had thought he had glimpsed was that of Javert.

At about eight o'clock a few evenings later, when he was giving Cosette a reading-lesson in his room, he heard the door of the house open and close. This was unusual. The old woman, the house's only other inhabitant, always went to bed at nightfall. Jean Valjean signed to Cosette to keep quiet. Someone was coming up the stairs. Jean Valjean blew out his candle.

He stayed silent and motionless, still seated in his chair with his back to the door and holding his breath. After a while, having heard nothing more, he turned cautiously round and saw through a crevice in the door a gleam of light. Someone with a candle was outside.

Several minutes passed and then the light vanished. But there was no sound of footsteps, which suggested that the person listening at the door had removed his shoes. Valjean flung himself fully clad on the bed and did not close his eyes all night.

At daybreak, when he was on the verge of falling asleep, he was aroused by the creaking of a door along the corridor and he heard footsteps. He leapt up and put an eye to his keyhole, hoping to catch a glimpse of his intruder. It was a man, as he had suspected, and this time he went past Valjean's room without stopping. The corridor was too dark for his face to be visible, but as he reached the top of the stairs he was silhouetted against the light coming from outside and Valjean had a full view of him from behind. He saw a tall man clad in a long tail-coat with a cudgel under his arm. A man with the formidable outline of Javert.

Clearly the man had used a key to enter the house. But who had provided him with one?

When the old woman came in at seven to do the room, Valjean looked hard at her but asked no questions. Her manner was unchanged. As she was sweeping the floor she said:

'Did monsieur hear someone come in last night?'

'Now you mention it, I did,' he answered casually. 'Who was it?'

'It was the new tenant. A Monsieur Dumont or Daumont – something like that.'

'And what kind of man is he, this Monsieur Dumont?'

She looked at him with her small, foxy eyes and said:

'He's a rentier – like you.'

The words may have had no special intention, but Valjean believed that he discerned one.

When the old woman had left, he made a roll of the coins he kept in a drawer, about a hundred francs, and put it in his pocket. Although he did this with care, so that the chink of money should not be heard, a five-franc piece fell out of his hand and rolled noisily across the floor.

At dusk he went downstairs and looked cautiously up and down the boulevard. It seemed to be entirely deserted.

He went upstairs again and said to Cosette, 'Come along!'

He took her by the hand and they left the house together.

Jean Valjean at once moved off the boulevard and into the side street, constantly changing direction and now and then turning back to put any possible pursuer off the scent. He felt reasonably sure that he was not being followed.

Cosette walked unquestioningly beside him. The hardships of the first years of her life had taught her a passive stoicism. Moreover, she had grown accustomed to the idiosyncrasies of the man and she felt safe in his protection.

Jean Valjean knew no more than she where they were going. He had no considered plan. He was not even sure that the man he had seen was Javert. But strange things had happened in the last few hours and he could not disregard them. They passed outside the police post in the Rue Pontoise, which was on the dark side of the street. A moment later instinct prompted him to look back. He was in time to see, by the light of the lantern over the doorway of the post, the figures of four men moving in his direction. They stopped and stood in a group as though consulting together. The one who appeared to be their leader turned and the moon shone full on his face, and Valjean now knew that it was Javert.

This was the end of uncertainty for Jean Valjean.

Increasing his speed, he came to the river embankment. Here he turned to take stock of his position. The embankment, like the streets he had passed through, was deserted. He breathed again.

At the Pont d'Austerlitz, a large cart came up, making for the right bank, and this was helpful to him; by walking beside it he could cross over in its shadow.

Across the river he saw timber yards a short distance to his right and decided to make for these. Between the walls of two of the yards there was a dark and narrow street, the Rue du Chemin-Vert-Saint-Antoine, which seemed exactly what he was looking for.

He was no longer walking fast, being obliged by Cosette to go more slowly. He picked her up and carried her, and she rested her head on his shoulder without speaking. He looked back from time to time, along the straight length of the lane behind him. The first two or three times he did this he saw and heard nothing and, somewhat reassured, he continued on his way. But then, as he turned his head again, he seemed to detect a distant movement amid the shadows through which he had passed.

He came to the boundary-wall of a lane crossing the end of the one he was following. He looked right. The new lane ran past a cluster of buildings and then came to a stop, ending in a high white wall that was clearly visible. To the left, however, it was open, debouching after a hundred yards or so into a wider street. Clearly he must go this way.

But as he was about to turn left he saw, standing at the end of the lane where it entered the street, a dark figure motionless as a statue.

The part of Paris which Valjean had now reached, situated between the Faubourg Saint-Antoine and La Rapee was known as 'le Petit-Picpus'. Whoever came from the Seine and reached the end of the Rue Polonceau, had to his left the length of the Rue Droit-Mur, with its wall directly facing him, and to his right a short extension of the same street, with no outlet, known as the Cul-de-sac Genrot.

This was where Valjean found himself.

Seeing the dark form at the corner of the Rue Droit-Mur and the Rue Picpus, he started back. There could be no doubt that the man was on the watch for him.

What was he to do? His retreat was cut off. The movement he had detected some distance behind him must mean Javert was there with the rest of his party. Valjean felt himself caught in a net that was slowly tightening.

The Rue Droit-Mur was almost entirely flanked on the left by a stark composite building made up of several sections which increased in height as they approached the Rue Picpus, so that the building was lofty at its far end but low at the end near the Rue Polonceau. Here, at the turning, it was nothing but a wall. But this wall was deeply recessed, so that anything within the recess was hidden from observers standing in the Rue Polonceau or the Rue Droit-Mur.

The branches of a lime tree hung over the wall. To Jean Valjean in his perilous situation, the apparent solitude and remoteness of the building had their attractions. He looked over it rapidly, feeling that if he could get inside he might be safe. Hope dawned on him.

The ivy-clad wall, above which the branches of the lime tree showed, must surely enclose a garden in which, despite the absence of foliage, they might be able to hide for the rest of the night.

At this moment a muffled, regular sound became audible in the distance. Valjean ventured to peer out of the recess. Some seven or eight soldiers in two files had just entered the far end of the Rue Polonceau. He caught the gleam of bayonets. They were coming his way.

The squad, at the head of which he could discern the tall figure of Javert, was advancing slowly and cautiously. This could only mean that Javert, having fallen in with a military patrol, had taken it under his command and that his own two men were marching in its ranks.

There was only one possible way out.

Jean Valjean had the singularity that he might be said to be doubly endowed, on the one side with the aspirations of a saint, on the other with the formidable talents of a criminal.

It will be recalled that among his other gifts Jean Valjean was a past master in the art of climbing walls without artificial aids, simply by muscular strength and dexterity using back, shoulders and knees in any angle or chimney. By these means he could climb as high as six storeys if necessary.

Valjean considered the wall at the point where the branches of the lime tree were visible above it. It was about eighteen feet high. The problem was Cosette. To carry her up to the top of the wall was impossible. A rope was what he needed, but he had none.

Extreme situations bring flashes which may blind or inspire us. Looking frantically about him, Valjean noticed the lamp bracket in the Cul-de-sac Genrot. These brackets were lowered for lighting by means of a stout cord. The reel on which the cord was wound was enclosed in an iron box to which the lamp-lighter had a key.

With the energy of desperation, Valjean darted across the end of the Rue Polonceau into the cul-de-sac, broke open the box with his knife and an instant later had rejoined Cosette. He had his length of rope.

Meanwhile the strangeness of their surroundings and the singular behaviour of Jean Valjean were beginning to distress Cosette.

'I'm frightened father,' she said. 'Who's that coming?'

'Quiet!' The hard-pressed man replied, 'It's Madame Thenardier. Leave everything to me. If you make a sound she'll hear you. She's coming to fetch you back.'

Then, with haste but without fumbling, he removed his cravat, passed it round Cosette under her armpits, tied the ends to one end of his rope, took the other end of the rope between his teeth and then climbed up the angle formed by the wall and the end of the building, doing so with as much ease and certainty as if he had stair-treads under his elbows and heels.

Cosette stared up in amazement, frozen to silence by the mention of Mme Thenardier. Then she heard his voice calling to her in a whisper:

'Stand with your back to the wall.' She did so. 'Don't make a sound and don't be afraid.'

She felt herself lifted off the ground. Before she had time to realize what was happening she too was on the wall. Jean Valjean seized hold of her and put her on his back. He had just slipped down on to the roof of the building when a hubbub of voices announced the arrival of the patrol. Javert bellowed:

'Search the cul-de-sac! I'll swear he's in the cul-de-sac!' Jean Valjean let himself slide down the roof, still with Cosette on his back, and with the help of the lime tree dropped to the ground. Whether from terror or bravery, Cosette had not uttered a sound. Her hands were slightly grazed.

Jean Valjean found himself in a rather strange garden, one of those that seem made to be seen only in winter and by night. It was oblong in shape, with a poplar-walk along the far side, tall shrubs at the corners, a few gnarled and stunted fruit trees, a melon patch with glass cloches gleaming in the moonlight and an old well-head.

He was standing beside the building whose roof he had used in his descent. The end of the garden was lost in mist and darkness. Any place more lonely and desolate it would have been hard to imagine. That the garden was deserted at that hour was understandable; but there was nothing about it to suggest that anyone ever walked there, even by day.

Outside they could hear the noise of the patrol, searching the cul-de-sac, the voice of Javert and his stream of imprecations mingled with words that they did not catch.

Time passed and the commotion seemed to be receding. Valjean bent over Cosette and found that she had fallen asleep with her head resting on a stone. He sat down beside her.

He now clearly perceived the truth that was henceforth to be the centre of his life, namely, that while she was there, while he had her near him, he would need nothing except for her sake and fear nothing except on her account. He sat thinking and only by degrees became aware of an odd sound that he had been unconsciously hearing for some time. It came from within the garden, the sound of a bell tinkling, faint but distinct, like a sheep-bell in the fields at night.

The sound caused him to turn his head and, peering, he saw that there was someone else in the garden. A person, seemingly a man, was walking amid the rows of cloches on the melon patch, pausing, stooping and straightening with regular movements as though spreading something over the ground. He appeared to be limping.

What was strange was that each of his movements was accompanied by this tinkle of a bell. Clearly it was attached to him; but what kind of man was it that was 'belled', like a wether or a cow?

While he was wondering about this he felt Cosette's hands. They were ice-cold.

'Oh God!' he exclaimed; and he said in a low voice, 'Cosette!' She did not open her eyes.

He shook her vigorously, but she did not wake.

'Is she dead?' he thought and stood upright, trembling from head to foot.

He reflected that sleep in the open air may prove fatal on a cold night. How could he warm her? How revive her?

He ran despairingly for the man in the melon patch. The man was bending down and did not see him. Valjean went up to him and said without preliminaries:

'A hundred francs!'

The man started and looked up.

'A hundred francs for you, if you can give me shelter for the night.'

The moonlight shone full on his tormented face.

'Why,' said the man, 'why, it's you, Pere Madeleine!'

The sound of his own name, spoken at that hour and in that place by an unknown person, caused Valjean to start in utter amazement. He had been prepared for anything except this. The speaker was a bent and crippled old man clad in working garments, with a leather kneeling-pad on his left knee to which a fair sized bell was fixed. His face, which was in shadow, was not clearly visible.

'In God's name, how did you get in, Pere Madeleine? It's as though you'd fallen from the sky. You'd have scared the life out of me if I hadn't recognized you.'

'Who are you and what is this place?' Jean Valjean asked.

'Do you mean to say you don't know me?'

'No. Nor do I understand how you know me.'

'You saved my life,' the old man said.

He turned, and the moonlight falling upon his face revealed the features of Fauchelevent, who had once been nearly crushed to death beneath a cart.

'Ah,' said Valjean. 'Yes I know you now.'

'So I should hope,' said the old man reproachfully.

'But what is this place?'

'It's the Convent of the Petit-Picpus.'

And then Valjean remembered. Chance, but it is better

to say Providence, had led him to the very convent in the Saint-Antoine quarter where old Fauchelevent, crippled after his accident, had been engaged as gardener on his recommendation.

'Now,' said Fauchelevent, 'perhaps you'll tell me, Pere Madeleine, how the devil you managed to get in here? You may be a saint but you're also a man, and men aren't admitted.'

'But you're here.'

'I'm the only one.'

'All the same,' said Jean Valjean, 'I've got to stop here.'

'Lord preserve us!' exclaimed Fauchelevent.

Valjean drew close to him and said in a grave voice:

'Pere Fauchelevent, I once saved your life. Well, now you can do as much for me.'

At this Fauchelevent burst out:

'I thank God if I can repay something of what I owe you. What do you want me to do?'

'I'll tell you. Have you a room?'

'I have a sort of cottage beyond the ruins of the old convent. No one ever comes near it. There are three rooms.'

'I must ask two things of you,' Valjean said. 'First, that you will tell no one what you know about me. And secondly, that you will not seek to know more than you already do.'

'Your affairs are no business of mine. I am yours to command.'

'Thank you. Now come with me. We must fetch the child.'

'Ah,' said Fauchelevent. 'So there's a child.'

Less than half and hour later Cosette, rosy once more in the warmth of a good fire, was asleep in the old gardener's bed.

The events of which we have witnessed the reverse side, so to speak, had come about in a very simple fashion.

When Jean Valjean escaped from prison in Montreuil-sur-mer, the police had supposed that he would make for Paris. Javert was summoned to Paris to assist in the search for Valjean and had played an important part in his recapture

His zeal and energy on that occasion had attracted the notice of M. Chapouillet, the secretary of the Prefecture. M. Chapouillet had him transferred from Montreuil-sur-mer to Paris.

Javert thought no more about Jean Valjean until in December 1823 his saw his name in a newspaper. His eye fell on a paragraph at the bottom of a page reporting the death of the convict Jean Valjean. The statement was so positive that he had no reason to doubt it and, reflecting that it was good riddance, he dismissed the matter from his mind.

In March 1824 a story reached him about an eccentric individual living in the parish of Saint-Medard who was known as 'the beggar who gives alms'. The man was said to be a person of independent means living with a small girl. An elderly beggar, a former beadle who was now a police informer, supplied further details. The man was a very queer customer, never went out except at night, never spoke to anyone except occasionally to the poor. He wore a wretched old yellow overcoat which was probably worth millions because its lining was stuffed with banknotes. In order to have a look at the queer customer Javert borrowed the ex-beadle's outer garments and the use of the pitch where he huddled every evening, intoning prayers and keeping his eyes open.

The 'suspect' duly appeared and gave the bogus mendicant money. Javert looked up as he did so, and Jean Valjean's shock when he thought he recognized the policeman was no greater than Javert's when he thought he recognized Jean Valjean.

He followed his man to the Gorbeau tenement and got the old woman to talk, which was no difficult matter. She confirmed the detail of the overcoat lined with millions. Javert rented a room in that tenement and occupied it that same evening. He listened at Valjean's door, hoping to hear the sound of his voice; but Valjean foiled him by keeping silent.

Jean Valjean fled the next day; but the sound of the five-franc piece that he let fall on the floor was overheard by the old woman, and she guessed that he intended to leave and hastened to warn Javert. When Valjean left the house that evening with Cosette, Javert was waiting for him, hidden behind the trees along the boulevard.

Why then, had he not at once arrested him? The reason was that he still had doubts.

So he continued tentatively to follow him until, some time later, by the light outside a tavern in the Rue Pontoise, he had a clear view of him and knew positively that this was Jean Valjean.

Then, with a demonic and sensual pleasure, he settled down to enjoy himself. He *played* his man, knowing that he had him, granting him a last illusion of freedom, relishing the situation like a spider with a fly buzzing in its web. His net was shrewdly cast, and he could close it when he chose. But when he reached the centre of his net he found that the fly had vanished.

Nevertheless, when he found that Jean Valjean had escaped him Javert did not lose his head. Convinced that his prey could not be far off, he scoured the district throughout the night. At daybreak he left two men on watch and he returned to Police Headquarters as shamefaced as the fox outwitted by a hen.

The convent of the Petit-Picpus-Saint-Antoine consisted of a number of buildings and a garden. The main building, taken as a whole, was a hybrid block of houses with a barred façade on the Petite Rue Picpus and a *porte-cochere*, No. 62, at its extreme end. It was into this establishment that Jean Valjean had fallen, in Fauchelevent's words, 'out of the sky'. After putting Cosette to bed he and Fauchelevent had a meal in front of a blazing fire and then, there being no other bed, they stretched out on bales of straw. Before closing his eyes, Valjean said, 'I shall have to stay here', and the words exercised Fauchelevent's mind for the rest of the night.

At daybreak, Pere Fauchelevent opened his eyes and looked at Monsieur Madeleine who, seated on his truss of straw, was watching Cosette while she slept. He sat up and said:

'Well, here you are. But how are we going to arrange for you to be here?'

The question summed up the situation, arousing Jean Valjean from his preoccupations, and the two men took counsel together.

'The fact is, Monsieur Madeleine, you've arrived at a fortunate moment – or unfortunate, I should say. One of the ladies is very ill – said to be dying, so the whole community has something on its mind and nobody is going to worry about us. That means that for today we shan't be disturbed, but I can't answer for tomorrow.'

'In any case,' said Jean Valjean, 'this cottage is tucked away behind some sort of ruin. There are trees. Surely it can't be seen from the convent?'

'True, and the nuns never come near it. But there are the children.'

At this point Fauchelevent was interrupted by the single note of a bell. He broke off and signed to Valjean to listen. The bell sounded again.

'So, she's dead,' he said. 'That's the death-knell. That bell will toll once a minute for the next twenty-four hours. Yes, the children play in the garden. They'd spot you in no time, and you'd have the whole lot squealing, "There's a man!"'

'I think I understand,' said Valjean. 'There's a boarding school.' The thought had instantly crossed his mind that it might be a place for the education of Cosette. He said aloud: 'The problem is to stay here.'

'No,' said Fauchelevent. 'The problem is to get out. If you're to be admitted you must come from outside. You can't just be found here like this. For me, you've fallen from Heaven, but that's because I know you. The nuns expect people to come in through the door. But why can't you go out the way you came in? I don't want to ask questions, but how did you get in?'

Jean Valjean had turned pale. The thought of returning to that dreadful street caused him to shudder.

'Impossible,' he said. 'Pere Fauchelevent, you must assume that I've fallen from the skies.'

'And I'm ready to believe it,' said Fauchelevent. 'No need to tell me anything. That child of yours is still asleep. What's her name?'

'Cosette.'

'Is she really yours – as it might be, your granddaughter?'

'Yes.'

'There'll be no trouble getting her out of here. There's a service-door to the outside yard. I knock and the door-keeper opens. It'll just be old Fauchelevent going out with his gardener's hod on his back. She'll be inside the basket, hidden under a piece of sacking. I'll take her to a friend of mine, an old woman who keeps a fruit-shop in the Rue du Chemin-Vert. Then the child can come back here with you. Because I'll find some way of getting you in. I'll have to. But how are you going to get out?'

Fauchelevent was still pondering when a bell rang and he hastily took his own bell off its nail and strapped it to his knee.

'That's for me. The prioress wants me. You wait here, Monsieur Madeleine, and don't move till I come back.'

He went out muttering, 'I'm coming, I'm coming', and Valjean saw him cross the garden as fast as his damaged leg allowed, glancing at his melon-patch as he passed.

When Fauchelevent returned to the cottage, Cosette was awake and Jean Valjean had seated her by the fire. At the moment when Fauchelevent entered he was pointing to the gardener's hod on the wall and saying:

'Listen carefully, my love. We have got to leave this place, but we shall come back here and be happy. The gardener will carry you out on his back in that basket. He will take you to a place where a lady will look after you until I come to fetch you. You must be very good and not say a word, if you do not want Madame Thenardier to catch you.'

Cosette nodded gravely.

Valjean looked round at Fauchelevent.

'Well?'

'Everything's arranged and nothing is. I've got leave to take you to the prioress, but before I can bring you in you've got to go out. That's where the trouble lies.'

Fauchelevent sat muttering, half to himself, 'There's another thing that worries me. I said I'd put earth in it, but that won't do. If it's packed tight it'll be too heavy, and if it's loose it'll shift about, it won't feel like a body. They'll suspect something.'

Valjean was staring at him, unable to follow any of this. The old man went on to explain the situation, the resolve of the Chapter that the dead nun should be interred in the chapel vault according to her wish and in defiance of regulations, the part which he was to play in the affair and a stratagem whereby he would present Valjean to the prioress as his brother and Cosette as his niece. But there remained the problem of the empty coffin.

'What coffin are you talking about?' asked Valjean.

'The municipal coffin. The doctor reports that a nun has died and the Municipality sends round a coffin, and the next day the pall-bearers come round with a hearse and take her off to the cemetery. But if they lift an empty coffin they'll know there's nothing in it.'

'Then you must put something in it.'

'Another dead body? I haven't got one.'

'A living body.'

'What do you mean?'

'Me,' said Jean Valjean.

'You!'

'Why not?' Valjean smiled one of his rare smiles which were like sunshine breaking through a winter sky.

'I have got to get out without being seen, and this is a way of doing it. But where will this empty coffin be?'

'In what is called the mortuary chamber, resting on trestles with a pall over it.'

'Who nails the coffin?'

'I do.'

'Will you be alone?'

'Yes.'

'Can you hide me in the chamber some time during the night when everyone's asleep?'

'Not in the chamber itself. But there's a closet where I keep my burial tools. I have a key to that.'

Fauchelevent sat back, cracking his finger-joints.

'It's impossible.'

'Nonsense. What is so difficult about putting a few nails in a coffin.'

'But how are you to breathe?'

'You must bore a few small holes in the lid over my mouth. And you need not nail the lid too tightly.'

'What worries me,' said Valjean, 'is what will happen at the cemetery.'

'Well, at least that's no problem,' said Fauchelevent. 'If you can survive the coffin I can get you out of the grave. The grave-digger's an old wine-bibber of my acquaintance, Pere Mestienne, a real soak. He'll be easy to handle. I say to him, "Come and have a glass while the Bon Coing is still open." I get him properly soused, which won't take long because he's always halfway there; and I say, "You go on home and I'll do the job for you." Either way there'll be only me and I'll soon have you out of the grave.'

Jean Valjean reached out his hand and Fauchelevent clasped it with a touching display of peasant devotion.

'Then that is settled, Pere Fauchelevent. We shall have no trouble.'

'Provided nothing goes wrong,' reflected Fauchelevent. 'But oh my Lord, if it does!'

On the following afternoon the rare pedestrians on the Boulevard du Maine removed their hats at the passing of an old-style hearse. The procession was making for the Cimetiere Vaugirard. The nuns of the Petit-Picpus had secured the right to be buried in their own corner and at nightfall. The grave-diggers, being thus obliged to work in the evening, were required to observe special rules. The gates were closed directly the sun sank behind the dome of the Invalides. If a grave-digger was still in the cemetery he could only get out by means of the special pass issued to him by the Municipality. There was a sort of letter-box in one of the shutters of the keeper's lodge. He thrust his card through this, and the keeper, hearing it drop, pulled the cord that opened the foot-gate. If he had forgotten to bring his card he shouted his name. In this event the grave-digger paid a fine of fifteen francs.

Fauchelevent was in a state of high delight. Everything had gone according to plan. What remained to be done was trifling. He had helped the rubicund Pere Mestienne, the grave-digger, to get drunk a dozen times in the past two years. Fauchelevent had no misgivings.

The procession pulled up at the gates, where the burial permit had to be shown. During the brief colloquy which ensued between the chief pall-bearer and the keeper, a stranger joined the party, taking his place beside Fauchelevent. He was some sort of workman, clad in a smock with large pockets and carrying a pickaxe under his arm.

Fauchelevent looked at him in some surprise and asked: 'Who are you?'

The man replied: 'I'm the grave-digger.'

The effect on Fauchelevent was as though he had been hit by a cannonball.

'The grave-digger! But – but Pere Mestienne is the grave-digger.'

'Used to be.'

'What do you mean?'

'He's dead.'

Fauchelevent had been prepared for anything except this, that a grave-digger should die. Yet the thing does happen.

Fauchelevent stared open-mouthed, finding scarcely the strength to stammer:

'But Pere Mestienne has always been the grave-digger.'

'Not any more. After Napoleon, Louis XVIII. After Mestienne, Gribier. My name is Gribier.'

Fauchelevent gazed wanly at this Gribier. He was a tall,

thin, sallow man with a face of flawless solemnity. He looked like a failed doctor who had taken up grave-digging. Fauchelevent burst out laughing.

'The things that happen! So Mestienne is dead, poor old Père Mestienne! But Pere Lenoir is still alive. Do you know Pere Lenoir? – the jug of wine on the counter, the flagon of good red Paris wine. Pere Mestienne is dead and I grieve for him. He enjoyed life. But you too, comrade, you enjoy life. Don't you? We must have a glass together in a little while.'

'Countryman, I have seven kids to feed. If they're to eat, I can't afford to drink.' He added with the impressiveness of a man who enjoyed turning a phrase: 'Their hunger is the enemy of my thirst.'

Fauchelevent thought: 'I'm done for.'

Jean Valjean had so arranged himself in the coffin that he could breathe just enough. His plan was going well and had done so from the start. Like Fauchelevent he counted on Pere Mestienne and he had no doubt of the outcome.

Suddenly he felt that he was standing on his head. The bearers and the grave-digger had failed to keep the coffin level and were lowering it head foremost into the grave. His momentary dizziness passed when he was motionless and again horizontal and knew that he was lying on the bottom.

He heard what was like the sound of rain pattering on the lid of the coffin and knew that it was holy water. He thought: 'This will soon be over. An hour at the outside.'

A voice intoned, '*Requiescat in pace*', and a boy's voice replied, '*Amen.*'

Jean Valjean, intently listening, presently heard the sound of departing footsteps.

But then there was a sound above his head that was like the thunder of an avalanche. It was made by a spadeful of earth falling on the coffin-lid.

A second followed and a third. The holes through which he breathed were being covered over.

A fourth spadeful fell.

There are things too strong for even the strongest man. Jean Valjean fainted.

At the graveside while Gribier was about to throw in the fourth spadeful, Fauchelevent's distracted gaze noticed something. Gribier's side-pocket had gaped open and the old man had a glimpse of something white inside. A light of inspiration gleamed in Fauchelevent's eye. While Gribier was still bowed over his shovel he slipped a hand into the open pocket and deftly removed the contents.

The fourth spadeful went in, and Fauchelevent then said in a voice of utmost calm:

'By the way, newcomer, have you got your card – it's nearly sunset.'

Gribier felt in his pocket. He then felt in his other pocket, in every part of his garments.

'It seems I must have forgotten it.'

'Fifteen francs fine,' said Fauchelevent.

Gribier turned green.

May all the saints preserve us! Fifteen francs!'

Gribier dropped his shovel.

This was Fauchelevent's moment.

'Come, come. No need to despair. I'm an old hand. I know all the ins and outs. I'll tell you what you can do. The gates will be shut in five minutes. But you've still got time to get out. I'll stay here and fill in the grave.'

'That's very good of you, countryman.'

'Then off you go,' said Fauchelevent.

Gribier departed at a run and Fauchelevent waited until the sound of his footsteps had died away.

'Pere Madeleine!'

There was no reply.

Trembling so much that he could hardly breathe, Fauchelevent used his chisel and hammer to lever up the lid of the coffin. The face of Jean Valjean shone whitely in the dusk, the eyes were closed.

Fauchelevent gazed down at him and murmured: 'He's dead!' Then he beat his breast and cried: 'So this is how I save him!'

He bent down over Jean Valjean, and suddenly he started back, recoiling as far as the narrow walls of the grave would allow. Valjean's eyes were open and he was looking up at him.

The sight of death is terrible, but the sight of resurrection is scarcely less so. Fauchelevent was for a moment turned to stone, not knowing whether he had to deal with the living or the dead.

'I fell asleep,' said Jean Valjean and sat up.

'Holy Mother of Heaven!' cried Fauchelevent. 'How you frightened me!'

'Let's get out of here quickly. But first a drop of something.' And he got out the flask that he had brought with him.

The flask completed what the fresh air had begun. After a gulp of *eau-de-vie* Valjean was himself again. He got out of the coffin and helped Fauchelevent to re-nail the lid.

They could take their time. The cemetery was closed. The old man took the spade and Valjean took the pick, and together they buried the empty coffin.

An hour later, when it was quite dark, the two men, with Cosette, knocked at the door of No. 62, Petite Rue Picpus.

Next morning two bells were to be heard tinkling in the garden. In short, Jean Valjean with his knee-strap and bell was now installed as a recognized member of the establishment under the name of Ultime Fauchelevent.

What had principally decided the matter was Cosette. The prioress had remarked, 'She will be plain', and made a place for her as a charity pupil at the school. This was entirely logical. The girl who knows herself to be pretty is less likely to become a nun, so the plain ones are much preferred.

As a pupil Cosette had to wear the school uniform. Jean Valjean kept the clothes she discarded, the mourning garments he had brought her when he took her away from the Thenardiers. He packed them together with a great deal of camphor and other aromatics in a small valise and this he kept on a chair by his bed, with the key always in his pocket. Cosette once asked him: 'Father, what is in that box that smells so nice?'

Cosette was allowed to spend an hour with him every day and, since he was very much better company than the nuns, she adored him. She would come running to the cottage when the hour struck, filling it with her presence, and Valjean would glow with a pleasure heightened by the pleasure he gave her. His whole heart was melted in gratitude and his love was magnified.

Thus the years passed and Cosette grew into girlhood.

THREE

Some eight or nine years after the events related, there was to be seen on the Boulevard du Temple and on the streets around the Chateau-d'Eau a boy aged eleven or twelve who went round in a pair of man's trousers that did not come from his father, and a woman's blouse that did not come from his mother, castaway garments bestowed on him out of charity by comparative strangers. He had a father and mother none the less; but his father never gave him a thought and his mother disliked him. He was one of those children who are most to be pitied, those who possess a parent but are still orphans. He was never happier than when he was in the streets, their very flagstones seeming to him less hard than his mother's heart.

Nevertheless, neglected though he was, it happened occasionally, two or three times a month, that the boy said to himself, 'I'll go and see mamma.' So then he headed for the river-embankment, crossed over and, passing through the working-class streets in the direction of the Salpetriere, arrived eventually – where? At no other place than the house numbered 50–52, the Gorbeau tenement.

The 'chief tenant' had died since the days of Jean Valjean, and had been replaced by another exactly like her. The replacement was Madame Bourgon.

The most squalid of all the present occupants of the tenement was a family of four, father and mother and two daughters, quite big girls, living together in the same garret.

At first glance there was nothing remarkable about this family except its state of extreme destitution. This was the family of our lively barefoot urchin. He went there to be greeted by poverty and wretchedness, and, which was worse, never a smile, by hearts as chilly as the room itself. When he entered they asked where he had come from and he answered, 'off the streets'; when he left they asked him where he was going and his answer was, 'back to the streets'. His mother asked, 'Why did you come here?'

His situation caused him no particular distress and he blamed no one. The fact is that he had no idea how parents ought to behave.

But the mother loved his sisters.

We have omitted to mention that on the Boulevard du Temple the boy was known as Gavroche. Why Gavroche? Perhaps for the same reason that had caused his father to adopt the name of Jondrette. To tear up the roots seems to be instinctive with some families of the very poor.

The Jondrettes' garret in the Gorbeau tenement was at the far end of the corridor. The cell next to theirs was occupied by a penniless young man called Monsieur Marius.

It is with Monsieur Marius that we are now concerned.

There are still a few former habitants of the Marais who remember a gentleman called Monsieur Gillenormand and take pleasure in recalling him.

M. Gillenormand was full of life in the year 1831. He was an idiosyncratic old gentleman and most decidedly a man belonging to another age, the complete picture of the somewhat aloof bourgeois of the eighteenth century, wearing his middle-class respectability with all the assurance of a marquis wearing his title. He was over ninety but still walked erect, talked loudly, saw clearly, took wine. He was frivolous, quick-witted and easily irritated, flying into a rage on the least provocation and generally against all reason.

Monsieur Gillenormand revered the Bourbons and held the year 1789 in horror. If any young man dared to praise the Republic in his hearing he turned purple in the face to the point of apoplexy. Monsieur Gillenormand had had two wives and a daughter by each of them. The younger had died at the age of thirty, having married a soldier of fortune who had served in the armies of the Republic and the Empire, been decorated at Austerlitz and promoted colonel at Waterloo. 'A disgrace to the family,' the old gentleman declared.

The elder daughter had never married and she kept house for her father.

There was another member of the household beside those two, a little boy whom Monsieur Gillenormand never addressed except in harsh terms and sometimes with a raised stick. The fact is, he adored him.

The boy was his grandson.

The little boy, whose name was Marius, knew that he had a father but that was all he knew. No one had told him more.

Twice a year, on New Year's Day and on the feast of St George, Marius wrote a letter to his father, dictated by his aunt, which might have been copied from a book on the art of letter-writing. This was all Monsieur Gillenormand would allow. The colonel replied with long, affectionate letters which the old man stuffed in his pocket without reading them.

Marius Pontmercy received the haphazard education of children of his class. When he grew too old for his Aunt Gillenormand, his grandfather entrusted him to a worthy tutor of unsullied classical innocence; thus his growing mind was subject first to a prude and then to a pedant. He did his years of high-school and read law at the university. He was a fanatical and austere royalist with little affection for his grandfather, whose frivolity and cynicism irked him, and with dark thoughts of his father.

In the year 1827, when Marius had just reached the age of seventeen, he came home one evening to find his grandfather awaiting with a letter in his hand.

'Marius,' said Monsieur Gillenormand, 'you are to go to Vernon tomorrow to see your father.'

Marius trembled slightly. Nothing could have been more unexpected, nor, it must be said, more disagreeable to him. Apart from his political reasons for disapproving of him, Marius was persuaded that his father had no affection for him: why else should he have abandoned him to the care of others? Feeling himself unloved, he gave no affection in return.

His grandfather continued:

'It seems that he's ill. He wants to see you.'

There was a pause.

'You'll have to start early,' Monsieur Gillenormand said. 'I understand there's a coach that leaves at six – it gets there by evening. You'll have to catch that. He says it's urgent.'

Marius might, in fact, have left that evening and been with his father the next morning, for there was a night-coach, but neither his grandfather nor he thought to inquire.

He reached Vernon at dusk next evening, when the candles were being lit, and asked the first person he met the way to the home of 'Monsieur Pontmercy'. Arrived at the house, he rang the bell and a woman carrying a small lamp opened the door to him.

'Monsieur Pontmercy?' said Marius.

She looked at him without speaking.

'Is this where he lives?'

She nodded.

'May I speak to him?'

She shook her head.

'But I'm his son. He's expecting me!'

'Not any longer,' she said, as she pointed to the door of a low-ceilinged room and he entered.

There were three men in the room, one standing, one on his knees and the third, in his nightshirt, lying on the floor. The first two were the doctor and a priest; the third was the colonel.

He had been attacked by brainfever three days before and had written to M. Gillenormand asking to see his son. He had grown worse, and that evening had risen from his bed, crying in delirium, 'My son is late. I must go to meet him.' He had collapsed in the antechamber and there had died. By the dim light of the candle a tear was to be discerned on the colonel's pallid cheek. The eye from which it came was sightless, but the tear had not yet dried: it was the measure of his son's delay.

Marius stood looking down at this man whom he was seeing for the first and last time. He reflected that this man was his father and now was dead, and he was unmoved. The grief he felt was no greater than the grief he would have felt in the presence of any dead man.

The colonel had left nothing. The sale of his possessions barely sufficed to cover the cost of the funeral. The house-keeper found a sheet of paper which she handed to Marius. It bore the following message, written in the colonel's hand.

For my son. The Emperor created me a baron on the field of Waterloo. Since the Restoration has refused me this title, paid for with my blood, my son will adopt it and bear it. It goes without saying that he will be worthy of it.

There was a further message on the other side.

My life was saved by a sergeant after Waterloo. His name was Thenardier. I believe that recently he kept an inn in a small village not far from Paris, Chelles, or Montfermeil. If my son should find him he will do Thenardier every service in his power.

Not from any sense of duty towards his father, but from that vague respect for the wishes of the dead which is so strong in men's hearts, Marius kept that missive.

Directly the funeral was over he returned to Paris and resumed his law studies, giving no more thought to his father than if he had never lived.

Marius clung to the religious habits of his childhood. He went regularly to hear Mass at Saint-Sulpice, in the little lady-chapel where he had always sat with his aunt; but one day in a fit of absentmindedness he seated himself unthinkingly behind a pillar on a velvet-upholstered chair bearing the name of 'Monsieur Mabeuf, churchwarden'. The service had scarcely begun when an old man approached him and said:

'Monsieur, that is my place.'

Marius hastily moved and the old man took his seat. But at the end of the service he again approached him.

'You must forgive me for having disturbed you, monsieur. You must have thought me uncivil. I should like to explain.'

'There's no need at all,' said Marius.

'There is indeed. I should like to tell you why I have a particular fondness for that place. It was from there that for some years, at intervals of two to three months, I watched an unhappy father who had no other opportunity of observing his son because he was debarred by a family compact from doing so. He came at the time when he knew the boy would be taken to Mass. The father concealed himself behind that pillar and watched the boy with tears in his eyes. He loved him deeply, as I could not help seeing. So the place has become as it were hallowed for me. I became acquainted with the unhappy man. He died, I believe, not long ago. He lived at Vernon. I forget his name – Pontmarie or Montpercy or something of that kind.'

'The name is Pontmercy,' said Marius, who had turned pale.

'Yes! That's it! But did you know him?'

'He was my father,' Marius said.

The old churchwarden stared at him and exclaimed:

'So, you're the child! Well, of course, you would be grown up by now. My dear lad, you had a father who greatly loved you.'

Marius offered the old man his arm and walked with him to his dwelling. The next day he went straight to the library of the School of Law and asked to see the file of the *Moniteur*.

He read the *Moniteur* and went on to read a number of histories of the Republic and the Empire. His first sight of his father's name in a Grande Armee bulletin put him in a fever of excitement for a week. He called upon generals under whom his father had served. He kept in touch with the churchwarden and learned from him something of his father's life in Vernon. In the end he formed a true picture of the gallant and gentle-hearted man who had been his father.

At the same time his ideas were undergoing a remarkable change. Hitherto the Republic and the Empire had to him been words of ill-omen, the Republic a guillotine in the dusk, the Empire a sword in the night. But when he looked closely he found that it was a night filled with stars –

Mirabeau, Vergniaud, Saint-Just, Robespierre, Camille Desmoulins, Danton, and then the rising of a sun that was Napoleon.

Marius perceived that hitherto he had understood his country no more than he had understood his father. Now he was filled with admiration for the one and adoration for the other.

He was overwhelmed with sorrow at the thought that there was no one except the dead to whom he could talk about what was on his mind. Why had his father died so soon, before age or justice or his son's love could reach him? There was a constant sob of grief in Marius's heart.

When in the course of his secret travail he had completely shed his former skin of a Bourbon-supporter to become wholly a revolutionary, profoundly a democrat and very nearly a republican, he visited an engraver and ordered a hundred visiting-cards bearing the name 'Le Baron Marius Pontmercy'. But since he knew no one, he kept them in his pocket.

Another inevitable consequence was that as he drew nearer to his father, so he moved further away from his grandfather. Marius was filled with resentment at the thought that Monsieur Gillenormand, for nonsensical reasons, had ruthlessly separated him from the colonel. In his newfound reverence for his father he came almost to hate the old man.

But none of this was apparent. Only that he grew more and more reserved and was seldom at home. His grandfather said:

'The boy's in love. I know the symptoms.'

'Where does he go?' his aunt wondered.

On one occasion he went to Montfermeil, obeying his father's injunction to look for the former Waterloo sergeant, the innkeeper Thenardier. But Thenardier had been sold up. Marius's inquiries kept him away from home for four days.

Marius returned home in the early morning. He went straight up to his room and, feeling the need to refresh himself with an hour at the swimming school, went straight off to the baths, having only stopped to shed his top-coat and the black ribbon which he wore round his neck.

Monsieur Gilllenormand, who like all elderly persons in good health had risen early, heard him come in. He hurried up to Marius's attic room meaning only to embrace him and perhaps, by adroit questioning, glean some notion of where he had been. But by the time he had climbed the stairs Marius had gone.

His bed had not been touched and the top-coat and black ribbon lay trustingly upon it.

'Better still,' said Monsieur Gillenormand.

A minute later he was in the drawing-room, where his daughter was busy with her cartwheel embroidery. He made a triumphal entry bringing with him the top-coat and the ribbon.

'Victory!' he cried. 'Now we shall get to the bottom of the mystery.'

A small case of black shagreen, something like a medallion, was attached to the ribbon. The old man examined it for some moments without opening it, savouring it greedily and angrily like a starving beggar witnessing the serving of a rich meal that is not for him.

'Do open it, father,' the old maid said.

The case opened with a spring catch. They found nothing in it but a carefully folded sheet of paper.

'Of course it's a love letter!' cried Monsieur Gillenormand, bursting into laughter.

'We must read it!' his daughter cried.

She put on her glasses and they read it together. What they read was Colonel Pontmercy's dying message to his son.

The effect of this on the old man and his daughter cannot be described. They were chilled as though by the presence of the dead. 'It's the bandit's handwriting, no doubt of that.'

The lady, after inspecting the document from every angle, replaced it in the case. At the same time something had fallen out of a pocket of the top-coat. A small, rectangular packet wrapped in blue paper. Mlle Gillenormand undid it. It contained Marius's hundred visiting-cards. She handed one of them to her father who read: Le Baron Marius Pontmercy.

The old man rang the bell for Nicolette. He picked up the ribbon, case and top-coat and tossed them into them middle of the room.

'Take those things away.'

A full hour passed in total silence. At length, Mlle Gillenormand said:

'Pretty!'

A few minutes later Marius appeared. Before he had even crossed the threshold his grandfather, who still had one of the visiting-cards in his hand, cried out in the sneering, bourgeois tone of voice which was so crushing in its effect:

'Well, well, well, well – so it seems you're a baron! My compliments. May I ask what this means?'

Marius flushed slightly.

'It means that I'm my father's son.'

Monsieur Gillenormand ceased to smile and said harshly:

'I am your father.'

'My father,' said Marius, speaking steadfastly with low-ered eyes, 'was a humble, heroic man who gallantly served the Republic of France and was great in the greatest chapter of human history.'

The high colour drained out of the old man's face until his cheeks were as white as his hair. He said with a smile that was almost calm:

'A baron like this gentleman and a bourgeois like myself cannot live under the same roof.'

Then, white and trembling, his forehead swelling in the terrible blaze of his wrath, he pointed a hand at Marius and cried:

'Clear out!'

Marius left the house.

He went off without saying where he was going, or know-ing himself, with thirty francs in his pocket, his watch and a few clothes in an overnight bag. Hailing a cab, he had himself driven at random to the Latin quarter.

What was to become of Marius?

Beneath the surface of that seemingly apathetic age there was a faint revolutionary stir. Gusts from the depths of '89 and '92 were again to be felt in the air. Youth, if we may be allowed the phrase, was on the move. Attitudes were changing, almost unconsciously, in accordance with the changing times. Royalists were becoming liberals, liberals were becoming democrats.

There did not yet exist in France such vast, widespread organizations as the German Tugenbund or the Italian Carbonari; but small, obscure cells were ramifying. The Cougourde was taking shape in Aix, and in Paris, along with similar bodies, there was the Society of Friends of the ABC.

The ABC Society was small in numbers, no more than a secret society in embryo. They had two meeting places in Paris, the one a drinking-place called Corinthe, near Les Halles, and the other a small cafe on the Place Saint-Michel, the Cafe Musain. The first was handy for the workers, the second for the students.

The councils of the ABC Society were held as a rule in a back room of the Cafe Musain. Most of the members were students having friendly relations with a number of workers. These are the names of the more important, those who have, to some extent, a place in history: Enjolras, Combeferre, Jean Prouvaire, Feuilly, Courfeyrac, Bahorel, Lesgle or Laigle, Joly, Grantaire. These young men formed a sort of family, united by friendship. All except Laigle came from the Midi.

On a certain afternoon, Laigle de Meaux stood voluptuously propped in the doorway of the Cafe Musain, idle except for his thoughts. Through the mists of his meditations, he drowsily perceived a two-wheeled vehicle moving slowly round the Place as though uncertain of its destination. Seated in the cab was a young man with a bulky travelling bag to which was affixed a card bearing in large black letters the name Marius Pontmercy.

The sight of this name aroused Laigle. He straightened himself and called:

'Monsieur Marius Pontmercy?'

The cab stopped. The young man, who seemed also to have been plunged in thought, looked up.

'I've been looking for you,' said Laigle de Meaux.

'What do you mean?' asked Marius, who had just left his grandfather's house and was now staring at somebody he had never seen before. 'I don't know you.'

'I don't know you either,' said Laigle. 'Weren't you at Law School the day before yesterday?'

'Possibly.'

'You certainly were.'

'Are you a student?' asked Marius.

'Yes, monsieur, I am a student like yourself, and the day before yesterday I chanced to drop in at the school. The professor was calling the roll. As you know, they're particularly tiresome on these occasions. If you fail to answer after your name has been called three times it is struck off the list. The professor was Blondeau. He had craftily begun the roll-call with the letter P, and I wasn't paying attention because that isn't my initial. But when he called "Marius Pontmercy" there was no reply. He repeated it more loudly, looking hopeful, and when there was still no reply he picked up his pen. I thought to myself, here is a good man about to be struck off. Here is a noble idler who enjoys life, and he must be saved. And so, when Blondeau repeated for the third time, "Marius Pontmercy," I answered, "Present!" In consequence, you were not struck off, but I was.'

'Why?' asked Marius.

'It's quite simple. With a diabolical cunning he switched back to the letter L. My name is Laigle. So Blondeau called out the name and I answered "Present!" upon which, looking at me with a tigerish satisfaction, he smiled and said, "If you are Pontmercy you cannot be Laigle." Having said which, he struck me off.'

'I'm mortified,' said Marius.

Laigle burst out laughing.

'And I'm delighted. I was in danger of becoming a lawyer and this has saved me. I would like to pay you a visit of gratitude. Where do you live?'

'In this cab,' said Marius.

At this moment Courfeyrac emerged from the cafe. Marius was smiling sadly.

'I have had it for two hours and I would like to get out of it. The fact is, I don't know where to go.'

'Monsieur,' said Courfeyrac, 'come to the place where I live.'

'I should have the priority,' said Laigle, 'but I don't live anywhere.'

Courfeyrac got into the cab and directed the driver to the Hotel de la Porte Saint-Jacques. By the evening Marius was installed in that hotel, in a room next to Courfeyrac's own.

Within a few days, Marius and Courfeyrac were friends. Youth is a time of quick resilience and the rapid healing of wounds. Marius found that in company with Courfeyrac he could breathe freely, a sufficiently novel experience.

One morning, Courfeyrac asked abruptly:

'By the way, have you any political views?'

'Of course,' said Marius, slightly ruffled.

'Well, what are you?'

'I'm a Bonapartist democrat.'

'A wary compromise,' commented Courfeyrac.

The next day he took Marius to the Cafe Musain. Murmuring with a smile, 'I must introduce you to the revolution', he led him into the back room used by the ABC Society and presented him to his friends with the words, 'A novice.'

Marius had fallen into a hornet's nest of lively minds. New vistas were opened up and since he could not get them in any perspective he was not sure that they were not visions of chaos. When he discarded his grandfather's views in favour of those of his father he had thought that his mind was made up; but now, in some perturbation and without wholly admitting it to himself, he began to suspect that this was not the case. His whole outlook began again to change; all his previous notions were called in question in a process of internal upheaval that he found almost painful. It seemed that his new friends held nothing sacred.

In his troubled state of mind, Marius gave little heed to certain prosaic aspects of life; but they were matters that could not be ignored. They brought themselves abruptly to his notice. The hotelkeeper came to his room and said:

'Monsieur Courfeyrac has vouched for you, has he not?'

'Yes.'

'But I need money.'

'Will you please ask Monsieur Courfeyrac if he can spare me a moment?'

Courfeyrac came to see him, and Marius told him what he had not thought of telling him until then, that for practical purposes he was alone in the world, having no parents.

'So what's to become of you?' asked Courfeyrac.

'I don't know,' said Marius.

'How much money have you?'

'Fifteen francs.'

'Do you want me to lend you some?'

'No – never.'

'Have you any jewellery?'

'A watch, gold. Here it is.'

'I know a second-hand dealer who will take your tail-coat and spare pair of trousers and I know a clockmaker who will buy your watch.'

'That's good.'

'No, it isn't good. What will you do when your money's gone? Do you know English or German?'

'No.'

'That's a pity. A friend of mine, a bookseller, is compiling a kind of encyclopaedia. You might have translated articles for it, from English or German. It's badly paid work, but one can live on it.'

'Then I'll learn English and German.'

'And in the meantime?'

'I'll live on my clothes and my watch.'

Marius left the Hotel de la Porte Saint-Jacques, not wanting to run further into debt.

Life became very hard for Marius. To have eaten his clothes and his watch was nothing; he had now to chew the cud of utmost necessity. It was a horrible time of days without food, nights without sleep, a hearth without a fire, and a future without hope. With all this he continued his law-studies and qualified as an advocate. Officially he shared Courfeyrac's chambers, which were presentable and contained a sufficient number of law-books, filled out with tattered novels, to constitute the library required by regulations. He had his letters sent to Courfeyrac's address.

Poverty is like everything else. In the end it becomes bearable. One continues to exist in a wretched sort of way that is just sufficient to sustain life. This is what happened to Marius Pontmercy.

He had got over the worst and the road ahead of him looked somewhat smoother. He learnt German and English and, thanks to Courfeyrac, who introduced him to his bookseller friend, he was able to fill the humble role of a literary 'devil'. The net result was an average income of seven hundred francs, on which he contrived to live, not too badly.

Marius was now twenty. It was three years since he had parted from his grandfather. Although he was now an advocate, he did not plead in the courts. Day-dreaming had given him a distaste for the law. The thought of consorting with attorneys, hanging about courts, chasing after briefs, was odious to him.

Marius enjoyed going for long walks – along the outer boulevards on the Champ de Mars, or in the less frequented streets around the Luxembourg. He would spend long periods contemplating the market gardens – vegetable plots, poultry scratching amid the dung. Strangers looked at him with surprise, and sometimes even with suspicion. But it was only an impecunious young man dreaming the hours away.

It was during one of these walks that he discovered the Gorbeau tenement and attracted by its cheapness and isolation, had rented a room there. He was known there only as Monsieur Marius.

During the past year or more he had noticed, on an alleyway in the Luxembourg garden, an elderly man with a very young girl, nearly always seated side by side on a bench at the more deserted end of the alleyway near the Rue de l'Ouest. Whenever Marius's meditative strolls took him in that direction, and this happened very often, he was likely to see them. The man, who was perhaps sixty, had a grave and serious look, his robust, wearied aspect conveying the impression that he had been a soldier. He looked good-natured but unapproachable, and he never returned the glance of a passer-by. His hair was very white.

The girl, when first Marius had noticed them, was aged thirteen or fourteen. She was skinny to the point of ugliness, awkward and insignificant, although her eyes promised to be beautiful. Her clothes were the mixture of too-old and too-young which is commonly seen on boarders at convent schools – a badly cut dress of coarse black merino. They seemed to be father and daughter.

Prompted by the girl's black clothes and the man's white hair, he had christened them 'Mlle Lanoire' and 'Monsieur Leblanc'. Thus for the first year Marius saw them almost daily in the same place at the same time. He liked the look of the man but took no interest in the girl.

But it happened in the second year, at precisely the point which our story has now reached, that Marius changed his itinerary, for no particular reason, and for some six months did not set foot in that alleyway. Then one day he went back and there was the same couple, seated on the same bench. But as he drew near them he was struck by a change. The man was the same, but the girl was not. What he now saw was a tall and beautiful creature, soft chestnut hair flecked with gold, a forehead of marble, cheeks like rose-petals, a pale sensitive skin, an exquisite mouth.

Marius could not see her eyes, which were modestly veiled by her long, chestnut lashes; but this did not prevent her from smiling as she listened to what the white-haired man was saying, and nothing could have been more alluring than that smile from beneath lowered lids.

She was no longer a schoolgirl in a plush hat and woollen dress. She had acquired taste as well as beauty and was now dressed with simple, unpretentious elegance.

The man, however, was unchanged.

Marius went by their bench. The girl looked up at him and their eyes met.

What message was to be read in her eyes? Marius could not have said. Nothing and yet everything. A spark had passed between them.

What he had encountered was not the frank innocent gaze of a child. There comes a day when every girl has this look in her eyes, and woe to him who encounters it! She looked steadily at him with a soft pensive glance that caused him to tremble from head to foot. Marius was in the first violent and entranced throes of a grand passion.

A single look had done it.

A whole month went by during which he went daily to the Luxembourg. Nothing was allowed to deter him. He was in a state of constant rapture, knowing that the girl saw him.

While still talking calmly and naturally to her father, she would bestow on Marius all the dreams and secret fervours of her virgin gaze.

But it seemed that Monsieur Leblanc had begun to suspect what was happening, because quite often when Marius appeared he got to his feet and they strolled on. He exchanged their usual bench for one at the other end of the alleyway to see whether Marius would follow them there. Marius failed to understand and made the mistake of doing so. Then Monsieur Leblanc became irregular in his visits and did not always bring his daughter with him. When this happened Marius did not linger, which was another mistake.

Marius took no account of these portents. One evening he found a handkerchief lying on a bench that Monsieur Leblanc and his daughter had just left. It was plain white and of fine material, and it seemed to him to be impregnated with the most exquisite of scents. He snatched it up with rapture. It bore the initials U.F. At that time Marius knew nothing whatsoever about the girl. The two letters were a first clue on which he at once proceeded to erect a scaffolding of surmise. Clearly the U stood for her Christian name – 'Ursula,' he thought. 'A delicious name!' He kissed the handkerchief and wore it next to his heart by day and kept it under his pillow at night.

In fact, the handkerchief belonged to the old gentleman and had simply fallen out of his pocket.

Thereafter he never appeared in the Luxembourg without his handkerchief, pressing it to his lips or clasping it to his breast. The girl could make nothing of this and showed as much by her expression.

'Such modesty!' sighed Marius.

Marius had already made two blunders, the first in continuing to haunt them after they had changed their bench, and the second in leaving the garden whenever Monsieur Leblanc went there alone. Now he was guilty of a third and far greater one. He followed his 'Ursula'. He found that she lived in the Rue de l'Ouest, in a modest-seeming house at the quiet end of the street. Thanks to this discovery he could add to the joy of seeing her in the Luxembourg the delight of following her home. But his appetite still grew.

One evening, having followed them to the house and seen them go in by the *porte-cochère*, he went in after them and boldly addressed the porter.

'Was that the gentleman on the first floor, the one who has just come in?'

'No, monsieur. He's the gentleman on the third floor.'

'What is his name?' asked Marius.

The porter looked hard at him and asked:

'Is monsieur connected with the police?'

This silenced Marius, but nevertheless he went off highly pleased with himself. He was making progress.

The next day Monsieur Leblanc and his daughter paid only a short visit to the Luxembourg, leaving early in the afternoon. Marius followed them home as usual; but when they reached the door Monsieur Leblanc, after standing aside to let the girl go in, turned and stared at him.

On the next day they did not come to the Luxembourg at all.

Again, on the following day, they did not appear.

Fearing to keep watch on the house by daylight, Marius went to the house as night was falling. There were no lights to be seen. Marius knocked at the *porte-cochère* and said to the porter:

'The gentleman on the third floor?'

'He's left.'

Marius reeled and asked feebly:

'Where has he gone?'

'I've no idea!'

'Didn't he leave an address?'

'No.'

The porter then recognized Marius. He glared at him and said:

'So it's you again! Well, you must certainly be a nark of some kind.'

Summer and autumn passed, and winter came. Neither Monsieur Leblanc nor the girl had set foot in the Luxembourg. Marius had but one thought, which was to see that enchanting face again. He had searched endlessly and everywhere, but without success. He was plunged in black despair. Work disgusted him, walking tired him, solitude bored him: the vast world of Nature, hitherto so filled for him with light and meaning, had become an emptiness. Everything, it seemed, had disappeared.

All human societies have what is known in the theatre as an 'under-stage'. During the years 1830–35 a quartet of villains,

Claquesous, Gueulemer, Babet and Montparnasse, ruled the underworld of Paris.

They were the setters of traps, the stabbers in the back. Persons desiring this kind of service, men with dark ambitions, applied to them. They were accustomed to meet at nightfall, a time of their awakening, in the wasteland near the Salpetriere. Here they took counsel together; with twelve hours of darkness ahead of them, they decided upon its use.

This four-man syndicate was known to the underworld by the name of '*Patron-Minette*'. One may sometimes deduce the nature of a play from the names of the characters; in the same way, one may get some idea of the nature of a gang. Here then are the names of the principal accomplices of Patron-Minette, names still to be found in the police archives:

Panchaud, alias Printanier, alias Bigrenaille

Brujon

Boulatruelle

Les-pieds-en-l'air

Demi-liard, or Deux-milliards

We may omit the rest, which were not the worst. Faces can be put to all those names. They stand, not only for individuals, but for types, each representing a variety of the misshapen fungi growing in the underworld of civilization.

Marius was still living in the Gorbeau tenement, indifferent to the people around him. As it happened, at that time the house was empty except for himself and the Jondrettes, the family of father, mother and daughters to none of whom he had spoken.

On one particular day that winter, it was 2 February, the ancient feast of Candlemas, Marius emerged from his own den as darkness was falling. It was time for dinner. Making for the Rue Saint-Jacques, he went slowly along the boulevard. Suddenly he was jostled in the mist by two shabbily dressed girls, breathlessly dashing in his direction as though they were running away from something. One was tall and thin, the other rather smaller.

The tall one was saying:

'The cops came along. They near as anything got me.'

The other said:

'I saw. I didn't half run for it.'

From which Marius gathered that, young as they were, they had had a brush with the gendarmes or the city police but had managed to escape.

He stood for a moment staring after them as they disappeared under the trees of the boulevard. Then, as he was about to continue on his way, he noticed a small, greyish object lying on the ground near him. He picked it up. It was a wrapping of sorts, evidently containing papers.

One of the girls must have dropped it as they passed. He turned and called after them but failed to make them hear, and so eventually, putting the package in his pocket, he went on to dinner.

When he undressed that night he found the package in his pocket, having forgotten about it, and it occurred to him that it might contain the girls' address, or that of the owner if it was not they who had dropped it.

He undid the wrapping, and found that it contained four letters, all addressed but also unsealed, and all smelling strongly of cheap tobacco.

The first was addressed to 'The Benevolent Gentleman outside the church of Saint-Jacques-du-Haut-Pas'.

Benevolent Sir,

If you will be so good as to accompany my daughter you will be the witness of a shattered life and I will show you my certificates. This letter in itself will, I know, cause your generous spirit to be inspired with a sense of lively benevolence, for the truly philosophical are always a prey to strong emotions.

I await your visit or your gift, if you are so kind as to make me one, and beg you to accept the sentiments of profound respect with which I subscribe myself,

> your most humble and obedient servant,
> P. Fabantou, artist of the drama

Having read the four letters, Marius found that he had not discovered what he wanted to know, since none bore the address of the writer. However, they were interesting in other respects. Although they purported to come from four different people, all were in the same handwriting, written on the same coarse, yellowed paper and impregnated with the same smell of tobacco; but there was nothing to indicate that they were the property of the two girls who had jostled him on the boulevard. He wrapped them up again, tossed them into a corner and went to bed.

The next morning there was a tap at his door.

'Come in,' said Marius without looking up from the papers on his writing-table. 'What is it, Ma'am Bougon?'

But the voice that answered, saying 'I beg your pardon, monsieur', was not that of Ma'am Bougon. It was more like the voice of a bronchitic old man, half-stifled, rendered husky as though by the drinking of spirits.

Marius looked up sharply and saw that his visitor was a girl, standing in the open doorway, facing the pallid light of the one small window in Marius's garret. She was a lean and delicate-looking creature, her shivering nakedness clad in nothing but a chemise and skirt. Bony shoulders emerged from the chemise, and the face above them was sallow and flabby. But what was tragic about the girl was that she had not been born ugly. A trace of beauty still lingered in the sixteen-year-old face, like pale sunlight fading beneath the massed clouds of a winter's dawn.

The face was not quite unfamiliar to Marius. He had a notion that he had seen her before.

'What can I do for you, mademoiselle?'

She answered in her raucous voice:

'I've got a letter for you, Monsieur Marius.'

So she knew his name. But how did she come to know it?

Without awaiting any further invitation she walked in, looking about her with a pathetic boldness at the untidy room with its unmade bed.

As he took the letter Marius noted that the large wafer sealing it was still damp. It could not have come very far. He read:

Most estimable young man!

My elder daughter will tell you that for two days we have been without food, four of us, including my sick wife. If I am not deceived in my trust in humanity I venture to hope that your generous heart will be moved by our affliction and that you will relieve your feelings by coming to my aid.

I am, with the expression of the high esteem we all owe to a benefactor of humanity,

Yours truly,
Jondrette

P.S. My daughter is at your service, dear Monsieur Marius.

This missive threw an immediate light on the problem that had been perplexing Marius. All was now clear. It came from the same source as the other letters – the same handwriting, the same paper, even the same smell of rank tobacco. He now had five letters, all the work of Jondrette – if, indeed, that was his real name.

During the time Marius had been living in the tenement he had paid little or no attention even to his nearest neighbours, his thoughts being elsewhere. Although he had more than once encountered members of the Jondrette family in the corridor or on the stairs, they had been to him no more than shadows of whom he had taken so little notice that he had failed to recognize the two daughters when they bumped into him on the boulevard; even now, in the shock of his pity and repugnance, he had difficulty in realizing that this must be one of them.

Marius sat pondering while he watched her. She drew near to his writing-table.

'Books!' she said.

A light dawned in her clouded eyes. She announced, with the pride in attainment from which none of us is immune: 'I know how to read, I can write too.' She dipped the pen in the ink and looked at Marius. 'I'll write something to show you.'

Before he could say anything she had written on a blank sheet lying on the table: 'Watch out, the bogies are around.'

She laid down the pen. 'No spelling mistakes. We've had some schooling, my sister and me. We haven't always been what we are now. We weren't brought up to be –'

But here she stopped and gazing with her dulled eyes at Marius she burst out laughing. In a tone in which the extreme of anguish was buried beneath the extreme of cynicism, she exclaimed: 'What the hell!'

She fell to examining Marius and said with a coy look:

'Do you know, Monsieur Marius, that you're a very handsome boy?'

Drawing nearer, she laid a hand on his shoulder.

'You never notice me, Monsieur Marius, but I know you by sight. It suits you, you know, having your hair untidy.'

She was striving to make her voice soft but could only make it sound more guttural. Marius drew gently away.

'I think, mademoiselle,' he said with his accustomed cold gravity, 'that I have something belonging to you. Allow me to return it.'

He handed her the wrapping containing the four letters. She clapped her hands and cried:

'We looked for that everywhere!'

Seizing it eagerly, she began to unfold it, talking as she did so:

'Heavens, if you knew how we'd searched, my sister and me! And so you're the one who found it.'

By now she had fished out the letter addressed to 'The Benevolent Gentleman outside the church of Saint-Jacques-du-Haut-Pas'.

'Ah, this is for the old boy who goes to Mass. Well, it's nearly time so I'd better run along and catch him. Perhaps he'll give me enough for our dinner. And do you know what that will mean? It will be breakfast and dinner for yesterday and the day before – the first meal for three days.'

This reminded Marius of why she had called upon him. He felt in his waistcoat pocket and succeeded in retrieving a five-franc piece.

'The sun's come out at last!' she cried, eagerly accepting the coin.

On her way to the door she noticed a crust of stale bread gathering dust on the chest of drawers. She snatched it up and started to devour it.

'It's good, it's tough – something to get your teeth into!' And she departed.

Marius had lived through five years of penury and deprivation, sometimes of great hardship; but, as he perceived, he had never known the meaning of utter destitution, until he encountered it in the person of that girl. To witness the abjection of men is not enough: one must also witness the abjection of women: and even this pales before the abjection of a child.

Marius was near to reproaching himself for his habit of abstraction and for the love-affair which until then had prevented him from giving a thought to his neighbours. Certainly they appeared utterly depraved, corrupt and odious; but it is rare for those who have sunk so low not to be degraded in the process, and there comes a point, moreover, where the unfortunate and the infamous are grouped together, merged in a single, fateful word. They are *les misérables* – the outcasts, the underdogs. And who is to blame? Is it not the most fallen who have most need of charity?

While he thus lectured himself Marius was staring at the wall which separated him from the Jondrettes. The wall was in fact no more than a lath-and-plaster partition with a few upright posts. Half-unconsciously Marius examined it while still pursuing his train of thought. Suddenly he stood up. In the upper part of the wall, near the ceiling, there was a triangular hole between three laths where the plaster had crumbled away. By standing on the chest of drawers one could see through it into the Jondrettes' garret. 'Let us see what these people are like,' said Marius, 'and how bad things really are.'

He got up on the chest of drawers, put his eye to the aperture and looked through.

*

Marius was poor and his own room was a barren place, but, as his poverty was high-minded so was his garret clean. The dwelling into which he looked was filthy, squalid and altogether noisome. Its only lighting came through the grimy, cobwebbed panes of a small dormer-window which admitted just sufficient light to make the face of a man look like that of a ghost. The walls had a leprous appearance, being covered with cracks and scars like a human face disfigured by some repellent disease.

Seated at a table, on which Marius could see a pen, paper and ink, was a small man of about sixty, lean, sallow-faced and haggard, with an expression of restless and wary cunning. He had a long, grey beard. He was clad above the waist in a woman's chemise, and below the waist in muddied trousers and a pair of top-boots from which his toes protruded.

He was smoking a pipe (there might be no food in the place, but there was still tobacco!) and busily writing – doubtless a letter similar to those Marius had already seen.

A burly woman who might have been aged forty or a hundred was squatting on bare heels by the fireplace. Although she was in a crouching position she was evidently a very tall woman, a giantess by comparison with her husband.

On one of the truckle-beds a skinny, pale-faced child, almost naked, was seated. This was presumably the younger sister of the one who had called on Marius. At first sight she appeared to be no more than eleven or twelve, but a second glance showed that she was at least fifteen.

Marius was about to get down from his post of observation when a sound caused him to stay where he was. The door opened abruptly and the elder girl came in.

Slamming the door behind her, she cried in triumph:

'He's coming!'

'Who's coming?' the father asked.

'The old gent, the philanthropist from the Eglise Saint-Jacques, he's following me.'

The man drew himself to his full height while a sort of radiance spread over his face. He said to the older girl:

'Is it cold out?'

'Bitterly cold. It's snowing.'

He turned to the younger girl, seated on the bed by the window, and bellowed at her:

'Move, you idle slut. Get down to the end of the bed and smash a window-pane.'

'Smash a window-pane?'

'You heard what I said.'

She stood up on the bed. By standing on tip-toe she could just reach the dormer window. In terrified obedience she punched it with her fist, and the pane broke and fell with a clatter to the floor.

The woman, who had so far not uttered a word, now stood up and said:

'My dear, what is all this for?'

'Get into bed,' he answered.

The peremptory tone admitted of no dispute. She flung herself heavily on their bed. At that moment a sob was heard.

'Now what's the matter?' the man demanded.

The younger girl, without emerging from the darkness of the corner where she was now crouched, held up a bleeding arm. She had taken refuge by her mother's bed and was crying. It was the mother's turn to start upright.

'There! She's cut herself breaking the window-pane.'

'Good. I thought she would.'

Tearing a strip off the chemise he was wearing, he rapidly bandaged the child's wrist. 'Better and better,' he said. 'Now we've got a torn shirt as well.'

Gazing about him to make sure that nothing had been overlooked, the man announced:

'Now we're ready for the philanthropist.'

At this moment there was a light tap on the door. The man dashed to open it, bowing almost to the ground as he did so.

'Please come in, my dear sir! My noble benefactor, please enter, with your charming young lady.'

An elderly man and a young girl appeared in the doorway; and Marius, still at his peep-hole, was seized with a wonderment that it is beyond the power of words to describe.

It was She.

She! Everyone who has ever loved will feel the force of that small word. In the luminous mist that suddenly clouded his vision Marius could scarcely distinguish the sweet face that had lighted his life for six months and then vanished, plunging him in darkness. And now the vision had reappeared – in this setting of unspeakable squalor!

The garret was so dark that to anyone coming from outside it was like entering a cavern. The newcomers therefore moved uncertainly, scarcely able to distinguish the objects around them, whereas they themselves were entirely visible to the denizens of the cavern, whose eyes were accustomed to the half-light. Monsieur Leblanc, with his kind, melancholy gaze turned to Jondrette, said:

'Monsieur, you will find a few things in the parcel – woollen stockings and blankets and suchlike.'

'Most noble sir, you overwhelm me,' said Jondrette.

Monsieur Leblanc said uncertainly:

'I see that you are greatly to be pitied, monsieur –' and he paused.

'Fabantou,' said Jondrette promptly. 'An actor, monsieur, who has had some success in his time, but now, alas, I am overwhelmed with misfortune. We are without food, monsieur, and without heating. A broken window – in this weather. My wife ill in bed, and our younger daughter injured.'

The child, distracted by the newcomers, was so absorbed in contemplating the young lady that her sobs had ceased.

'Bawl, can't you?' muttered Jondrette under his breath, and, operating with the dexterity of a pickpocket, he gave her wrist a smart pinch. It drew a loud yell from her, and the lovely girl whom Marius had christened Ursula started forward.

'Oh, the poor child!' she exclaimed.

For some moments Jondrette had been gazing intently at the 'philanthropist', as though he were trying to remember something. He then resumed his lament.

'And do you know what is going to happen to us

tomorrow? Tomorrow is the last day our landlord will allow us. If by this evening I have not paid in full we shall all be turned out – turned out into the street without shelter from the snow and rain! That is the position, monsieur. I owe four quarters' rent, a whole year, making sixty francs!'

Monsieur Leblanc got a five-franc piece out of his pocket and laid it on the table; and Jondrette found a moment to whisper in his daughter's ear:

'See that? The bastard! What the devil's the good of five francs?'

Monsieur Leblanc meanwhile was taking off the brown overcoat he wore over his blue tail-coat. He laid it across the back of the chair and said:

'Five francs is all I have left on me at the moment. But I'll take my daughter home and come back this evening. I think you said you need the money by this evening.'

Jondrette's face was suddenly and wonderfully illumined. He replied eagerly:

'Quite right, most worthy sir. I have to be at my landlord's by eight o'clock.'

'Then I'll come at six and I'll bring you the sixty francs.'

Taking his daughter's arm, Monsieur Leblanc turned towards the door. But as they were in the act of leaving the elder Jondrette girl exclaimed:

'Monsieur, you're forgetting your overcoat.'

Jondrette darted a blistering look at her, accompanied by a massive shrug of the shoulders. Monsieur Leblanc said smiling:

'I hadn't forgotten. I'm leaving it here.'

'My protector!' cried Jondrette. 'Allow me to accompany you to your fiacre.'

'In that case you had better put the coat on,' said Monsieur Leblanc. 'It is really very cold.'

The visitors left the room together, with Jondrette leading the way.

*

Marius had missed nothing of the foregoing scene, and yet in a sense he had seen nothing. His eyes had been intent upon the girl. His only thought when she had departed was to follow on her footsteps until at least he had found out where she lived and ran no risk of losing her again. But on the verge of opening his door, he hesitated. Monsieur Leblanc would probably not yet have got back to his fiacre. If he should look round and see Marius in that house he might well take fright and again find the means of eluding him.

He hovered in perplexity, and at length, deciding that he must run the risk of being seen, he left his room. He arrived on the boulevard just in time to see a fiacre turn the corner, heading back into Paris. It was already a long way ahead, and there seemed to be no way of overtaking it. Certainly he could not do so on foot. He went back to the tenement in despair.

He might have reflected that Monsieur Leblanc had promised to return that evening, and at this time he might be more successful in his efforts to track him down; but such was his state of dejection that the thought scarcely occurred to him.

As he was about to enter the house he saw Jondrette, enveloped in the 'philanthropist's' overcoat, standing in conversation with one of those sinister individuals known as 'gateway prowlers'. Despite Marius's melancholy preoccupations, the thought crossed his mind that the man Jondrette was talking to resembled a certain Panchaud, alias Bigrenaille, who had been pointed out to him by Courfeyrac and was regarded in the quarter as a dangerous night-bird.

Marius went into his garret, pushing the door behind him. But the door did not shut, and turning, he saw that a hand was holding it ajar. It was the elder Jondrette girl.

'So, it's you again,' said Marius almost harshly. 'What do you want now?'

She did not reply but stood thoughtfully regarding him, seeming to have lost all her earlier assurance.

'Monsieur Marius,' she said, 'you seem upset. What is the matter?'

'There is nothing the matter with me.'

'You were generous this morning. Be kind now. You gave me money for food, now tell me what your trouble is. Is there nothing I can do for you? You have only to say.'

He drew closer to her, a drowning man clutching at a straw.

'Well, you brought that gentleman here, with his daughter. Do you know their address?'

'No.'

'Can you find out for me?'

'Get you the address of the beautiful young lady?'

The note of sarcasm irritated Marius. He said impatiently:

'The address of father and daughter. *Their* address.'

She looked hard at him.

'What will you give me?'

'Anything you want.'

'Then I'll get it.'

She abruptly withdrew, closing the door behind her.

Marius dropped on to a chair and leaned forward with both elbows on his bed and his head in his hands, rendered almost giddy by the thought of all that had happened in so brief a time. But suddenly he started up.

The harsh voice of Jondrette was loudly raised next door, speaking words that instantly intrigued him.

'I tell you I'm sure. I recognized him.'

To whom else could he be referring, if not to Monsieur Leblanc? Without another thought Marius leapt rather than climbed on to the chest of drawers and again stood peering through his spy-hole into the Jondrettes' lair.

Nothing had changed except that the woman and the two girls had undone the parcel and were now wearing stockings and vests. Two new blankets lay on the beds.

Jondrette, who had evidently just come in, was still gasping with the chill of the outside air. The girls were seated on the floor by the fireplace. The woman was huddled on one of the beds staring in astonishment while her husband strode up and down the room. She asked hesitantly:

'Really? Are you sure?'

'Of course I'm sure. It's eight years, but I recognized him all right. Do you mean to say you didn't?'

'No.'

'He's scarcely aged in eight years. He's better dressed, that's all. . .' He broke off to address the two girls. 'Clear out, you two.'

The girls got submissively to their feet. As they reached the door Jondrette took the elder by the arm and said with particular emphasis:

'You're to be back here at exactly five o'clock. Both of you. I'm going to need you.'

Left alone with his wife, Jondrette said:

'And I'll tell you another thing. That girl . . .'

Marius was now in a state of feverish expectation, but Jondrette had bent over the woman and was talking in a whisper. Straightening up, he concluded:

'That's who she is.'

'*Her*?' said the woman. 'Impossible! Our daughters barefoot and that one in satin and fur and ankle boots!'

'I tell you it is. You'll see. This is going to make our fortune. It's all arranged. I've been talking to people. He's coming at six, bringing the sixty francs. At six, when the fine fellow next door goes off to dine and old mother Bougon's out on a cleaning job. There won't be a soul in the place. The girls will keep watch, you'll help us, and he'll cough up.'

'But supposing he doesn't?'

Jondrette made a gesture. 'We'll know what to do about it.'

For the first time Marius heard him laugh, a cold, soft laugh that made him shudder. Jondrette went to a cupboard and got out an old cap which he put on his head after brushing it with his sleeve.

'I've got to go out again. There are some other men I've got to see, real good 'uns.' He stood in thought for a moment, with his hands in his trouser pockets, and then exclaimed: 'You know, it's a bit of luck he didn't recognize me. It's the beard that saved me.'

Pulling his cap down over his eyes, he left the room; but a moment later the door opened again and his crafty, savage face appeared round it.

'Something I meant to tell you. You're to have a charcoal fire going.'

The door closed again, and this time Marius heard Jondrette's footsteps go rapidly along the corridor and down the stairs.

Despite his addiction to daydreaming Marius was capable of firm and decided action.

'These wretches must be dealt with,' he told himself.

None of the riddles that perplexed him had been answered. Only one thing was clear from the conversation he had overheard, and this was that some kind of trap was being prepared, the nature of which he did not know but which represented a serious threat to the girl in all likelihood and her father for certain.

There was only one thing to be done. He wrapped a scarf round his neck, put on his hat and stole out of the house as quietly as though he were walking barefoot on grass.

The nearest police post was No. 14 Rue de Pontoise. Marius asked to see the Superintendent of Police.

'The superintendent isn't here,' said the desk-clerk. 'There's an inspector sitting in for him.'

He was shown into the superintendent's office. A tall man in a big greatcoat was standing on the other side of a metal grille with his back to a large stove.

'What do you want?' he asked with no attempt at civility.

'Are you the Commissaire de Police?'

'He's away. I'm acting for him.'

'This is a highly confidential matter.'

'Well, tell me about it.'

'And very urgent.'

'Then talk fast.'

His cool terseness was at once disconcerting and reassuring; he inspired both awe and confidence. Marius accordingly told his story in full, beginning with the statement that he was Marius Pontmercy, lawyer. A gentleman whom he knew only by sight was to be lured that evening into a trap. He had heard about the business because the man planning it occupied the room next to his own in the house where he lived. The villain in question was a man named Jondrette, but he would have accomplices, probably gateway prowlers, among them a certain Panchaud. The trap was to be sprung at six o'clock that evening in a house in the most deserted part of the Boulevard de l'Hopital, No. 50–52.

The mention of this number caused the inspector to look up sharply.

'Would it be the room at the end of the corridor?'

'Yes,' said Marius in surprise. 'Do you know the house?'

The inspector was silent for a moment, staring thoughtfully at the floor. 'It seems I do,' he said, talking less to Marius than to himself. 'Looks like Patron-Minette's mixed up in it.'

The words struck Marius.

He was silent again, and then muttered:

'I know the place all right. Nowhere in it to hide.'

He looked hard at Marius.

'Would you be scared?'

'What of?'

'These men.'

'No more than you,' said Marius coolly. He was beginning to notice that this policeman never addressed him as sir.

'But what are you proposing?'

Plunging with a single movement his two enormous hands into the capacious pockets of his greatcoat, he brought out two very small pistols.

'Take these,' he said briskly. 'They're both loaded. Go back home and hide in your room so that they think you're out. Keep watch through that hole you spoke of. When they arrive, let them start their business, and when you think it's gone far enough fire a shot. Then I'll take charge. But not too soon, understand. They've got to start, there's got to be evidence. You're a lawyer. You know what I mean.'

Marius took the pistols.

'And now there's no time to be lost. The party's at seven, you said?'

'Six,' said Marius.

'Well, that still gives me time, but only just. Don't forget what I told you. One pistol-shot.'

'I'll do it,' said Marius and turned to leave the room.

'One other thing,' the inspector said. 'If you should need me before then you'd better come here or send someone. The name's Javert.'

Marius made all speed back to No. 50–52. He sat down on his bed and thought of the forces mustering in the shadows, the march of crime on the one side and of justice on the other. He was not afraid, but he could not think without a tremor of what was so soon to happen.

It had stopped snowing. The moon, growing steadily brighter, had now risen above the mist, and its rays, mingled with the white reflection of the fallen snow, flooded his room with a cavernous light. A light was burning in the Jondrettes' lair. Marius could see through the hole in the partition a ruddy glow which looked to him like a blood-red eye. Certainly it did not look like the light of a candle. Then he heard voices.

'What's the time?' said Jondrette.

'Getting on for six. The half hour has struck at Saint-Medard.'

'Time for the girls to go on watch,' said Jondrette. 'Listen to me, you two.' A sound of whispering followed.

A moment later Marius heard the barefeet of the two girls going along the corridor and the sound of the front door closing indicated that they had gone out.

Marius decided that it was time for him to return to his post of observation and, within an instant, moving with the suppleness of youth, he was back on the chest of drawers with his eye to the peep-hole.

The aspect of the Jondrette dwelling was singularly changed. He could now account for the strange light he had seen. A candle was burning in a tarnished candlestick, but this was not its source; the garret was flooded with the glare of a fair-sized brazier standing in the hearth and filled with glowing charcoal. The brazier itself was red hot, and the blue flame on top of the charcoal helped him to discern the outline of the chisel which had been thrust into it. In a corner by the door, as though put there for a specific purpose, were two piles of objects, one a heap of what looked like scrap-iron and the other a pile of rope. The den, thus illumined, looked more like a smithy than a gateway to the inferno; but Jondrette by the same light looked more like a demon than a blacksmith.

Jondrette had lit his pipe and sat smoking. He was still wearing the overcoat bestowed on him by Monsieur Leblanc. Suddenly he raised his voice:

'I've just thought of something. He'll be bound to come in a fiacre in this weather. Light the lantern and go downstairs with it and wait at the front door. Open the door directly you hear the cab draw up. Light him up the stairs, then run down again, pay off the cab, and send it away.'

'What about the money?'

Jondrette felt in his pocket and handed her a five-franc piece.

'Where does this come from?' she exclaimed.

'From him next door, this morning,' said Jondrette with dignity.

She hurried out again, leaving the man alone.

Jondrette twisted the chisel in the burning charcoal and moved an old screen in front of the hearth to hide the brazier. Then he bent over the pile of rope as though inspecting it. Marius now realized that what he had supposed to be nothing but rope was in fact a well-made rope ladder with wooden rungs and two iron hooks to hang it by.

Of a sudden a distant, melancholy sound caused the windows to vibrate, slightly. Six o'clock was striking at the church of Saint-Medard.

Jondrette noted each stroke with a nod of his head. Then he began to pace the room, stood listening at the door, paced and listened again, then returned to his chair. Scarcely had he seated himself than the door opened.

His wife stood in the corridor, her hideous grimace of welcome lighted from below by one of the apertures in the dark-lantern.

'Please to come in, monsieur,' she said.

'My noble benefactor, enter!' cried Jondrette, hastily rising.

Monsieur Leblanc appeared. His serene bearing lent him a singular dignity. He placed four louis on the table.

'That is for your rent and urgent requirements, Monsieur Fabantou,' he said. 'We have to consider what else is needed.'

'May God reward you, most generous sir,' said Jondrette; and in a swift aside to his wife: 'Get rid of the cab.'

She vanished, and had reappeared by the time Jondrette with many bows and fulsome expressions of gratitude had seated Monsieur Leblanc. She gave him a nod.

Monsieur Leblanc's first act when he was seated was to look round at the two empty beds. 'How is the hurt child?' he asked.

'Not well,' said Jondrette with a smile of mournful gratitude. 'Her sister has taken her to the hospital to have the wound dressed.'

'Madame Fabantou seems to have recovered,' said Monsieur Leblanc, glancing at the Jondrette woman, who was standing between him and the door as though guarding the exit.

'She's desperately ill,' said Jondrette. 'But what is one to do? She has so much courage, you see. She's more than a woman – she's an ox.'

The elegant compliment drew a simper from the lady and she exclaimed coyly:

'You always flatter me, Monsieur Jondrette.'

'Jondrette?' said Monsieur Leblanc. 'I thought your name was Fabantou?'

'It's either,' said Jondrette promptly. 'Jondrette is my stage name.'

He gave his wife a look which Leblanc failed to notice.

'My most noble patron,' said Jondrette gazing tenderly at Monsieur Leblanc with eyes not unlike those of a boa-constrictor, 'I have a picture for sale. Perhaps you will allow me to show it to you.'

He rose and picking up the panel leaning against the wall turned it round and left it leaning there.

'What on earth is it?' asked Monsieur Leblanc.

'It is a masterpiece, my dear sir,' cried Jondrette. 'A picture I cherish. But I have been reduced to such straits that I am forced to part with it!'

Monsieur Leblanc, while examining the picture, also glanced round. There were now three strangers present, standing by the door, all bare-armed, motionless and with blackened faces. Catching the direction of Monsieur Leblanc's glance, Jondrette said:

'They're all neighbours. They're furnacemen; they have dirty faces because they do dirty work. Don't worry about them, noble benefactor, but buy my picture. What do you consider it is worth?

Monsieur Leblanc was looking closely at him, like a man now on his guard.

'It's an old inn-sign,' he said. 'It's worth about three francs.'

Jondrette continued to talk, 'If you do not buy my picture, noble benefactor, then I shall have no recourse but to throw myself into the river. The other day I went down the steps by the Pont d'Austerlitz . . .'

But suddenly the dull eyes flamed; the little man drew himself up and became terrifying. Taking a step towards Monsieur Leblanc, he shouted:

'But never mind all that! Don't you know me?'

The door of the garret was suddenly flung wide to admit three men in dark smocks wearing black paper masks. The first was thin and carried a long, iron-studded cudgel. The second, a species of colossus, was carrying a butcher's pole-axe. The third grasped a huge key stolen from some prison-door.

It seemed that this was what Jondrette had been awaiting. There was a rapid exchange of dialogue between him and the man with the cudgel.

'Is everything ready?' Jondrette asked.

'Yes,' the thin man replied.

'But where's Montparnasse?'

'The pretty boy stopped to chat to your daughter.'

'Which one?'

'The older.'

'The fiacre's ready?'

'Yes.'

The ruffians whom Jondrette had described as furnace-men had meanwhile gone to the heap of scrap-iron. One had taken up a pair of shears, the second a pair of tongs, and the third a hammer.

It seemed to Marius that the time was very near when he must give the alarm, and he raised his right hand with the pistol, pointing it upwards. Jondrette, having concluded his colloquy with the man with the cudgel, turned back to Monsieur Leblanc and repeated his question.

'Don't you recognize me?'

Monsieur Leblanc looked steadily at him.

'No.'

Jondrette drew close to the table. Crouching like a wild beast about to spring, he cried:

'My name isn't Fabantou or Jondrette either. My name is Thenardier! I'm the innkeeper from Montfermeil. Thenardier, d'you hear? Now do you recognize me?'

A slight quiver passed over Monsieur Leblanc's face, but he answered calmly and without raising his voice:

'No more than before.'

Marius did not hear this reply. At the sound of Thenardier's name he had trembled so violently as to have to lean against the partition for support. His right arm, raised to fire the warning shot, sank slowly to his side. Jondrette in disclosing his identity had not shaken Monsieur Leblanc, but he had shattered Marius. Monsieur Leblanc might not know the name, but Marius knew it. A name linked with that of his father in his prayers. And now, here he was, Thenardier, his father's rescuer – a bandit, a monster in the act of committing an abominable crime, the nature of which was still not fully clear but which looked like murder. And the murder of whom, in God's name! . . . Could Fate have played any more scurvy trick than this? Two voices seemed to ring in his ears, that of the girl pleading for her father and that of the colonel commending Thenardier to his care. His senses were reeling and he felt his knees grow weak.

Meanwhile Thenardier was stalking up and down in a sort of frenzied triumph. Then, turning to Monsieur Leblanc, he spat at him:

'So I've caught up with you at last, my noble philanthropist, my wealthy buyer of dolls! You got the better of me once! You must have thought I was a fine fool when you got away with the brat. You were the stronger that day in the forest. But now it's my turn. I hold the cards now, and you're done for. I want money, a lot of money, the devil of a lot, or else, by God, I'll do for you!

'Well,' he said, 'have you anything to say before we go to work on you?'

Monsieur Leblanc said nothing. Amid the ensuing silence a hoarse voice proclaimed:

'If there's any chopping to be done, I'm your man!'

A huge, grimy face loomed up by the doorway. It was the face of the man with the pole-axe.

'Why have you taken your mask off?' Thenardier shouted furiously and, in shouting at the man, he turned his back on the prisoner.

Monsieur Leblanc took instant advantage of this. Moving with astonishing speed, he was half-way through the window when six powerful hands laid hold of him and dragged him back.

The commotion brought in the rest of the gang, who had been clustered in the corridor. One of the men, whom Marius now recognized as Panchaud (alias Bigrenaille), was flourishing a species of bludgeon.

It was too much for Marius. 'Forgive me, father,' he

murmured and his finger sought the trigger. But as he was about to fire Thenardier cried:

'Don't hurt him!'

Far from enraging Thenardier, the prisoner's desperate bid to escape had sobered him.

'Don't hurt him,' he repeated, and in doing so unwittingly scored a success. Marius delayed the firing of the shot.

Meanwhile a prodigious struggle was in progress. Monsieur Leblanc had felled two of his assailants to the ground. He was now kneeling with a knee on two other men, who lay groaning under the pressure. But the remaining four, gripping him by the arms and neck, prevented him from rising.

Eventually they managed to drag him on to the bed nearest the window, treating him now with respect.

'Search him,' said Thenardier.

Monsieur Leblanc made no further resistance. They searched him. He had nothing on him except a leather purse containing six francs and a handkerchief. Thenardier put the handkerchief in his pocket. Then going across to the corner by the door, picked up a bundle of rope and tossed it to them.

'Tie him to the foot of the bed,' he said.

They roped him solidly, standing upright, to the post furthest from the window, and nearest to the hearth.

When this was done Thenardier went over to the fireplace and moved the screen, unmasking the glowing brazier in which the red-hot chisel was plainly discernible, its surface flecked with small points of light. Then he resumed his seat facing Monsieur Leblanc.

'To continue,' he said. 'I was wrong to fly into a rage the way I did. I lost my head and talked extravagantly. For example, I said that I intended to demand a great deal of money, an enormous amount. But that would not be reasonable. However rich you may be, you have expenses, as who has not? I have no wish to ruin you. All I am asking is two hundred thousand francs.'

Monsieur Leblanc said nothing. Thenardier continued:

'You will, of course, point out that you haven't got

two hundred thousand francs on you. I am not so foolish as to have expected it. At the moment I am only asking one thing, that you will write a letter that I shall dictate.'

Thenardier turned to Bigrenaille. 'Untie the gentleman's right arm.'

The man did so, and when the prisoner's right hand was free Thenardier dipped the pen in the ink and passed it to him.

'I will now dictate.'

Monsieur Leblanc held the pen poised. 'My dear daughter –' Thenardier began, and at this the other started and stared at him. 'No,' said Thenardier. 'Better make it, My dearest daughter.' Monsieur Leblanc wrote accordingly, and he went on: 'You are to come at once.' Then he broke off. 'I suppose you address her as *tu*?'

'Who?' asked Monsieur Leblanc.

'The girl, of course,' said Thenardier. 'The child – the Lark.'

Monsieur Leblanc said without the least sign of emotion: 'I don't know what you're talking about.'

'Never mind,' said Thenardier and resumed his dictation: '. . . come at once. The bearer of this note will bring you to me. And now you must sign it. What is your name?'

'Urbain Fabre,' the prisoner replied.

With a catlike movement Thenardier plunged his hand in his pocket and whipped out the handkerchief taken from Monsieur Leblanc. He held it up to the light of the candle, inspecting it for initials.

'U.F.,' he said. 'That's right. Urbain Fabre. Well, sign the letter U.F.'

The prisoner did so.

'And now give it to me. It needs two hands to fold it, so I'll attend to that myself. Good,' said Thenardier. 'Now you must address it.'

The prisoner reflected for a moment, then took up the pen and wrote:

'To Mademoiselle Fabre, care of Monsieur Urbain Fabre, 17 Rue Saint-Dominique-d'Enfer.'

Thenardier snatched up the letter with a sort of feverish excitement. 'Wife,' he called, and she hurried forward. 'Here it is. You know what you have to do. There's a fiacre down below. Get off at once and come back quick as you can.'

He turned to the man with the pole-axe.

'As you've taken your mask off you might as well go with her. Get up behind the fiacre. You know where it's waiting?'

'Yes,' said the man and, dropping his pole-axe, he followed the woman out of the room.

In less than a minute they heard the cracking of a whip, which rapidly died away.

Marius waited in a state of anxiety. The puzzle was more mystifying than ever. Who was the 'child' whom Thenardier had called 'the Lark'? The prisoner had seemed quite unaffected by the mention of the Lark. Was it his 'Ursula'? At least the riddle of the initials was now resolved. The U.F. stood for Urbain Fabre, and Ursula was not Ursula. This was the one thing that was clear to Marius.

'At least,' he reflected, 'if she is the Lark I shall know it, because the woman is going to bring her here. That will settle the matter. I will sacrifice my life to save her, if need be.'

Nearly half an hour passed. Thenardier seemed lost in his own dark thoughts. The prisoner did not move. Nevertheless it seemed to Marius that now and then a slight, furtive sound came from his direction.

At length the silence was broken by the sound of the house-door opening and closing. The prisoner stirred in his bonds.

'Here she is,' said Thenardier.

And a moment later the woman rushed into the room, flushed and breathless, her eyes glaring.

'It was a fake address!' she cried.

Her escort, following her in, picked up his pole-axe.

'A fake?' Thenardier repeated.

'There's no Monsieur Urbain Fabre at 17, Rue Saint-Dominique! They've never heard of him! The old man's been fooling you, Monsieur Thenardier.'

Marius breathed again. So the girl at least was safe. Thenardier turned to the prisoner and said slowly, and in a voice of singular ferocity:

'A false address. What did you expect to gain by that?'

'Time!' cried the prisoner in a ringing voice, and at the same moment he shook off the ropes that bound him. They had been cut. He was now only tied to the bed by one leg.

Before the other men had had time to realize what was happening he had reached out a hand to the brazier and then again stood upright. Thenardier, the woman, and the party of ruffians, clustered in stupefaction at the other end of the room, saw him defiantly facing them, holding the red-hot chisel by its wooden handle above his head.

It was revealed at the judicial inquiry into the affair at the Gorbeau tenement that the police, when they searched the garret, found a large coin which had been cut and worked in a particular fashion. It was one of those marvels of craftsmanship fashioned with the patience engendered by imprisonment. The wretch determined to escape contrives to slice a copper coin in two thin sheets; and then cuts a thread so that the two sheets can be screwed together, forming a box. Within the box a watchspring is concealed; and a watchspring, properly handled, will cut through a thick rope or an iron bar. It is probable that the prisoner managed to conceal it in his hand while he was being searched and later unscrewed it when his hand was freed. He had used the saw to cut through the bonds, which would explain the slight sounds and furtive movements noticed by Marius; but he could not bend down for fear of giving himself away, and so had not been able to cut the rope binding his left leg.

The prisoner now addressed them.

'You're a poor lot,' he said, 'but my own life is not much worth defending. As for making me talk – or making me write anything I don't want to write . . . look!'

He drew up the sleeve covering his left arm and, holding it out, pressed the red-hot chisel against the bare skin.

The hiss of burnt flesh was audible, and a smell associated with torture-chambers spread through the room. Marius was sickened with horror, and even the ruffians gasped. But the expression of this remarkable elderly man scarcely altered.

'Poor fools,' he said, 'you need no more fear me than I fear you.' Withdrawing the chisel from his arm, he flung it through the open window, and the horrid implement vanished in the darkness. 'Now you can do what you like with me.'

He was quite defenceless.

'Get hold of him,' said Thenardier.

Two of the men grasped him by the shoulders. Marius heard a sound of whispering immediately below him, so close to the partition that he could not see the speakers.

'There's only one thing for it –'

'Slit his throat!'

'That's it!'

Husband and wife were taking counsel together. Thenardier walked slowly over to the table and got out the knife.

Now the peril was imminent and Marius could delay no longer. He gazed wildly about him in the extremity of despair and suddenly he started. A brighter ray of moonlight, falling on the writing-table immediately behind him, shone upon a sheet of paper. It bore the sentence scrawled by the Thenardier girl that morning to prove that she could write:

'Watch out, the bogies are around.'

Instantly he saw what he must do. This was the means of saving both victim and assassin. Kneeling down, he reached for the paper. He softly detached a piece of plaster from the partition, wrapped the page round it, and flung it through the aperture so that it landed in the middle of the Thenardiers' room.

He was just in time. Thenardier, having overcome his last misgivings or scruples, was advancing upon the prisoner when he was checked by a sudden exclamation from his wife:

'Something fell!' she cried.

'What do you mean?'

She darted forward, picked up the small missive, and handed it to her husband.

'How did this get here?' he asked.

'Through the window, of course!'

Thenardier hastily unfolded the paper and studied it by the light of the candle.

'It's Eponine's handwriting, by God!' He signed to his wife to read the message and said in a hoarse voice: 'Quick. The ladder. We'll leave the mouse in the trap and clear out!'

'How do we go?' asked Bigrenaille.

'Through the window. If Ponine threw the message in that way it means that side of the house isn't guarded.'

The rope-ladder was swiftly unrolled and let down from the window, with its hooks secured to the window-ledge. The prisoner paid no attention to what was going on, seeming plunged in thought, or in prayer.

Directly the ladder was ready Thenardier called to his wife, 'Come on!' but Bigrenaille grabbed him roughly by the collar.

'Not so fast, my old joker. We go first.'

'You're being childish,' said Thenardier. 'We're wasting time. They can't be far off.'

'Then,' said one of the men, 'we'll draw lots for who's to go first.'

'Are you crazy?' spluttered Thenardier. 'We've got the law on our heels and you want to draw lots out of a hat!'

'Perhaps you would like to borrow my hat,' said a voice from the doorway.

They swung round and saw that it was Javert. He stood there holding out his hat with a smile.

Javert had posted his men at nightfall and had taken up his own position behind the trees on the other side of the boulevard. Waiting for the signal, he had been considerably perturbed by the coming and going of the fiacre. Finally he lost patience, and being now convinced that he had uncovered a hornet's nest and that his luck was in – for he had recognized several of the men who entered the house

– he had decided to go in without waiting for the pistol-shot.

He had arrived at the crucial moment. The startled desperadoes snatched up the weapons they had just let fall and clustered together in readiness to defend themselves.

Javert replaced his hat on his head and advanced two paces into the room with his stick under his arm and his sword still in its sheath.

'Take it easy,' he said. 'There are fifteen of us. No point in turning it into a brawl.'

Bigrenaille produced a pistol from under his smock and thrust it into Thenardier's hand, murmuring as he did so:

'That's Javert, a man I'm afraid to shoot at. Will you dare?'

'By God I will!' said Thenardier.

He levelled the weapon at Javert, who was not more than three paces away from him. Javert looked steadily at him and simply said:

'Better not. It won't fire anyway.'

Thenardier pulled the trigger. The pistol did not fire.

'What did I tell you?' said Javert.

Bigrenaille flung down the bludgeon he was carrying.

'You're the king of devils!' he cried. 'I give in.'

Javert looked round at the others.

'And the rest of you?'

They nodded.

'Good,' said Javert, and, turning, he shouted: 'You can come in now.'

A party consisting of *sergents de ville* armed with swords and policemen with truncheons entered the garret.

'Handcuff the lot of them,' ordered Javert.

The woman, stared down at her manacled hands and those of her husband, and sank weeping to her knees.

'My daughters!' she cried.

'We've got them,' said Javert.

Three men with masks and three with blackened faces, still had the look of ghosts.

'Leave the masks on,' said Javert. Looking them over like Frederick the Great reviewing his troops at Potsdam, he greeted them in turn: 'Good evening to you, Bigrenaille – Brujon – Deux-milliards . . .' And to the masked men: 'How nice to see you, Gueulemer – Babet – Claquesous.'

He then noticed the prisoner, who from the time the police had entered the room had stood with his head bowed and without speaking a word.

'Untie the gentleman,' he said. 'But no one's to leave until I give the order.'

After which he seated himself at the table, methodically wiped the pen and trimmed the candle, and taking a sheet of official paper from his pocket set to work on his preliminary report. But after writing the opening lines, which were no more than a routine formula, he looked up.

'Ask the gentleman to step forward.'

The police stared about them.

'Well, where is he?' Javert demanded.

He was gone. The prisoner – Monsieur Leblanc, Monsieur Urbain Fabre, the father of Ursula or the Lark – had disappeared.

The door was guarded, but the window was not. The rope-ladder was still swinging.

On the evening following these events a youngster who seemed to have come from the Pont d'Austerlitz hurried along a narrow street in the direction of the Fontainebleau barrier. It was dark. The boy was pale and thin and wretchedly clad, wearing cotton trousers in that month of February, but he was singing at the top of his voice.

At the corner of the Rue du Petit-Banquier an old woman was ferreting in a garbage-heap by the light of a street lamp. The boy bumped into her and started back.

'Blimey, I thought it was an enormous – an ENORMOUS dog!'

The old woman straightened up angrily.

'Little demon!' she shouted. 'If I hadn't been bending I know where I'd have put my foot.'

'Now then!' said the boy, already some way past her. 'Perhaps I wasn't all that wrong after all.'

Spluttering with indignation, she recognized him.

'So it's you, you little pest!'

'Why, it's the old dame,' said the boy. 'Good evening, Ma Bougon. I've come to call on my ancestors.'

The old woman responded with a grimace, unfortunately wasted in the darkness, which was a wonderful mixture of malice, decay and ugliness.

'There's no one there, stupid.'

'Why, where's my father?'

'In prison – at La Force.'

'You don't say! And my mother?'

'She's in the Saint-Lazare.'

'Well, what about my sisters?'

'They're in the Madelonnettes.'

The boy scratched his head, stared at Ma'am Bougon, and whistled.

'Ah, well!'

Then he turned on his heels and she stood watching while he disappeared beyond the black shapes of the elms shaking in the winter wind, his clear young voice again raised in song.

> The merry monarch Coupdesabot
> Was plump and very short, and so
> He went out shooting on a pair
> Of stilts to make the people stare,
> And spread his legs to let them through,
> And charged the customers *deux sous*.

After witnessing the unexpected outcome of the plot of which he had warned Javert, Marius slipped out and went to Courfeyrac, who was no longer the unshakeable inhabitant of the Latin Quarter but 'for political reasons' had gone to live in the Rue de la Verrerie.

'I've come to lodge with you,' Marius said, and Courfeyrac said: 'You're welcome.'

Marius returned to the tenement, paid his rent and departed leaving no address.

Marius had two reasons for this prompt removal. In the

first place, he now had a horror of that house in which he had encountered a form of social ugliness that was perhaps even more repulsive than the evil rich: namely, the evil poor. The second reason was that he did not want to be involved in the criminal proceedings which must surely ensue, when he would have been obliged to testify against Thenardier.

Javert assumed that the young man, whose name he had not noted, had taken fright and bolted, or possibly had not even gone back to his lodging at the time when the trap was sprung.

Two months passed. Marius was deeply unhappy. He had had a brief, shadowy glimpse of the girl with whom he had fallen in love and the elderly man whom he presumed to be her father and at the moment when he had thought to draw near them a puff of wind had borne them away like shadows. He no longer even knew the girl's name, which he thought he had discovered. Certainly it was not Ursula, and 'the Lark' was only a nickname. And what was he to make of the man? He was both heroic and two-faced. Why had he run away? Was he in fact the girl's father? And was he really the man Thenardier claimed to have recognized? . . . A string of unanswerable questions which, however, did nothing to diminish the angelic charm of the girl he had seen in the Luxembourg. Marius was in utter despair.

So the days drifted by, bringing nothing new.

Javert's triumph in the Gorbeau tenement had seemed complete but was not. In the first place, and it was his chief vexation, he had not laid hands on the victim of the plot. The prospective victim who escapes is even more suspect than the prospective murderer, and it seemed likely that this person, if he represented so rich a haul for the band of ruffians, must have been no less valuable a capture for the authorities.

Montparnasse had also escaped. Montparnasse had in fact run into Eponine when she was keeping watch and had gone off with her, deciding that he was more in a mood to amuse himself with the daughter than play hired assassin for the father. It was a fortunate impulse and he was still at large. As for Eponine, Javert had picked her up later and she had gone to join her sister in the Madelonnette prison.

Criminals do not cease their activities because they have fallen into the hands of the law; they are not to be deterred by trifles. To be imprisoned for one crime does not prevent the planning of the next.

Towards the end of February 1832 one of the night warders peered through the peep-hole in the door of Brujon's dormitory. He saw Brujon sitting up in bed and writing something by the dim light of the wall-lamp. He went in and Brujon was sent back to solitary for a month, but they were not able to discover what he had been writing.

What is certain is that the next day a '*postillon*' was flung from the Cour Charlemagne into the Lions' Den, clearing the intervening five-storey building. A *postillon* is convict slang for a carefully kneaded lump of bread which is flung over a prison roof from one courtyard into another. Whoever picks up the missile will find a message inside it. If it is picked up by a prisoner, he passes it on to the person it is intended for; if by a warder it is passed on to the police. On this occasion the *postillon* was delivered to the right address, although the addressee was at the time in a solitary-confinement cell. He was none other than Babet.

The message contained in the lump of bread was as follows:

'Babet. There's a job in the Rue Plumet. Garden with a wrought-iron gate.' This was what Brujon had written the previous night.

Although he was under close surveillance, Babet contrived to get the message passed from the La Force prison to a woman called Magnon. This Magnon by visiting Eponine could serve as a link between the prisons.

As it happened, the Thenardier daughters were released on the day she went to visit Eponine, the preliminary investigation having disclosed insufficient evidence to warrant their detention. When Eponine came out, Magnon handed her Brujon's note and asked her to spy out the land. Eponine, accordingly, went to the Rue Plumet, and after a careful study of the house and its inhabitants called upon Magnon. She gave her a 'biscuit', to be passed on to Babet, the term, in the recondite jargon of the underworld, signifies 'no good'.

Thus a criminal operation conceived by Brujon in the prison of La Force was still-born.

But it happens often enough that, thinking to plan one event, we set in motion another.

One morning Marius was seated on a parapet overlooking the stream, the Riviere des Gobelins. Suddenly a voice spoke, a voice known to him.

'Ah! There he is!'

He looked up and recognized the unhappy girl who had called upon him one morning, the elder Thenardier daughter, Eponine, whose name he had subsequently learned.

She was contemplating Marius with a look of pleasure on her pale face and something that was almost a smile.

'So at last I've found you!' she finally said. 'If you only knew how I've been looking for you. For six whole weeks. You aren't living in the tenement any more?'

'No,' said Marius.

'Where are you living now?'

Marius did not answer.

'You don't seem very glad to see me.'

Marius still said nothing, and after a pause she exclaimed:

'Well, I could make you look happy if I wanted to!'

'How?' said Marius. 'What do you mean?'

'You weren't so unfriendly last time.'

'I'm sorry. But what do you mean?'

She bit her lip and hesitated as though wrestling with some problem of her own. Finally she seemed to make up her mind.

She looked steadily at him.

'I've got the address.'

Marius turned pale.

'You mean –'

'The address you wanted. The young lady – you know . . .'
She spoke the words with a deep sigh.

Marius jumped down from the parapet where he had been sitting and took her by the hand.

'You know it? You must take me there. You must tell me where it is. I'll give you anything you ask.'

'It's right on the other side of town. I shall have to take you. I don't know the number, but I know the house.' She withdrew her hand and said in a tone of sadness that would have wrung the heart of any beholder, but of which Marius in his flurry was quite unconscious: 'Oh, how excited you are!'

A thought had struck Marius and he frowned. He seized her by the arm.

'One thing. Your father. Eponine, you must swear to me that you'll never tell him where it is.'

She was gazing at him in astonishment.

'All right, I promise. What difference does it make to me?'

'Now take me there.'

'This minute?'

'Yes, this minute.'

'Well, come along.'

She walked a few paces and then stopped.

'By the way, you remember you promised me something?'

Marius felt in his pocket. All he had in the world was a five-franc piece. He got it out and thrust it into her hand, and she opened her fingers and let the coin fall to the ground. She looked sombrely at him.

'I don't want your money,' she said.

Round about the middle of the last century a judge of the High Court and member of the Parliament of Paris, having a mistress and preferring to conceal the fact – for in those days great aristocrats were accustomed to parade their mistresses, but lesser mortals kept quiet about them – built himself a small house in the Faubourg Saint-Germain, in the unfrequented Rue Blomet, now the Rue Plumet.

The house was a two-storey villa and in the front was a garden with a wide wrought-iron gate to the street. The garden was about an acre in extent, and this was all that could be seen from the street; but behind the villa there was a narrow courtyard, with, on its far side, a two-room cottage with a cellar. This cottage communicated, by a concealed door, with a very long, narrow, winding passageway, which emerged, by another concealed door, in the Rue de Baby-lone, in what was virtually another quarter, half-a-mile away.

In October 1829 a gentleman getting on in life had rented the property as it stood and had quietly moved in with a young girl and an elderly servant, more in the manner of an interloper than a man taking possession of his own house.

This unobtrusive tenant was Jean Valjean, and the girl was Cosette. The servant was an unmarried woman named Toussaint whom Jean Valjean had saved from the work-house. He had rented the property under the name of Monsieur Fauchelevent, of private means.

But why had Jean Valjean left the Petit-Picpus convent? What had happened?

The answer is that nothing had happened.

Jean Valjean, as we know, was happy at the convent, so much so that in the end it troubled his conscience. Seeing Cosette every day, and with the sense of paternal responsibil-ity growing in him, he brooded over her spiritual well-being, saying to himself that she was his and that nothing could take her from him, that certainly she would become a nun. But as he thought about this he began to have misgivings. He told himself that the child had a right to know something about the world before renouncing it. It might be that eventually, finding that she regretted her vows, Cosette would come to hate him. It was this last thought, almost a selfish one, that he found intolerable. He resolved to leave the convent.

Having made up his mind he awaited a favourable oppor-tunity, and this soon came. Old Fauchelevent died.

Jean Valjean applied to the prioress for an audience and told her that, his brother's death having brought him a modest legacy, he wished to leave the convent, taking his daughter with him. In this fashion he and Cosette departed.

When they did so he himself carried the small valise of which he had always kept the key in his possession. He kept it always in his bedroom. Cosette laughed at it, calling it 'the inseparable' and saying that it made her jealous.

Valjean did not return to the outside world without profound apprehension. He discovered the house in the Rue Plumet and hid himself in it, going by the name of Ultime Fauchelevent. But at the same time he rented two apartments in Paris so as to have a place of retreat and not be taken at a loss as he had been on the night when he had so miraculously escaped from Javert. Both apartments were modest and of poor appearance and were situated in widely separated parts of the town, one being in the Rue de l'Ouest and the other in the Rue de l'Homme-Arme.

Properly speaking, his home was in the Rue Plumet.

Cosette and the servant occupied the villa. Valjean himself lived in the sort of porter's lodge across the yard, with a mattress on a truckle-bed, a plain wooden table, two rush-bottomed chairs, a few books on a shelf and never any fire.

In the Rue de Babylone door there was a box designed for the reception of letters and newspapers; but since the present occupants of the villa were accustomed to receive neither, the only use of this former receptacle of *billets-doux* was for the reception of tax demands and notices concerned with guard-duty. For Monsieur Fauchelevent, gentleman of private means, was a member of the Garde Nationale, not having been able to slip through the meshes of the census of 1831. The municipal inquiries had penetrated even into the Petit-Picpus convent.

Accordingly, three or four times a year Jean Valjean donned his uniform and did his spell of duty – very readily, it may be said, because this was a trapping of orthodoxy which enabled him to mingle with the outside world without otherwise emerging from his solitude.

One detail, however, must be noted. When Valjean went out with Cosette he could easily be mistaken for a retired officer. But when he went out alone, which was generally at night, he always wore workman's clothes and a peaked cap which hid his face. Was this from caution or humility? It was from both. Cosette, accustomed by now to the strangeness of his life, scarcely noticed her father's eccentricities. She wholeheartedly loved her father – that is to say, Jean Valjean – with an innocent, confiding love which made of him the most charming and desirable of companions. Monsieur Madeleine had read a great deal. Jean Valjean continued to do so, and had in consequence become an excellent talker. He discoursed upon whatever came into his head, drawing upon his wide reading and his past suffering. And Cosette listened while she gazed about.

Where Jean Valjean was, there was contentment; and since he did not frequent the villa or the garden she was happier in the paved back-yard, happier in the cottage with its rush-seated chairs than in her own richly furnished drawing-room. Jean Valjean would sometimes say, delighted at being thus pursued, 'Now run along and leave me in peace.'

Cosette had only vague recollections of her childhood. It seemed to her that she had begun her life in a kind of limbo from which Jean Valjean had rescued her, and that childhood had been a time of beetles, snakes and spiders. It sounds strange, but in her profound ignorance as a convent-bred child she had come to believe that her mother had been almost non-existent. She did not even know her name, and when she asked Valjean he would not answer. If she repeated the question he merely smiled, and once, when she persisted, the smile was followed by a tear. Thus did Valjean by his silence hide the figure of Fantine in darkness. Was it from instinctive prudence, from respect for the dead, or from fear of surrendering that name to hazards of any memory other than his own?

Otherwise Valjean was content and he thanked God from the depths of his heart for having caused him, unworthy wretch that he was, to be so loved by a creature so innocent.

One day when Cosette was in the garden she heard old Toussaint say: 'Has Monsieur noticed how pretty Mademoiselle is growing?' She did not hear her father's reply, but Toussaint's words filled her with amazement. She ran up to her bedroom and looked hard at herself in the glass. She uttered a cry, delighted by what she saw.

She was beautiful as well as pretty. Her figure had filled out, her skin was finer and there was a new splendour in her blue eyes.

Jean Valjean, for his part, had a sense of profound, indefinable unease. For some time he had been apprehensively watching this growing radiance of Cosette's beauty, a bright dawn to others but to himself a dawn of ill-omen. He saw it as a portent of change in their life together, a life so happy that any change could only be for the worse. 'Such loveliness!' he thought. 'So what will become of me?'

The first signs of change were not slow to appear.

From the morrow of the day on which she had said to herself 'I am beautiful!' Cosette began to give thought to her appearance. In less than a month she was not merely one of the prettiest women in Paris, which is saying a great deal, but one of the best dressed, which is saying even more.

It was at this point that Marius, after a lapse of six months, again saw her in the Luxembourg. Cosette in her solitude, like Marius in his, was ready to be set alight.

On that day Cosette's gaze drove Marius wild with delight, while his gaze left her trembling. From that day on they adored each other.

It happened now and then that Valjean caught a glimpse of Marius. His demeanour was anything but natural, he was awkward in his concealments and clumsy in his boldness.

Cosette, for her part, was giving nothing away. Without knowing precisely what was happening to her, she knew that something had happened and that it must be kept secret.

There is a law applying to those youthful years of agitation and turmoil, those frantic struggles of first love against first impediments: it is that the girl never falls into any trap and the young man falls into all of them. Jean Valjean opened a secret campaign against Marius which Marius, in the spell of his youthful passion, quite failed to perceive. Valjean devised countless snares. He changed the time of their visits, came to the garden alone, dropped his handkerchief; and Marius was caught out every time. To every question-mark planted under his nose by Valjean he responded with an ingenuous 'yes'.

Valjean, who had thought himself no longer capable of any malice, now felt the return of an old, wild savagery, a stirring in the depths of a nature that once had harboured much wrath.

At these moments a strange and sinister light shone in his eyes, not that of a man looking at a man, or an enemy facing an enemy, but of a watchdog confronting a thief.

We know what followed. Marius continued to act absurdly. He followed Cosette and Valjean moved out of the Rue de l'Ouest, swearing never again to set foot in that street or in the Luxembourg. They returned to the Rue Plumet.

Cosette uttered no complaint. She said nothing, asked no questions; she was at the stage when our greatest fear is of discovery and self-betrayal. Jean Valjean had had no experience of those particular troubles, the only attractive ones and the only ones he had never known. That is why he did not grasp the true gravity of Cosette's silence. But he did see that she was unhappy, and this perturbed him. It was a case of inexperience meeting with inexperience.

He tried once to sound her. He asked:

'Would you like to go to the Luxembourg?'

A flush rose on her pale cheek.

'Yes.'

They went there but Marius was not to be seen. Three months had passed, and he had given up going there. When on the following day Valjean again asked if she would like to go there Cosette said sadly and resignedly, 'No.'

Thus by degrees the shadows deepened over their life. There remained to them only one distraction, one which had once been a source of happiness – the feeding of the hungry and the gift of clothing to those who were cold. During those visits to the poor, on which Cosette often accompanied Jean Valjean, they regained something of the warmth that had formerly existed between them. It was at this period that they visited the Jondrettes.

On the day following that visit Jean Valjean walked into the villa with his usual air of calm but with a large, inflamed and suppurating wound resembling a burn on his left fore-arm, for which he accounted in an off-hand way. It led to his being confined to the house with a fever for more than a month. He refused to see a doctor, and when Cosette begged him to do so he said, 'Call a vet if you like.'

Cosette nursed him so devotedly and with such evident delight in serving him that all his former happiness was restored, the fears and misgivings all dispelled, and he reflected as he gazed at her, 'Oh, most fortunate wound!'

Such was his happiness that his discovery that the so-called Jondrettes were in reality the Thenardiers scarcely troubled him. He had made good his escape and covered his tracks, and what else mattered? They were now in prison, and therefore, he assumed, no longer able to harm anyone.

Spring came, and the garden at that time of year was so delightful that Valjean said to Cosette, 'You never go in it, but I want you to' . . . 'Why then,' said Cosette, 'I will.'

So to humour her father she resumed her walks in the garden, but generally alone, for Valjean seldom entered it, as we know, probably because he was afraid of being seen through the gate.

There was a stone seat in the garden, close by the railing along the street, sheltered by a hedgerow from the gaze of the passer-by but so near to it that it might have been touched, at a pinch, by anyone reaching an arm through the railing and the hedge. Cosette was sitting on it one evening that April when Valjean was out.

The breeze was freshening. She got up and walked slowly round the garden, through the dew-soaked grass, reflecting idly that she should wear thicker shoes when she went out at that time or she would catch cold.

She returned to the bench, but as she was in the act of sitting down she suddenly had that feeling that sometimes comes to us, of someone behind her. She looked round and started to her feet.

It was he.

He was bareheaded and he looked pale and thinner. Cosette, near to fainting, did not utter a sound. She drew slowly away, because she felt herself drawn towards him. He did not move.

In withdrawing Cosette found herself with her back to a tree, and she leaned against it. Without it she would have fallen.

Then he began to speak, in that voice that she had never heard before, speaking so softly that it was scarcely raised above the rustle of the leaves.

'Forgive me for being here. I have been in such distress, I could not go on living the way things were, and so I had to come. Do you perhaps recognize me? You mustn't be afraid. It's a long time ago, but do you remember the day when you first looked at me – in the Luxembourg, nearly a year ago. If you knew how I adore you! Forgive me for talking like this, I don't know what I'm saying, perhaps I'm annoying you?'

'Mother!' she murmured, and sank down as though she herself were dying.

He caught her as she fell and clasped her tightly in his arms without knowing that he did so. He held her, trembling. She took his hand and laid it against her heart. He stammered:

'Then – you love me?'

She answered in a voice so low that it was scarcely to be heard: 'Of course! You know I do.'

He fell back on to the bench with her at his side. A kiss, and all was said.

And gradually they began to speak. Pure as disembodied spirits, they told each other about themselves, their dreams and how they had come to love each other at a distance and their despair when they no longer saw each other.

When they had finished, when everything had been said, she laid her head on his shoulder and asked:

'What is your name?'

'My name is Marius. And yours?'

'Cosette.'

You will have gathered that Eponine, having recognized the girl behind the wrought-iron gate in the Rue Plumet, whither she had been sent by Magnon, had led Marius to it.

Following that blessed and hallowed hour when a kiss had sealed the lovers' vows, he went there every evening.

Jean Valjean suspected nothing.

But meanwhile complications were looming.

One evening when Marius was just about to turn into the Rue Plumet a voice spoke to him.

'Good evening, Monsieur Marius.'

He looked up and saw Eponine.

The encounter gave him a shock. He had not given the girl a thought since the day she had led him to the Rue Plumet; he had not seen her again, and the memory of her had completely slipped his mind. He had every reason to be grateful to her; he owed his present happiness to her, yet it embarrassed him to meet her.

He said awkwardly:

'Oh, it's you, Eponine.'

'Why do you speak to me in that cold way? Have I done something wrong?'

'No,' he said.

Certainly he had nothing against her – far from it. It was simply that, with all his warmth bestowed on Cosette he had none for Eponine.

He stayed silent and she burst out, 'But why – ?' But then she stopped. It seemed that words had failed the once so brazen and heedless creature. She tried to smile but could not. She said, 'Well . . .' and then again was wordless, standing with lowered eyes.

'Good night, Monsieur Marius,' she said abruptly, and left him.

The next day was 3 June 1832, a date which must be set down because of the grave events, now impending, that loomed like thunder-clouds over Paris. Marius was going the same way as on the previous evening, when he saw Eponine coming towards him past the trees on the boulevard. Two days in succession was too much. He turned sharply off the boulevard and made for the Rue Plumet by way of the Rue Monsieur.

This caused Eponine to follow him as far as the Rue Plumet, a thing which she had not previously done.

So, without his knowing it, she followed him, and saw him slip through the wrought-iron gate into the garden. 'Well! He's going into the house!' she concluded, and, testing the bars of the gate, rapidly discovered his means of entry.

As though taking up guard duty, she sat down on the step at the point where the stone gatepost adjoined the neighbouring wall. It was a dark corner which hid her entirely. She stayed there for more than an hour without moving. At about ten o'clock six men entered the Rue Plumet. They came in single file, walking at some distance from one another and skirting the edge of the street like a scouting patrol. The first of them stopped at the wrought-iron gate, where he waited for the rest to catch up.

The sixth man proceeded to examine the gate as Eponine had done an hour before and was not slow to discover the bar loosened by Marius. But as he was about to wrench it aside a hand emerging from the darkness seized him by the arm. He felt himself thrust backward and the lanky figure of a girl rose up before him.

The man recoiled with the shock of the unexpected, exclaiming:

'Who the devil are you?'

'Your daughter.'

The man was Thenardier.

At this the five other men, Claquesous, Gueulemer, Babet, Montparnasse and Brujon, gathered round them, moving silently, without haste and without speech, in the slow, deliberate manner that is proper to creatures of the night.

'What are you doing here? Have you gone crazy?' cried Thenardier. 'Have you come to try and put me off?'

Eponine laughed.

'I'm here because I'm here, dearest father. Aren't I even allowed to sit down in the street? You're the one who shouldn't be here. What's the use of coming here when it's no good? I told Magnon it was a biscuit. So you're out again?'

Thenardier grunted.

'Yes, I'm not inside any more. And now, clear out.'

'It was very clever of you to get out. You must tell me how you did it. And mother – where is she? You must tell me about mother.'

'She's all right,' said Thenardier. 'Now clear out.'

'But I don't want to go,' said Eponine and she tightened her grip on him.

'This is getting silly,' said Babet.

'You can see we've got a job to do,' said Gaulemer.

Eponine said very sweetly, 'Don't you remember, Monsieur Babet and Monsieur Gueulemer, that I was sent to look this place over? I swear there's nothing for you here.'

'Go to the devil!' exclaimed Thenardier. 'When we've ransacked the house from top to bottom we'll know if there's anything worth having.'

She stood with her back to the gate, facing the six men, all armed to the teeth and went on in a low, resolute voice:

'If you try to get into the garden, if you so much as touch this gate, I'll scream the place down. I'll rouse the whole neighbourhood and have the lot of you pinched.'

'She will, too,' muttered Thenardier.

Eponine nodded vigorously, adding, 'And my father for a start!'

Thenardier moved towards her.

'You keep your distance,' she said.

He drew back, 'What's got into her?' And he spat the word at her: 'Bitch!'

She took a step towards them.

'My God, do you think I'm scared? I'm used to starving in summer and freezing in winter. What do I care if my body's picked up in the street tomorrow morning, beaten to death by my own father – or found in a year's time in the ditches round Saint-Cloud or the Ile des Cygnes, along with the garbage and the dead dogs?

'I've only got to yell, you know, and people will come running. There are six of you, but I'm the public.'

Having said which she sat down again on the step. She sat swinging her foot with an air of indifference. Through the rents in her tattered garment her thin shoulder-blades were to be seen. It would be hard to conceive a picture more determined or more surprising.

The six ruffians, disconcerted at being kept at bay by a girl, withdrew.

At the bend of the street they paused to exchange a few cryptic words.

'Where are we going to sleep tonight?'

'Under the town.'

'Have you the key to the grating, Thenardier?'

'Maybe.'

Eponine, intently watching, saw them move off the way they had come. She got up and stole along behind them, keeping close to walls and housefronts until they reached the boulevard. Here they separated, and melted like shadows into the night.

While that human watchdog was guarding the gate, and the six ruffians were giving in to a girl, Marius was with Cosette.

Never had the night been more starry and enchanting and never before had Marius been more enraptured and entranced. But he had found Cosette unhappy. She had been weeping and her eyes were red. It was the first cloud in their clear sky.

'My father said this morning that he has business to attend to and we may have to leave this place.'

Marius trembled.

'I don't understand what you mean.'

'He said that he had to go on a journey and we would go together. We must be ready within a week, and perhaps we should be going to England.'

'Cosette, are you going?'

'But what else can I do?' she cried, wringing her hands.

'So you are going?'

'But if my father goes . . .'

Marius looked away from her but then, looking back at her, he found that she was smiling.

'Marius, how silly we're being! I've got an idea.'

'What is it?'

'If we go you must come too. I'll tell you where, and you must meet me there, wherever it is.'

'How can I possibly do that?' Marius cried. 'It takes money to go to England, and I haven't any. I haven't told you, Cosette, but I'm a pauper. You only see me at night and you give me your hand; if you saw me by daylight you'd give me alms. England! I can't even afford a passport.'

He got up and stood with his face pressed to the trunk of a tree. Finally he turned.

'Cosette, I have never given anyone my word of honour because it frightens me to do so. I feel my father watching me. But I give you my most sacred word of honour that if you leave me I shall die.'

These words were uttered with so much quiet solemnity that she trembled.

'Now listen,' he said. 'Don't expect me here tomorrow.'

'Why not?'

'Not until the day after.'

'A whole day without seeing you! But that's dreadful!'

'We must sacrifice a day for the sake of our whole lives.'

'While I think of it,' said Marius, 'you must have my address in case you need it. I'm living with this friend of mine, Courfeyrac, at 16, Rue de la Verrerie.'

He got a penknife out of his pocket and scratched it on the plaster of the wall – 16, Rue de la Verrerie.

Cosette was intently watching him.

'Tell me what you're thinking, or how shall I sleep tonight?'

'I'm thinking this – that God can't possibly mean us to be separated. I shall be here the evening after tomorrow.'

While he had stood reflecting with his face against the tree-trunk, Marius had had an idea – one that alas he himself thought hopeless and impossible. He had taken a drastic decision.

Monsieur Gillenormand had now passed his ninety-first year. He was still living with his daughter in the old house which he owned in the Rue des Filles-du-Calvaire. He was, we may recall, one of those veterans cast in the antique mould who await death upright, burdened but not softened by age.

An evening came – it was the 4th of June, but that did not prevent him from having a fire blazing in the hearth – when Monsieur Gillenormand was thinking of Marius with both affection and bitterness. His bald head had sunk on to his chest, and he was gazing with grievous, exasperated eyes into the fire.

And while this mood was on him his old man-servant Basque entered the room and asked:

'Will monsieur receive Monsieur Marius?'

Monsieur Gillenormand started upright, ashen-faced and looking like a corpse revived by a galvanic shock. All the blood seemed to have been drained out of his body. He said in a very low voice:

'Show him in.'

Marius stood uncertainly in the doorway. The shabbiness of his clothes was not apparent in the half-darkness of the room. Nothing of him was clearly visible but his face, which was calm and grave but strangely sad.

'Monsieur,' said Marius, 'I know that I am not welcome here. I have come to ask for only one thing, and then I will go away at once.'

'You're a young fool,' the old man said. 'Who said you were to go away?'

It was the nearest he could get to the words that were in his heart.

'Monsieur,' said Marius, with the expression of a man about to jump off a precipice, 'I have come to ask your consent to my marriage.'

The old man burst out:

'So I suppose you've got some sort of position. What do you earn as a lawyer?'

'Nothing,' said Marius in a voice of almost savage firmness and defiance.

'Nothing? Well then I take it the girl is rich.'

'No richer than I am.'

'Well, what's her name?'

'Mademoiselle Fauchelevent.'

'Pshaw!' said the old man.

'So that's it.'

'So you said to yourself, "I'll have to go and see him, that old fossil. It's too bad I'm not yet twenty-five. I wouldn't have to worry about him and his consent. As it is, I'll go there and crawl to him, and the old fool will be so happy to see me that he won't care who I marry." That's what you think, isn't it? Well, my lad, you can do what you please. Marry your Pousselevent or Coupelevent or whatever her name is. But as for my consent, the answer is, never!'

'Grandfather –'

'Never!'

The tone in which the word was uttered robbed Marius of all hope. He rose, picked up his hat and walked resolutely towards the door. Here he turned, bowed deeply to his grandfather, straightened himself and said:

'I shall ask nothing more of you, monsieur. Farewell.'

The old man stayed motionless for some moments, unable to speak or breathe. Finally he croaked pitifully:

'What have I done to him? He's going away again. Oh, my God, my God, this time he'll never come back!'

At about four o'clock on the afternoon of that same day, Jean Valjean had been seated alone on the shady side of one of the more isolated slopes of the Champ de Mars. He was again on easy and happy terms with Cosette, his earlier anxieties having been put to rest; but during the past week or so other things had occurred to trouble him. One day as he walked along the boulevard he had seen Thenardier. Thanks to his disguise the latter had not recognized him, but since then he had seen him several times, often enough to convince him that Thenardier was now frequenting that part of the town. This had prompted him to take a major decision. Thenardier was the embodiment of all the dangers that threatened him.

Besides which, Paris was in an unsettled state, and for anyone with something to hide the present political unrest had the disadvantage that the police had become more than usually obtrusive, and might, in their search for agitators, light upon someone like Jean Valjean.

The upshot was that, after due consideration, Jean Valjean had decided to leave Paris, and even France. He had warned Cosette that he wanted to leave within a week. And now he sat on the grass in the Champ de Mars turning it all over in his mind.

While he was thus engaged he saw, by the shadow cast by the sun, that someone was standing on the ridge of the slope at his back. He was about to turn when a scrap of folded paper fell on his knee, seeming to have been tossed over his head. Unfolding it, he read two words, pencilled in capital letters:

'CLEAR OUT'

He got up quickly, but now there was no one on the slope. Looking about him he saw a queer figure, too tall for a child but too slight for a man, clad in a grey smock and drab-coloured corduroy trousers, scramble over the parapet.

Valjean went home at once, his mind much exercised.

Marius dejectedly left his grandfather's house. He had gone there with only a gleam of hope; he left in utter despair.

He wandered aimlessly though the streets, thinking of nothing that he could afterwards remember. At two in the morning he returned to Courfeyrac's lodging and flung himself fully dressed on his mattress.

When he awoke he found that Courfeyrac, Enjolras, Feuilly and Combeferre were all in the room seeming very agitated.

Courfeyrac asked him:

'Are you coming to the funeral of General Lamarque?'

For all they meant to him, the words might have been Chinese.

He went out some time after them, having put in his pocket the pistols Javert had loaned him on the occasion of the affair in February, which he had never returned. They were still loaded. It would be difficult to say what thought at the back of his mind prompted him to do this.

He roamed about all that day without knowing where he went.

At moments, as he strayed along the frequented boulevards, it struck him that there was a strange hubbub in the town, and he emerged from his preoccupations to wonder, 'Are people fighting?'

At nightfall, at nine o'clock precisely in accordance with his promise, he was in the Rue Plumet, and as he drew near the wrought-iron gate he forgot all else.

Marius slipped through the gate and hurried into the garden. Cosette was not in the place where ordinarily she awaited him. He crossed the shrubbery and made for the recess by the steps. 'She'll be there,' he thought – but she was not there. Looking up he saw that all the shutters were closed. He explored the garden and found it empty. Returning to the house, half-crazed with love and grief and terror, he banged with his fists on the shutters. He banged and banged again, regardless of the risk that a window might open to reveal the scowling face of her father. He gave up banging and began to shout, 'Cosette! Cosette, where are you?' There was no reply. There was no one in the house or garden, no one anywhere.

Suddenly he heard a voice calling through the trees, apparently from the street.

'Monsieur Marius!'

He looked up.

'Who's that?'

'Is that you, Monsieur Marius?'

'Yes.'

'Monsieur Marius, your friends are waiting for you at the barricade in the Rue de la Chanvrerie.'

The voice resembled the husky croak of Eponine. Marius ran to the gate, shifted the loose bar and, thrusting his head through, saw someone who looked like a youth vanish at a run into the darkness.

By the spring of 1832, although for three months cholera had chilled men's spirits and in some sort damped their state of unrest, Paris was more than ripe for an upheaval. The town was like a loaded gun, needing only a spark to set it off. The spark, in June 1832, was the death of General Lamarque.

Lamarque was a man of action and of high repute. Under the Empire and the Restoration he had possessed the two forms of courage required by those two epochs – courage on the battlefield and courage in the debating chamber. He was as eloquent as he had been brave.

His death, which was not unexpected, had been feared by the people as a loss, and by the Government as a pretext. It was a day of national mourning, and, like all other bitterness, mourning may be transformed into revolt. That is what happened.

The rebellion, arising out of the clash between civilians and the military in front of the Arsenal, was a moment of terrible recoil. The crowd broke ranks and scattered, some uttering bellicose cries, others in the pale terror of flight. The river of humanity filling the boulevards overflowed to left and right, breaking up into lesser streams with a sound like the bursting of a dam. At this moment a ragged small boy, coming down the Rue Menilmontant with a sprig of flowering laburnum which he had picked on the heights of Belleville, noticed in a stall outside an antique shop an old cavalry pistol. Throwing away his flowers, he snatched it up, shouted to the proprietress, 'Missus, I'm borrowing your thingumajig!' and made off with it.

Gavroche was going to war. Not until he reached the boulevard did he notice that the pistol had no hammer.

Gavroche, having arrived at the Marche Saint-Jean, where the police post had already been put out of action, proceeded to join forces with a party led by Enjolras, Courfeyrac, Combeferre and Feuilly.

A tumultuous crowd was following them, composed of students, artists, navvies and dock-labourers, armed with cudgels and bayonets, and a few with pistols in their belts.

The column turned into the Rue de la Verrerie. Gavroche, now in the forefront, was singing some doggerel with the full strength of his lungs, so that his voice rang out like a trumpet-call.

> 'Now that the moon is risen high
> Into the forest let us fly,'
> Said Charlot to Charlotte.

Their numbers were steadily increasing. They were joined in the Rue des Billettes by a tall, grey-haired man whose bold, vigorous appearance impressed Enjolras and his friends, although none of them knew him. Gavroche, still striding along at the head of the column, had not noticed him.

They went past Courfeyrac's door in the Rue de la Verrerie. 'Good,' said Courfeyrac. 'I came out without my purse and I've lost my hat.' Leaving the party, he ran upstairs to his room, picked up his purse and an old hat, and also seized a large, square box about the size of a suitcase which was hidden under his dirty linen. As he hurried down again the concierge called to him:

'There's someone waiting to see you.'

'Who is it?'

'I don't know.'

'Well, where is he?'

'In my lodge.'

At this moment a youth, who seemed to be some sort of workman, slight of figure, wearing a torn smock and patched velveteen trousers, came out of the lodge and said:

'I'm looking for Monsieur Marius.'

'He's not here.'

'Will he be back this evening?'

'I couldn't tell you. I certainly shan't be here myself,' said Courfeyrac.

The youth looked hard at him and asked:

'Where are you going?'

'I'm going to the barricades.'

'Shall I come with you?'

'If you want to,' said Courfeyrac. 'The streets are open to everyone.'

He ran off to rejoin his friends, and when he had caught up with them gave two of them his box to carry. It was some time before he noticed that the youth had followed him.

A makeshift crowd does not always go where it first intended; it is borne on the wind. They passed by Saint-Merry and presently, without quite knowing why, found themselves in the Rue de la Chanvrerie.

Dismay gripped the whole street when the newcomers poured in. Casual loiterers took to their heels. In the twinkling of an eye doors were bolted and windows shuttered and an old dame had rigged a mattress across her window as a protection against musket-fire. Only the tavern remained open, for the good reason that the party made straight for it.

The newspapers of the day, which reported that the 'almost unassailable' barricade in the Rue de la Chanvrerie reached the level of the second storey, were in error. The fact is that it was nowhere more than six or seven feet high, and so constructed that the defenders could shelter behind it or peer over it or climb on top of it by means of four piles of superimposed paving-stones arranged to form a broad flight of steps. The outer side of the barricade, consisting of paving-stones and barrels reinforced by wooden beams and planks interlaced in the wheels of the cart and the overturned omnibus, had a bristling, unassailable appearance. A gap wide enough for a man to pass through had been left at the end furthest from the tavern to afford a means of exit. The shaft of the omnibus had been set upright and was held in position with ropes. It had a red flag affixed to it which fluttered over the barricade.

The small Mondetour barricade was not visible from that side, being concealed behind the tavern. Between them the two barricades constituted a formidable stronghold.

When both barricades were completed and the flag had been hoisted, a table was brought out of the tavern and Courfeyrac climbed on to it. Enjolras brought out the square box and Courfeyrac opened it. It was filled with cartridges, and at the sight of these even the stoutest hearts quivered and there was a momentary silence. Courfeyrac, smiling, proceeded to pass them out. A barrel of powder was placed handy to the door and kept in reserve.

Meanwhile, a fairy-light had been set on the small barricade, and on the larger one a wax torch of the kind that one sees on Mardi-Gras.

Night fell, but nothing happened. The prolonged pause was a sign that the Government was taking its time and assembling its forces. Fifty men were awaiting the onslaught of sixty thousand.

Enjolras was seized with the impatience that afflicts strong characters on the threshold of great events. He went to look for Gavroche, who was now making cartridges in the downstairs room.

Gavroche was very much preoccupied at that moment, but not precisely with cartridges. The man who had joined them in the Rue des Billettes had come into the downstairs room and seated himself at the table in the darkest corner. He had been issued with a large-bore musket, which was now propped between his knees. Gavroche, drawing nearer, walked round the detached and brooding figure with extreme caution. At the same time communing with himself

– 'I'm seeing things . . . Could it possibly be . . . ? No, it can't be!'

It was at this moment that Enjolras came up to him.

'You're small enough,' Enjolras said. 'You won't be noticed. I want you to slip into the streets, and come back and tell me what's going on.'

'Well, that's fine. I'll do it. You trust the little'uns, guv'nor, but keep an eye on the big'uns. For instance, that one there.' He had lowered his voice as he nodded towards the man from the Rue des Billettes.

'He's a police spy, a copper's nark.'

'You're sure?'

'He picked me up less than a fortnight ago by the Pont Royal, where I was having a stroll.'

Enjolras hurriedly left the room and returned almost instantly with four men. Enjolras then went up to him and asked:

'Who are you?'

The abrupt question caused the man to start. Looking hard into Enjolras's eyes, he seemed to discern exactly what was in his mind, and smiling the most disdainful, unabashed and resolute of smiles he answered:

'I see how it is . . . Yes, I am.'

'You're a police informer?'

'I'm a representative of the law.'

'And your name?'

'Javert.'

Enjolras nodded to the four men. Before Javert had time to move he was seized and stood upright with his hands tied behind his back and bound to the wooden pillar in the centre of the room that had given the tavern its original name. Enjolras said:

'You will be shot two minutes before the barricade falls.'

'Why not now?' Javert inquired with the utmost composure.

'We don't want to waste ammunition.'

Enjolras gestured to Gavroche. 'You! Get started. Do what I told you.'

'I'm off,' said Gavroche.

But at the door he paused.

'Anyway, let me have his musket. I'm leaving you the musician, but I'd like to have his trumpet.'

He made them a military salute and slipped happily through the gap in the large barricade.

Almost immediately after the departure of Gavroche, Courfeyrac caught sight of the slim young man who that morning had come to his lodging in search of Marius. This youth, who had a bold and heedless air, had come to join them.

The voice summoning Marius in the dusk to join the barricade on the Rue de la Chanvrerie, had sounded to him like the voice of Fate. He wished to die and here was the means; his knock on the door of the tomb was answered by a hand tendering him the key. There is a fascination in the melancholy inducements that darkness offers to the despairing. Marius parted the bars of the gate, as he had done so many times before, and leaving the garden behind him said, 'So be it!' As it happened, he was already armed, having Javert's pistols on him. The youth he thought he had discerned in the shadows had vanished.

The clock of Saint-Merry had struck ten, and Enjolras and Combeferre had seated themselves with their carbines near the narrow breach in the main barricade. They were not talking; both were listening with ears strained to catch the least, most distant sound of marching feet.

Suddenly the brooding silence was broken by the sound of a gay young voice, raised in an improvised ditty to the tune of '*Au clair de la lune*', and ending with a cockcrow.

'It's Gavroche,' said Enjolras.

Running footsteps echoed down the empty street, a figure nimble as a circus clown scrambled over the omnibus and Gavroche, very much out of breath, leapt down from the barricade.

'They're coming! Where's my musket?'

An electric stir ran through the defenders and there was a sound of hands snatching up weapons.

'Would you like my carbine?' Enjolras asked.

'No, I want the big musket,' said Gavroche. He meant Javert's musket.

Every man took up his action station. Forty-three defenders, among them Enjolras, Combeferre, Courfeyrac, Bossuet, Joly, Bahorel and Gavroche, knelt behind the main barricade with muskets and carbines thrust through gaps between the paving-stones, alert and ready to fire. Six others, commanded by Feuilly, waited with loaded muskets at the windows on the two upper floors of the tavern.

There was a pause, as though both sides were waiting. Suddenly a voice called out of the darkness, the more awesome because no speaker was to be seen, so that it sounded like the voice of the darkness itself:

'Who's there?'

At the same time they heard the clicking of muskets being cocked. Enjolras responded in lofty and resonant tones:

'The French Revolution!'

'Fire!' ordered the voice, and an instant glare of light shone upon the front of the houses.

A hideous blow shook the barricade. Bullets ricocheting back off the houses behind them wounded several of the defenders. The effect of that first discharge was stupefying, its sheer weight enough to make the boldest man think twice. They were evidently confronted by, at the least, a whole regiment.

Gavroche, keeping watch, thought he saw men moving stealthily towards the barricade. He shouted:

'Watch out!'

A dense glitter of bayonets was now visible on the other side of the barricade. The tall forms of Municipal Guardsmen surged in, some climbing over the omnibus and others coming by way of the breach. Gavroche was forced to give ground, but he did not run away.

It was a critical instant, like the moment when floodwaters

rise to the topmost level of an embankment and begin to seep over. In another minute the stronghold might have been taken.

Bahorel sprang towards the first man to enter and shot him at point-blank range; a second man killed him with a bayonet-thrust. Courfeyrac was felled by another man and called for help. The biggest of all the attackers, a giant of a man, bore down with his bayonet on Gavroche. Raising Javert's heavy musket, the boy took aim and pulled the trigger. Nothing happened. Javert had not loaded the musket. The Municipal Guardsman laughed and thrust at the youngster with his bayonet.

But before the bayonet could reach Gavroche the musket fell from the man's hands and he himself fell backwards with a bullet in his forehead. A second bullet took the man assailing Coufeyrac in the chest and laid him low.

Marius had entered the stronghold.

Crouched at the turning of the Rue Mondetour, Marius had witnessed the beginning of the battle. The killing of Bahorel, Courfeyrac's call for help, the threat to Gavroche; friends to be rescued or avenged. He had rushed into the melee with a pistol in either hand, and one had saved Gavroche, the other Courfeyrac.

He was now weaponless, having flung away his discharged pistols; but he had seen the keg of powder near the door in the lower room of the tavern. While he was looking at it, a soldier levelled his musket at him, but as he was in the act of firing a hand was thrust over the muzzle, diverting it. The person who had flung himself forward was the young workman in corduroy trousers. The ball shattered his hand and perhaps entered his body, for he fell; but it did not touch Marius. It was an episode in misted darkness, half-seen rather than seen. Marius was scarcely aware of it.

The rebels, shaken but not panic-stricken, had rallied. Muskets were levelled on both sides at point-blank range; they were so close that they could talk without shouting. At this point, when the spark was about to be struck, an officer in a stiff collar and large epaulettes raised his sword and said:

'Lay down your arms!'

'Fire!' ordered Enjolras.

The two volleys rang out simultaneously, and the scene was enveloped in thick, acrid smoke filled with the groans of the wounded and the dying. When it had cleared both sides could be seen, diminished but still in the same place, re-charging their weapons in silence. But suddenly a ringing voice cried:

'Clear out or I'll blow up the barricade!'

All heads were turned to stare in the direction of the voice.

Marius, seizing the powder-keg in the tavern, had taken advantage of the smoke-filled lull to slip along the barricade until he reached the structure of paving-stones in which the torch was fixed. To detach the torch and set the powder-keg in its place had taken him only the time he needed to bend down and then stand upright.

'If you blow up the barricade,' a sergeant called, 'you'll blow up yourself as well!'

'And myself as well,' said Marius, and lowered the torch towards the keg.

But there was no longer anyone on the barricade. The attackers had made off in a disorderly stampede, leaving their dead and wounded behind. It was a rout, and the fortress had been relieved.

His friends flocked round Marius, and Courfeyrac flung his arms about his neck.

'So you've come! I'd be dead otherwise,' said Courfeyrac.

'I'd have copped it too,' said Gavroche.

'Where is the leader?' Marius asked.

'You're now the leader,' Enjolras said.

Marius thought of the smaller barricade and went to inspect it. The Mondetour alleyway, and the small streets running into it, were entirely quiet.

As he was leaving, having concluded his inspection, he heard his own name faintly spoken in the darkness.

'Monsieur Marius!'

He started, recognizing the husky voice that two hours previously had called to him through the gate in the Rue Plumet. But now it was scarcely more than a whisper. Although he peered hard into the darkness he could see nothing.

'I'm at your feet,' the voice said.

Looking down, Marius saw a dark shape crawling over the cobbles towards him. The gleam of the lamp was enough to enable him to make out a smock, a pair of torn corduroy trousers, two bare feet and something that looked like a trail of blood. A white face was turned towards him and the voice asked:

'Don't you recognize me?'

'No.'

'Eponine.'

Marius bent hastily down and saw that it was indeed that unhappy girl, clad in a man's clothes.

'How do you come to be here? What are you doing?'

'I'm dying,' she said.

Marius cried, as though starting out of sleep:

'You're wounded! I'll carry you into the tavern.'

He tried to get an arm underneath her to raise her up, and in doing so touched her hand. She uttered a weak cry.

'Did I hurt you?'

'A little.'

'But I only touched your hand.'

She lifted her hand for him to see, and he saw a hole in the centre of the palm.

'What happened?' he asked.

'A bullet went through it.'

'A bullet? But how?'

'Don't you remember a musket being aimed at you?'

'Yes, and a hand was clapped over it.'

'That was mine.'

Marius shuddered.

'What madness! You poor child! Still, one doesn't die of a wounded hand.'

'The ball passed through my hand but it came out through my back. It's no use trying to move me. I'll tell you how you can treat my wound better than any surgeon. Sit down on that stone, close beside me.'

Marius did so. She rested her head on his knee and said without looking at him:

'Oh, what happiness!'

For a moment she was silent, than with an effort she turned to look at Marius.

'You know, Monsieur Marius, it vexed me when you went into that garden. That was silly, because after all I'd shown you the way there, and anyway I should have known that a young gentleman like you –' She broke off, and passing from one unhappy thought to another: 'You think I'm ugly, don't you?' She went on: 'No one will get out of this place alive. And I'm the one who brought you here! You're going to die. I was expecting it, and yet I put my hand over that musket barrel. How queer. But I wanted to die before you did. I dragged myself here when I got hurt. I've been waiting for you, Monsieur Marius.'

At this moment the voice of Gavroche rang out in another burst of song.

Eponine had raised herself on one arm and was listening. She looked up at Marius. 'That's my brother. He mustn't see me. He'd scold.'

'Your brother?' Marius repeated, while in the bitterest depth of his heart he recalled the obligation to the Thenard-ier family laid upon him by his father.

Marius made a movement.

'Oh, don't go!' she said. 'It won't be long.'

She was sitting almost upright, but her voice was very low. At moments she struggled for breath. Raising her face as near as she could to Marius's, she said:

'Look, I can't cheat you. I have a letter for you in my pocket. I was asked to post it, but I didn't. I didn't want you to get it. But you might be angry with me when we meet again. Because we shall all meet again, shan't we? Take your letter.'

With a convulsive movement she seized Marius's hand and guided it to her pocket.

Marius took out the letter, and she made a gesture of satisfaction and acceptance.

'Now you must promise me something for my trouble . . .' She paused.

'What?' asked Marius.

'Do you promise?'

'Yes, I promise.'

'You must kiss me on the forehead after I'm dead . . . I shall know.'

She let her head fall back on his knees; and then she was motionless. He thought that the sad soul had left her. But then she slowly opened her eyes and said in a voice so sweet that it seemed already to come from another world:

'You know, Monsieur Marius, I think I was a little bit in love with you.'

She tried to smile, and died.

Marius kept his promise. He kissed the pale forehead. It was no act of infidelity to Cosette, but a deliberate, tender farewell to an unhappy spirit.

He had trembled as he took the letter Eponine had brought him. Instantly sensing its importance, he longed to read it. But first he laid her gently on the ground, feeling that he could not read it beside her dead body.

Going into the tavern, he unfolded it by the light of a candle.

My dearest,

Alas, father insists that we must leave here at once. We go tonight to No. 7 Rue de l'Homme-Arme, and in a week we shall be in England.

Cosette 4th June

What had happened may be briefly told: Eponine was responsible for everything. After the evening of 3 June she had had two things in mind: to frustrate the plan of her father and his friends for robbing the house in the Rue Plumet, and to separate Marius and Cosette. She had exchanged clothes with a youth who thought it amusing to go about dressed as a woman. It was she who had given Jean Valjean the note warning him to change his address. Cosette, shattered by this unexpected blow, had hurriedly written her letter to Marius. But how was it to be posted? While she was debating the matter Cosette had caught sight of Eponine through the garden gate, wandering in her male attire up and down the street. Thinking she had to do with a young workman, she had given her five francs and the letter. Eponine had put the letter in her pocket and the next day, the 5th, had gone to Courfeyrac's lodging. She had waited there for Marius, but when Courfeyrac told her that he and his friends were going to the barricade a sudden impulse had seized her – to plunge into that death and take Marius with her.

Marius covered Cosette's letter with kisses. So she still loved him! He thought for a moment that now he must not die, but then, he thought, she was going with her father to England, and his grandfather had refused to consent to their marriage. Nothing was changed in the fate that pursued them.

But he reflected that he had two duties to perform. He must send Cosette a last message of farewell; and he must save that poor little boy, Thenardier's son, from the disaster that so nearly threatened them all.

He got out a sheet of paper, and with a pencil wrote the following lines:

Our marriage was impossible. I went to my grandfather, and he refused his consent. I have no fortune; neither have you. I hurried to see you but you were no longer there. You remember the pledge I gave you. I shall keep it. I shall die. I love you. When you read this my soul will be very near at hand and smiling at you.

Having nothing with which to seal the letter he simply folded the paper in four and addressed it.

Then after a moment's reflection he wrote on another sheet of paper:

'My name is Marius Pontmercy. My body is to be taken to the house of my grandfather, M. Gillenormand, 6 Rue des Filles-du-Calvaire, in the Marais.'

He returned the wallet to his jacket pocket and called to Gavroche.

'Will you do something for me?'

'Anything you like,' said Gavroche. 'Lord love us, if it weren't for you I'd have copped it.'

'I want you to deliver this letter. You must leave here at once.'

'Yes, but look here,' said the valiant Gavroche, 'the barricade may be taken while I'm away.'

'The chances are that they won't attack again until daybreak, and the barricade won't fall until noon.'

'Well, then,' said Gavroche, 'why shouldn't I deliver the letter tomorrow morning?'

'It would be too late. By then all the streets round us will be guarded and you'd never get out. You must go at once.'

'Very well,' he said. And went off at a run down the narrow Rue Mondetour.

The thought that had decided Gavroche was that the Rue de l'Homme-Armé was not far off, and that he could deliver the letter and be back in plenty of time.

Cosette had not left the Rue Plumet without protest, but the abrupt warning to Valjean to change his abode, flung at him by a stranger, had so alarmed him as to make him overbearing. He had thought that his secret was discovered and that the police were after him. Cosette had been forced to give way.

In their departure from the Rue Plumet, so hasty as to be almost flight, Jean Valjean had taken nothing with him except the cherished box of child's clothing which Cosette had nicknamed his 'inseparable'. It was only with difficulty that Toussaint had obtained permission to make up a few packages of clothes. One of these contained Valjean's National Guard uniform. Cosette had taken nothing but her letter-case and blotter. Valjean, as a further precaution, had arranged for them to leave at nightfall, which had allowed her time to write her letter to Marius. It was dark when they reached the Rue de l'Homme-Arme.

They went to bed in silence.

Panic, such is human nature, may die down as irrationally as it arises. Scarcely had they reached their new dwelling than Valjean's alarm subsided until finally it had vanished altogether. He was almost light-hearted when he got up next morning.

As for Cosette, she had asked Toussaint to bring her a cup of soup in her bedroom and she did not appear until the evening. At about five o'clock Toussaint set a dish of cold chicken on the table and Cosette deigned to attend the meal, out of deference to her father.

This done, and saying that she had a headache, Cosette bade her father good night and went back to her bedroom. Valjean sat with his elbows on the table, basking in his present security. He got up presently and began to walk up and down the room, from the door to the window and back, feeling more and more at ease.

But as he paced slowly up and down the room something suddenly caught his eye. He came face to face with the mirror hanging at an inclined angle over the sideboard, and, reflected in it, he read the following lines:

My dearest,

Alas, father insists that we must leave here at once. We go tonight to No. 7, Rue de l'Homme-Arme, and in a week we shall be in England.

Cosette 4th June

Jean Valjean stood aghast.

Cosette when they arrived had put her blotting-book on the dresser, and in her distress had forgotten to remove it, leaving it open at the page on which she had blotted her letter to Marius, and the mirror, reflecting the reversed handwriting, had made it clearly legible. It was simple and it was devastating.

Of all the torments he had suffered in his long trial by adversity, this was the worst. Alas, the supreme ordeal – indeed the one true ordeal – is the loss of the beloved.

It is true that the poor, ageing man loved Cosette only as a father; but the emptiness of his life had caused this paternal love to embrace all others.

Now, when he realized that another possessed her heart and that he was no more than the father, the intensity of his pain was past enduring. His thoughts flew instantly to Marius. He did not know the name, but he promptly placed the man, the youthful stranger in the Luxembourg.

Having decided in his mind that this young man was at the bottom of it all, Jean Valjean, the man who had redeemed himself, turned his inward vision upon himself: and a ghost rose before his eyes – hatred.

There are actions which arise, without our knowing it, from the depths of our thought. No doubt it was owing to an impulse of this kind that a few minutes later Valjean was out in the street. He was seated, bareheaded, on the kerbstone outside the house.

Darkness had fallen.

How long did he stay there? Probably he himself did not know.

The street was empty. Vague sounds of distant tumult, tocsins and fanfares, were to be heard and a sudden burst of firing sounded from the direction of the market, followed by a second, even more violent. Probably this was the attack on the Rue de Chanvrerie barricade which Marius had repulsed.

The sound of footsteps caused him to raise his head. By the light of the street-lamp he saw a youthful figure approaching. Gavroche had arrived in the Rue de l'Homme-Arme.

He was gazing at the housefronts, apparently in search of a number. All were locked and barred. After trying five or six houses in vain he shrugged his shoulders and commented:

'Well, blow me!'

Jean Valjean, who in his present state of mind would not have addressed or answered any other person, was irresistibly moved to question this lively small boy.

'Well, youngster, what are you up to?'

'What I'm after is that I'm hungry,' said Gavroche crisply; and he added, 'Youngster yourself.'

Valjean felt in his pocket and produced a five-franc piece. Startled by the size of the offering, Gavroche stared at the coin, charmed by its whiteness as it glimmered faintly in his hand. He had heard of five-franc pieces, he knew them by reputation, and he was delighted to see one at close quarters. Something worth looking at, he thought, and did so for some moments with pleasure.

'You're all right,' said Gavroche. He put the coin in one of his pockets, and with a growing assurance, asked: 'Do you live in this street?'

'Yes. Why?'

'Would you mind telling me which is Number Seven?'

'Why do you want to know?'

Gavroche was brought up short, feeling that he had already said too much. He ran a hand through his hair and said cryptically:

'Because.'

A thought occurred to Jean Valjean. Acute distress has these moments of lucidity. He asked:

'Have you brought me the letter I've been waiting for?'

'You?' said Gavroche. 'But you're not a woman.'

'A letter addressed to Mademoiselle Cosette. I'm to give it to her. May I have it?'

Gavroche fished in another pocket and got out the folded sheet of paper.

'Well, here you are.' Gavroche handed over the letter. 'That letter comes from the barricade in the Rue de la Chanvrerie, to which I am now returning. Good night, citizen.'

Whereupon Gavroche departed – or, better, returned like a homing pigeon to its nest.

Jean Valjean went back into the house with Marius's letter. We cannot be said to read when in a state of violent emotion. Our eyes skip the beginning, hurrying on to the end. With a feverish acuteness we grasp the general sense. In the letter written by Marius, Jean Valjean was conscious only of the following: 'I shall die . . . When you read this my soul will be very near . . .'

The effect of these words was to kindle in him a horrid exaltation. His problem was solved, more rapidly than he had dared to hope. Without any action on the part of Jean Valjean, this 'other man' was about to die. Once again he would have Cosette to himself, without any rival, and their life together would continue as before. He had only to keep this letter in his pocket. Cosette would never know what had happened to that other man. 'I have only to let things take their course. If he is not yet dead, he will certainly die.'

But having assured himself of this, Valjean's gloom returned; and presently he went downstairs and roused the porter.

About an hour later he left the house again, clad in the full uniform of the National Guard and fully armed. The porter had had no difficulty in finding in the neighbourhood the means to complete his equipment. With a loaded musket and a pouch filled with cartridges he set off for Les Halles.

Dawn rouses the spirits as it does the birds. Heady prognostications ran from group to group in a kind of grim and gay murmur resembling the buzz of war in a hive of bees.

Enjolras returned from his cautious patrol of the surrounding darkness. He stood for a moment listening to this exuberance. Then he said:

'The whole Paris army is involved. A third of it is concentrated on us, besides a contingent of the Garde Nationale. We shall be attacked within the hour. As for the populace, we've nothing to hope for – not a single faubourg or a single regiment. They have failed us.'

The effect of these words on the gossiping groups was like that of rainfall on a swarm of bees. All were silent. There was a moment of inexpressible terror, overshadowed by the wings of death.

But it swiftly passed. A voice from one of the groups cried:

'Then we'll build the barricade up to twenty feet high, citizens, and defend it with our dead bodies. We'll show the world that if the people have deserted the republicans, the republicans have not deserted the people!'

The speech, releasing men from their private terror, was greeted with a roar of strange satisfaction, triumphant in tone.

'To the death! We'll all stay here.'

'Why all?' asked Enjolras. 'The barricade is sound. Thirty men can hold it. Why sacrifice forty?'

'Because no one wants to leave,' was the reply.

'Citizens,' cried Enjolras. 'The Republic is not so rich in men that it can afford to waste them. If it is the duty of some of us to leave, that duty should be carried out like any other.'

'Besides,' a voice said, 'it's all very well to talk about leaving, but we're surrounded.'

'Not on the side of Les Halles,' said Enjolras. 'The Rue Mondetour is clear. You can get to the Marche des Innocents.'

'And there we'll be taken,' said another voice. 'They'll smell powder, and we'll be shot.'

Without replying Enjolras touched Combeferre's shoulder and the two of them went into the tavern. They re-emerged a minute later, Enjolras carrying the four uniforms stripped off the bodies of the dead soldiers and Combeferre with their belts and helmets.

'Anyone can pass through the soldiers' ranks wearing these,' Enjolras said. 'They'll do for four of you.' He dropped the uniforms on the ground.

Their stoical audience still showed no sign of obeying.

Marius suddenly spoke:

'I agree there must be no unnecessary sacrifice. And there is no time to be lost. Some of you have families –

mothers, wives and children. Those men must leave at once.'

No man stirred.

'I beseech you,' said Marius.

And then, touched by Marius's plea, the heroic defenders began to denounce one another. 'You're a father of a family. You're keeping two sisters.'

'Citizens,' said Enjolras, 'this is the Republic, where universal suffrage prevails. You must decide by vote who is to go.'

He was obeyed. Within a few minutes five men had been selected and they stepped out of the ranks.

'Five!' exclaimed Marius. 'But there are only four uniforms.' He looked down at the four uniforms.

As he did so a fifth uniform was added to the heap, as though it had fallen from the clouds.

Looking round, Marius recognized Monsieur Fauchelevent.

Jean Valjean had entered the stronghold.

No one had noticed Valjean when he appeared, all eyes being intent on the five men and the four uniforms. Valjean had stood listening, and, grasping the situation, had silently stripped off his uniform and dropped it on the pile.

The sensation was enormous.

'Who is this man?' demanded Bossuet.

'At least,' said Combeferre, 'he's ready to save another man's life.'

Marius said authoritatively:

'I know him.'

This was enough for them. Enjolras turned to Jean Valjean.

'Citizen, you are welcome.' And he added, 'You know that we are about to die.'

Valjean, without replying, helped the man he had saved to put on his uniform.

When the men restored to life had departed, the thoughts of Enjolras turned to the man condemned to death. He went into the tavern and asked:

'Do you want anything?'

Javert replied:

'When are you going to kill me?'

'You must wait. At the moment we need all our ammunition.'

'I'm not at all comfortable,' said Javert. 'It was scarcely kind to keep me lashed to this pillar all night. You can tie me up as much as you like, but you might at least let me lie on a table.'

At Enjolras's order, four of the rebels released Javert from the pillar, walked him to the table and, stretching him out on it, tied him to it securely with a rope passed round his body.

While they were doing this a man appeared in the doorway and stood staring with a singular fixity at Javert. The shadow he cast caused Javert to turn his head. He looked round and recognized Jean Valjean. He gave no sign of emotion. Coolly averting his gaze, he simply said, 'So here we are!'

As on the previous evening, all eyes were intent on the end of the street, which was now bathed in daylight. There was a rattling of chains and a clatter of massive wheels over the cobbles – a sort of solemn commotion heralding the approach of more sinister ironmongery.

A piece of artillery came in sight.

In a matter of instants the gun was ready for action, its wheels straddling the gutter in the middle of the street, its formidable mouthpiece pointing at the barricade. The discharge was awaited with tense anxiety.

The blow fell, accompanied by a roaring explosion; and a cheerful voice cried:

'I'm back!'

Gavroche had reappeared at the precise moment that the ball ploughed into the barricade, having scrambled over the small barrier. His arrival made more impression than did the cannon-ball, which simply buried itself in the rubble.

The defenders crowded round Gavroche, but he had no time to tell them anything. Marius, trembling, dragged him aside.

'Why have you come back here?'

'If it comes to that,' said Gavroche, 'why are you here at all?' And he surveyed Marius with his customary effrontery, his eyes widening with the glow of his achievement.

'Did you at least deliver my letter?'

Gavroche was feeling somewhat remorseful about that letter. In his haste to get back to the barricade he had got rid of it rather than delivered it. He feared Marius's rebuke. So he took the easiest way out: he lied outrageously.

'Citizen, I gave the letter to the doorkeeper. The lady was asleep. She'll get it when she wakes up.'

Marius had sent the letter with two objects in mind, to bid farewell to Cosette and to save Gavroche. He had to content himself with having accomplished only one of them.

But the thought of the letter reminded him of the presence of Monsieur Fauchelevent in the stronghold, and it occurred to him that the two things might be connected. Pointing to Monsieur Fauchelevent, he asked:

'Do you know that man?'

'No,' said Gavroche.

It will be remembered that he had encountered Jean Valjean after dark. Marius's suspicions were dispelled.

All this time Enjolras in his redoubt was watching and intently listening. He caught a sound that he thought he recognized, the rattle of grape-canisters. He saw the leader of the gun-crew readjust his aim, pointing the gun-muzzle slightly to the left.

'Heads down and get back to the wall,' shouted Enjolras. 'All of you down on your knees.'

But the gun was fired before the order could be carried out, and they heard the hideous whistle of grape-shot. The gun was aimed at the narrow breach between the end of the barricade and the house wall. The bullets ricocheted off the wall, killing two men and wounding three. If it went on like that the barricade would cease to be tenable. It was not proof against grape-shot.

'Stuff that gap with a mattress,' ordered Enjolras.

'There isn't one to spare,' said Combeferre. 'The wounded are using them all.'

Jean Valjean, seated on a kerbstone at the corner of the tavern with his musket between his knees, had thus far taken no part in the proceedings. Now, however, he got to his feet.

It will be recalled that when the party had entered the Rue de la Chanvrerie an old woman in one of the houses had rigged a mattress outside her window as a precaution against bullets. It was an attic window six storeys above ground, and the house was situated just outside the barricade.

'Will someone lend me a double-barrelled carbine?' said Valjean.

Enjolras passed him his own. Jean Valjean took aim and fired, and one of the cords parted, leaving the mattress hanging by the other. He fired again, and the mattress slid between the two poles and fell into the street.

There was a burst of applause from the defenders and someone cried:

'There's your mattress.'

'Yes,' said Combeferre, 'but who's going to fetch it?'

The mattress had fallen outside the barricade and the soldiers were keeping up a steady fire. The bullets buried themselves harmlessly in the barricade; but the street in front of it was a place of hideous danger.

Jean Valjean went out through the breach, dashed through the hail of bullets, picked up the mattress and, carrying it on his back, brought it into the stronghold. He then used it to block the breach, fixing it against the house wall in a position where the gunners could not see it.

Then the defenders awaited the next salvo of grape, which was not slow in coming; but this time there was no ricochet. The mattress had had the desired effect; it had damped the spread of the bullets.

'Citizen,' said Enjolras to Jean Valjean, 'the Republic thanks you.'

Joly was laughing as he marvelled:

'How immoral that a mattress should prove so effective! A triumph of submissiveness over aggression!'

Seated on a paving-stone near Enjolras, Courfeyrac exclaimed: 'Here's another!'

And indeed a second cannon had been brought into action. The gunners rapidly manoeuvred it into position alongside the first.

It was the beginning of the end.

A minute later both pieces fired together, accompanied by a volley of musketry from the supporting troops.

'We really must abate this nuisance,' said Enjolras, and he shouted: 'Open fire on the gunners.'

Everything was in readiness. The barricade, so long silent, burst furiously into flame, six or seven volleys following one another. The street was filled with blinding smoke, but after a few minutes the bodies of two-thirds of the gunners could be discerned. Those still on their feet continued with rigid composure to serve the guns, but the rate of fire slackened.

'Good!' said Joly to Enjolras. 'A success.'

Enjolras shrugged his shoulders.

'Another quarter of an hour of that kind of success and we shan't have ten cartridges left.'

It seemed that Gavroche must have heard those words.

Courfeyrac suddenly perceived someone crouched in the street just beyond the barricade. Gavroche, having fetched a basket from the tavern, had slipped out through the break and was calmly engaged in filling it with ammunition from the pouches of the men killed in the previous assault.

'What are you doing?' demanded Courfeyrac.

Gavroche looked up perkily.

'I'm filling my basket.'

'Come back at once!'

'All in good time,' said Gavroche, and moved further along the street.

Smoke filled the street like fog. This state of affairs was very helpful to Gavroche. Under cover of the smoke, and thanks to his small size, he could move some distance into the street without being seen. He looted the first seven or eight pouches without being in much danger, creeping along on hands and knees, wriggling from one body to the next and emptying pouches and cartridge-belts like a monkey cracking nuts.

As he moved further along the street the veil of smoke grew thinner, so that presently the soldiers and men of the Garde Nationale clustered at the corner of the street were able to discern something moving in the haze. He was ransacking the pouch of a sergeant lying near a kerbstone when the body was hit by a bullet.

'Blazes!' said Gavroche. 'Now they're killing dead men.'

A second bullet struck a spark from the near-by cobbles and a third overturned his basket. Looking up, Gavroche saw that it had come from the street-corner. He got to his feet, and standing erect with his hands on his hips, his eyes fixed on the men of the Garde Nationale, he sang:

> They're ugly at Nanterre,
> It's the fault of Voltaire;
> And stupid at Palaiseau,
> All because of Rousseau.

Then he picked up his basket, retrieved the cartridges that had fallen out of it without losing one, and moved still nearer to the attackers to loot another pouch. A fourth bullet narrowly missed him. He sang:

> I'm no lawyer, I declare,
> It's the fault of Voltaire.
> I'm nothing but a sparrow,
> All because of Rousseau.

Every shot inspired him to another verse. He was neither child nor man but a puckish sprite, invulnerable in battle. The bullets pursued him, but he was more agile than they. The urchin played his game of hide-and-seek with death, and whenever the dread spectre appeared he tweaked its nose.

But at length a bullet caught him, better aimed than the rest. Gavroche was seen to stagger, and then he collapsed.

A cry went up from the barricade. But, a Paris urchin touching the pavement, is a giant drawing strength from his mother earth. Gavroche had fallen only to rise again. He sat upright with blood streaming down his face, and raising his arms above his head and gazing in the direction of the shot, he again began to sing:

> I have fallen, I swear
> It's the fault of Voltaire,
> Or else this hard blow
> Has been dealt by –

He did not finish the verse. A second ball from the same musket cut him short. This time he fell face down and moved no more. His gallant soul had fled.

Marius had dashed out beyond the barricade with Combeferre behind him. But it was too late. Gavroche was dead. Combeferre brought back the basket of ammunition while Marius brought back the boy. When he returned to the stronghold with the body in his arms his face, like that of Gavroche, was covered with blood. A bullet had grazed his scalp without his noticing it.

Suddenly, in between two volleys Enjolras sprang to his feet and gave the following order in a ringing voice:

'Paving-stones are to be brought into the house to reinforce the first floor and attic window-sills. Half the men to stand by with muskets, the rest to bring in the paving-stones. There's not a minute to be lost.'

A squad of sappers with axes over their shoulders appeared in battle-order at the end of the street. They could only be the head of a column, surely an attacking column, since the sappers, whose business was to break down the barricade, always preceded the soldiers who had to climb over it.

Enjolras said to Marius: 'We are the two leaders. I shall give the last orders inside while you keep watch on the outside.'

Marius took up his post of observation on top of the barricade.

Having thus made his plans, Enjolras turned to Javert.

'I haven't forgotten you,' he said. Putting a pistol on the table, he went on, 'The last man to leave this place will blow out this spy's brains.'

'Here?' someone asked.

'No. We don't want his body to be mixed up with our own. Anyone can get over the small barricade in the Rue Mondetour. He's to be taken there and executed.

At this point Jean Valjean intervened. He had been in the main group of defenders. He now left them and said to Enjolras:

'A short time ago you thanked me. Do you think I deserve a reward?'

'Certainly.'

'Then I will ask that I may be allowed to blow that man's brains out.'

Javert looked up and, seeing Valjean, made a slight movement of his head.

'All right. You can have the spy.'

When Jean Valjean was alone with Javert he undid the rope, then took him by the belt of his greatcoat, much as one takes an animal by its halter, and tugging him behind him led him out of the tavern. Valjean had a pistol in his other hand.

Thus they crossed the interior of the stronghold, while its defenders, intent upon the coming attack, had their backs to them. Only Marius saw them pass, and that sinister pair, victim and executioner, reflected the sense of doom in his own spirit.

Jean Valjean with some difficulty helped Javert, bound as he was, to climb over the barricade leading to the Rue Mondetour, without letting go of him for an instant. Having done so they were in the narrow alleyway, where the corner of the house hid them from the insurgents.

'Take your revenge,' said Javert.

Valjean got a clasp-knife out of his pocket and opened it.

'A knife-thrust!' exclaimed Javert. 'You're quite right. That suits you better.'

Jean Valjean cut the halter round Javert's neck, then the

ropes binding his wrists and ankles; then, standing upright, he said:

'You're free to go.'

Javert was not easily taken aback but, with all his self-discipline, he could not conceal his amazement.

'I don't suppose I shall leave here alive,' Valjean went on. 'But if I do, I am lodging at No. 7, Rue de l'Homme-Armé, under the name of Fauchelevent.'

A swift tigerish grimace curled the corner of Javert's lip.

'Number seven,' he repeated.

He re-buttoned his greatcoat and with folded arms, he marched off in the direction of the market. Valjean stood watching him.

When Javert had vanished from sight Valjean fired the pistol into the air.

Then he went back into the stronghold and said, 'It's done.'

In the meantime the following had occurred.

Marius, more concerned with what was happening outside the stronghold, had paid little attention to the spy tied up in the obscure downstairs room of the tavern; but when he saw him in full daylight he recalled the police inspector in the Rue de Pontoise. Not only did he recall his face but he remembered his name, 'Javert!' Perhaps there was still time to intercede in his favour.

Marius started forward, but at this moment there was the sound of a pistol-shot and Jean Valjean returned saying, 'It's done.'

A chill pierced Marius to the heart.

Suddenly a drum beat the charge.

The attackers had the advantage of numbers; the rebels had the advantage of position. Nevertheless, being constantly reinforced and expanding under the hail of bullets, the attacking column inexorably moved forward and now, little by little and step by step, the army was compressing the barricade like the screw of a wine-press.

They fought body to body, hand to hand. They were one against sixty. Feuilly, Courfeyrac, Joly, all were killed;

Combeferre, pierced by three bayonet thrusts while he was picking up a wounded soldier, had only time to look up to the sky before he died.

Marius, still fighting, was so covered with wounds, particularly on the head, that his face was smothered with blood as though he had a red scarf tied round it.

When only two of the leaders were left alive, Marius and Enjolras at either end of the barricade, the centre, which for so long had been sustained by Courfeyrac, Feuilly and Combeferre, gave way.

A supreme assault was launched, and this time it succeeded. The mass of soldiery, bristling with bayonets and advancing at the double, was irresistible, and the dense front line of the attacking force appeared amid the smoke on top of the barricade. This time all was over. The rebels beat a hasty retreat.

Enjolras stood now in the interior courtyard of the stronghold, his back to the tavern, a sword in one hand, a carbine in the other, defending the door against the attackers, and cried to his men, 'This is the only door.' Covering them with his body, defying a battalion single-handed, he let them pass behind him. They hastened to do so; and Enjolras, using his carbine as a cudgel to batter down the bayonets that threatened him, was the last to enter.

Marius had stayed outside. A ball had shattered his shoulder-blade. He felt himself grow dizzy and he fell. At this moment, when his eyes were already closed, he felt himself grasped by a vigorous hand, and in the moment before he sank into unconsciousness he had just time to think, mingled with the memory of Cosette, 'I'm taken prisoner. I shall be shot.'

Marius was indeed a prisoner, and of Jean Valjean. It was Valjean's hand that had grasped him as he fell, and whose grip he had felt before losing consciousness.

The attack at that moment was so intensely concentrated upon Enjolras and the door of the tavern that no one saw Valjean carry Marius's unconscious form across the stronghold and vanish round the corner of the house.

Here Jean Valjean stopped, lowered Marius to the ground, and with his back to the wall stood looking about him.

The situation was appalling. For perhaps two or three minutes this corner of wall might afford them shelter; but how to escape from the inferno?

To his right was the low barricade, an obstacle easily surmounted; but beyond the barricade a row of bayonets was visible, those of the soldiers posted to block this way of escape. And on Valjean's left was the field of battle.

It was a situation such as only a bird could have escaped from.

Valjean looked at the house opposite, at the barricade and then at the ground. As he looked something like a possibility emerged. He saw, a few feet away, an iron grille let into the street. Beneath the bars was a dark aperture, something like a chimney flue. Valjean leapt forward, all his old experience of escape springing like inspiration into his mind. To raise the grille, lift Marius's inert body on to his shoulder and to climb down into this fortunately shallow well; all this only took a few minutes.

Valjean, with the still unconscious Marius, found himself in a long subterranean passage, a place of absolute peace, silence and darkness.

Like a subdued echo above his head he could still hear the formidable uproar which accompanied the capture of the tavern.

Jean Valjean was in the Paris sewer. The trap-door of salvation had suddenly opened beneath him. A gust of fetid air told him where he was.

The truth is that they were less safe than Valjean supposed. Other dangers, no less fearful, might await them. Valjean had moved from one circle of Hell into another. After walking fifty paces he had to stop. A question had arisen. The passage ran into another, so that now there were two ways he might go. Which to choose – left or right? How was he to steer in that black labyrinth? But the labyrinth provides a clue – its slope. Follow the slope and you must come to the river.

Jean Valjean instantly realized this. He thought that he was probably in the sewer of Les Halles, and that if he went left, following the slope, he would arrive within a quarter of an hour at some outlet to the Seine between the Pont-au-Change and the Pont-Neuf – appear, that is to say, in broad daylight in the most frequented part of Paris, perhaps even at a crossroads. Arrest would then be certain. It was better to press deeper into the labyrinthine darkness, trusting to chance to provide a way out. He moved upwards, turning to the right.

When he had turned the corner into the new passageway the distant light from the hatch vanished completely and he was blind. Marius's arms were round his neck while his feet hung down behind. He held both arms with one hand, following the wall with the other. Marius's cheek was pressed against his own and stuck to it, since it was bleeding; he felt the warm stream trickling beneath his clothes. But the faint breathing in his ear was a sign of life. Thus he went darkly on, like some creature of the night.

It was perhaps three o'clock in the afternoon when he reached the ring sewer. He was at first astonished by the suddenly increased width, finding himself in a passageway where his outstretched hands could not touch both walls nor his head the roof. But here the question arose – to go up or down? He felt that time was running out and that he must at all costs try to reach the Seine. That is to say, downward; and he turned to the left.

Instinct served him well. Descent was the way of safety. A little way beyond an effluent which probably came from the Madeleine, he stopped. A large hatchway gave a light that was almost bright. With the gentleness of a man handling a wounded brother, Valjean laid Marius down at the edge of the sewer. He laid a hand on his chest and found that his heart was still beating. Tearing strips off his own shirt, he bandaged Marius's wounds as best he could.

Then, bending over the unconscious form in that dim light, he stared at him with inexpressible hatred.

He found two objects in Marius's clothing, the piece of bread left from the day before and his wallet. He ate the bread and, opening the wallet, found on the first page the lines Marius had written.

Valjean pored over the message, memorizing the address; then he replaced the wallet in Marius's pocket. He had eaten and regained his strength. Taking Marius on his back with his head on his right shoulder, he resumed his downward path. Valjean did not know what part of the town he was passing under or how far he had come. He pressed on, feeling his way in the darkness, which suddenly became terrible.

He found that he was moving in water, and that what he had under his feet was not stone but sludge. Jean Valjean had come to a pit. These were numerous under the Champs-Elysees, which because of its excessive fluidity did not lend itself to the work of construction and conservation. The darkness was greater here than anywhere else. It was a hole of mud in a cavern of night.

Valjean felt the surface slip away from under him, water on top, sludge beneath. He had to go on. Marius was at death's door and he himself exhausted. He felt himself sinking. Only his head was now above water, and his two arms carrying Marius. In old paintings of the flood there is one of a mother carrying her child in this fashion.

He made a last desperate effort, thrusting a foot forward, and it rested upon something solid – only just in time. In fact this foothold, reached at the supreme moment, was the other end of the floor, which had sagged under the weight of water but without breaking, and, climbing its slope, Valjean was saved.

If he had not left his life in that pit, he seemed certainly to have left his strength there. The final effort had exhausted him. But if his strength was flagging his will was not. He went on despairingly, but almost quickly, until suddenly, looking up, he saw in the far distance a light, and this was no cavern light, but the clear white light of day.

He saw the way of escape and he was no longer conscious of fatigue or of the weight of Marius; his muscles were revived, and he ran rather than walked. As he drew nearer he saw the outlet more plainly. It was a pointed arch, less high than the ceiling, which was growing gradually lower.

But when he reached it, Valjean stopped short. It was an outlet, but it offered no way out. The arch was closed with a stout grille, fastened with a huge, rusty lock. And beyond the grille was open air, daylight, the river. All Paris, all liberty, lay beyond it; to the right, downstream, the Pont d'Iena, to the left the Pont des Invalides. One of the most deserted spots in Paris, a good place to escape from after dark. Flies came and went through the grille.

It was perhaps half past eight in the evening. Valjean set Marius down by the wall, where the floor was dry; then, going to the grille, he seized it with both hands. But his frantic shaking had no effect. He tried one bar after another hoping to find one less solid that might be used as a lever. But no bar shifted. He had no way of opening the gate. He turned his back to the grille and sank on to the floor beside the motionless form of Marius, his head sunk between his knees. It was the last extreme of anguish. Of whom did he think in that moment? Not of himself or of Marius. He thought of Cosette.

While he was in this state of despair a hand was laid on his shoulder and a low voice said:

'We'll go halves.'

Valjean had not heard a sound. He looked up and saw a man standing beside him.

The man was clad in a smock. His feet were bare and he carried his shoes in his hand, having removed them so that he might approach Valjean in silence. Unexpected though this, meeting was, he knew the man instantly. It was Thenardier.

Jean Valjean had his back to the light, and was anyway

so begrimed and blood-stained that even in the brightest light he would have been unrecognizable.

He saw at once that Thenardier did not know him. The two men contemplated one another in the dim light, each taking the measure of the other. It was Thenardier who broke the silence.

'How are you going to get out?'

Valjean made no reply. Thenardier went on:

'No way of unlocking the door. But you've got to get away from here.'

'How do you mean?'

'You've killed a man. All right. I have a key.' Thenardier pointed at Marius and went on: 'I don't know you but I'm ready to help you.'

Valjean began to understand. Thenardier supposed him to be a murderer.

'You won't have killed that man without looking to see what he has in his pocket. Give me half and I'll unlock the door.' He produced a large key from under his smock. Providence had come to his rescue in a horrid guise.

Thenardier was haggard, slightly threatening but friendly. He did not seem quite at his ease, talking furtively in a low voice. Valjean reflected that there might be other footpads hidden somewhere near, and that Thenardier did not want to share with them.

'Let's have it. How much did the chap have on him?'

Valjean searched his pockets. He had only a little change in his waistcoat pocket, a mere thirty francs.

'You didn't kill for much,' said Thenardier.

He began familiarly to pat Valjean's pockets and those of Marius, and Valjean, anxious to keep his back to the light, did not stop him. While searching Marius, Thenardier, with a pickpocket's adroitness, managed to tear off a fragment of material which he hid in his smock without Valjean's noticing. But he found no more money.

'It's true,' he said. 'That's all there is.'

Forgetting what he had said about sharing, he took the lot. He again produced the key.

'Well, pal, you'd better go out. It's like a fair, you pay when you leave. You've paid.' And he laughed.

Thenardier opened the gate just enough to allow Valjean to pass through, closed it after him, turned the key in the lock and then vanished into the darkness.

And Valjean was outside.

He laid Marius on the bank. The darkness, stench and horror were all behind him. He was bathed in pure, fresh air and surrounded by silence, the delicious silence of sunset in a clear sky.

For some moments he was overwhelmed by this serenity and then, recalled to a sense of duty, he bent over Marius and sprinkled a few drops of water on his face from the hollow of his hand. Marius's eyelids did not move, but his open mouth still breathed.

Valjean was again about to dip his hand in the water when he had that familiar sense of someone behind him. He looked sharply round. A tall man in a long coat, with folded arms and a cudgel in his right hand, was standing a few paces away. In the half-darkness it seemed a spectral figure; but Valjean recognized Javert.

After his unhoped-for escape from the rebel stronghold the inspector had immediately returned to his duties, which entailed keeping watch on the right bank near the Champs-Elysees, a spot which had been attracting the notice of the police. Seeing Thenardier, he had followed him.

The gate so obligingly opened for Valjean was a stratagem on the part of Thenardier. With the instinct of a hunted man, Thenardier had sensed that Javert was there and he wanted to distract him. What could be better than to supply him with a murderer?

Javert did not recognize Valjean, who, as we have said, looked quite unlike himself. Without unfolding his arms, he asked:

'Who are you?'

'Myself.'

'Who is that?'

'Jean Valjean.'

Javert put the cudgel between his teeth and leaning forward clapped his hands on Valjean's shoulders, seizing them in a vice-like grip. Staring hard, he recognized him. Jean Valjean stayed unresisting.

'Inspector Javert,' he said, 'you have got me. In any case, since this morning I have considered myself your prisoner. I did not give you my address in order to escape from you. But grant me one thing.'

Javert did not seem to hear. Finally, as though in a dream, he murmured:

'What are you doing here? Who is this man?'

'It is about him I wished to speak,' said Valjean. 'You may do what you like with me, but help me first to take him home. That is all I ask.'

Javert's face twitched. But he did not refuse. Bending down, he took a handkerchief from his pocket, soaked it in water, and bathed Marius's blood-stained forehead.

'He was at the barricade,' he muttered, 'the one called Marius.'

'He's wounded,' said Valjean

'He's dead,' said Javert.

'No. Not yet. He lives in the Marais with a relative whose name I forget.' He felt in Marius's jacket, found the wallet and handed it to Javert.

There was still just light enough to read by, Javert studied the words and grunted.

'Gillenormand, 6 Rue des Filles-du-Calvaire.' Then he shouted:

'Coachman!'

A fiacre had been waiting 'just in case'. In a very short time it had come down the ramp and Marius had been placed on the back seat, while Javert and Valjean sat in front. The fiacre drove off rapidly along the quay in the direction of the Bastille. The dark interior of the fiacre, when it passed under a street lamp, was momentarily lighted and the three tragic figures were thrown into relief – the seeming corpse, the spectre and the statue.

*

It was quite dark when they reached 6 Rue des Filles-du-Calvaire. Javert got out first and questioned the porter in a brisk, official tone.

'Anyone live here called Gillenormand?'

'Yes. What do you want of him?'

'We're bringing back his son.'

'His son?' exclaimed the porter in amazement.

'He's dead.'

Valjean, at whom the porter had been staring with horror as he stood, ragged and covered in mud in the background, shook his head.

'He was at the barricade,' said Javert, 'and here he is.'

'At the barricade!'

'He got himself killed. Go and wake his father.' The porter awakened Basque. Basque awakened Nicolette, who awakened Aunt Gillenormand. They let the old man sleep on, thinking that he would know soon enough.

Marius was taken up to the first floor and laid on an old settee in Monsieur Gillenormand's sitting-room. Basque went in search of a doctor and Valjean felt Javert's hand on his arm. He understood and went downstairs, with Javert close behind him. They got back into the fiacre.

'Inspector,' said Jean Valjean, 'grant me one last favour.'

'What is it?' Javert asked harshly.

'Let me go home for a minute. After that you can do what you like with me.'

Javert was silent for some moments, his chin sunk in the collar of his greatcoat. Then he pulled down the window in front of him.

'Drive to No. 7 Rue de l'Homme-Arme,' he said.

At the entrance to the Rue de l'Homme-Arme, the fiacre stopped, since the street was too narrow to admit vehicles. Javert and Valjean got out.

They walked along the street which was deserted. Valjean knocked on the door of No. 7 and it was opened.

'Go up,' said Javert. He had a strange expression, as though it cost him an effort to speak. 'I'll wait for you here.'

Valjean looked at him. This was little in accordance with his usual habits. But, since Valjean had resolved to give himself up and be done with it, this did not greatly surprise him. He entered the house and went upstairs.

On the first floor he paused. The sash window was open. As in many old houses the staircase looked on to the street and was lighted at night by the street lamp immediately outside. Perhaps automatically, or simply to draw breath, Valjean thrust out his head. He looked down into the street. Javert had gone.

Javert had walked slowly away from the Rue de l'Homme-Arme, walking for the first time in his life with his head bowed; his whole person bore the imprint of uncertainty.

Walking through the silent streets, he took the shortest way to the Seine, finally arriving near the police post in the Place du Chatelet.

Javert leaned with his elbows on the parapet, his chin resting on his hands. Something new, a revolution, a disaster, had occurred to him, and he had to think it over.

He could see two ways ahead of him, and this appalled him, because hitherto he had never seen more than one straight line.

To owe his life to a man wanted by the law and to pay the debt in equal terms; to have accepted the words, 'You may go', and now to say, 'Go free', this was to sacrifice duty to personal motive. And now what was he to do?

Only one proper course lay open to him – to hurry back to the Rue de l'Homme-Arme and seize Valjean. Something prevented him. What was it? All the principles on which his estimate of man had been based were overthrown. Behind Valjean loomed the figure of Monsieur Madeleine, and they merged into one, into a figure deserving of veneration. Something dreadful was forcing its way into Javert's consciousness – admiration for a convicted felon. He did not for a moment deny that the law was the law. What more simple than to enforce it? But when he sought to raise his hand to lay it on Valjean's shoulder an inner voice restrained him: 'You will deliver up your deliverer? Then go and find

Pontius Pilate's bowl and wash your hands!' He felt himself diminished beside Jean Valjean.

But his greatest anguish was the loss of certainty. He was forced to admit that infallibility is not always infallible, that there may be error in dogma, that judges are men and even the law may do wrong. All was chaos; and he, Javert, was in utter disarray. There were only two ways out. To go determinedly to Jean Valjean and return him to prison; or else . . .

The place where Javert stood was where the river flows in a dangerous rapid. He looked down. There was a sound of running water, but the river itself was not to be seen. What lay below him was a void, so that he might have been standing at the edge of infinity. He stayed motionless for some minutes, staring into nothingness. Abruptly he took off his hat and laid it on the parapet. A moment later a tall, dark figure, which a passer-by might have taken for a ghost, stood upright on the parapet. It leaned forward and dropped into the darkness.

There was a splash, and that was all.

Marius lay for a long time between life and death, in a state of fever and delirium. Finally on 7 September, three months to the day after Marius had been brought to his grandfather's house, the doctor announced that he was out of danger. But because of the damage to his shoulder-blade he had to spend a further two months resting on a chaise-longue.

Marius, during all his convalescence, had but one thought in mind, that of Cosette. He did not know what had happened to her or to himself. Vague pictures lingered in his mind – Eponine, Gavroche, the Thenardiers, and the friends who had been with him at the barricade. The appearance of Monsieur Fauchelevent in that sanguinary affair was a riddle to him. He did not know how he had come to be saved, and no one could tell him. Past, present and future, all were befogged in his mind. There was but one clear, fixed point: his resolve to find Cosette.

He did not conceal the difficulties from himself. He

thought that any mention of Cosette would lead to the old quarrel revived. So he hardened his heart in advance.

One day Marius, whose strength was now almost quite restored, sat up with clenched fists and glared at his grandfather.

'There is something I have to say to you.'

'What is it?'

'I want to get married.'

'But of course,' said the old man, laughing.

'How do you mean – of course?'

'That's understood. You shall have your little girl. She comes here every day in the shape of an elderly gentleman who asks for news of you. Since your injury she has spent her time weeping and making bandages. I know all about her. You didn't think of that, did you? You expected me to play the tyrant and ruin everything. Not a bit of it – Cosette is yours. Be so good as to get married, my dear sir. And be happy, my dear, dear boy.'

Having said which the old man burst into tears. He clasped Marius's head to his chest and they wept together.

'Father!' cried Marius.

'At last you love me!' the old man said.

Cosette and Marius saw one another again. All the household, including Basque and Nicolette, were assembled in Marius's room when she entered. Standing behind Cosette was a white-haired man, grave but nevertheless smiling. It was 'Monsieur Fauchelevent' – that is to say, Jean Valjean. He was standing somewhat apart from the others. Monsieur Gillenormand bowing said:

'Monsieur Tranchelevent . . .' He did not do it on purpose; but inattention to proper names was one of his aristocratic habits. 'Monsieur Tranchelevent, I have the honour, on behalf of my grandson, Baron Marius Pontmercy, to ask for your daughter's hand in marriage.'

Monsieur Tranchelevent bowed.

'Then that is settled,' said the old man, and turning to Marius and Cosette with arms upraised he said: 'My children, you are free to love one another.'

He took their hands in his own.

'So enchanting, this Cosette. It's a pity she'll only be a baroness, she should be a marquise. But now I come to think of it, more than half of all I possess is tied up in an annuity. My poor children, what will you do after my death in twenty years' time?'

A quiet voice said: 'Mademoiselle Euphrasie Fauchelevent has six hundred thousand francs.'

It was Jean Valjean who had spoken. Hitherto he had not uttered a word, but had stood silently contemplating the happy group.

'Six hundred thousand?' exclaimed the old man. 'That settles matters very nicely, does it not. This young rogue of a Marius, he finds a millionairess in his dreamland.'

But as to Marius and Cosette, they were gazing into each other's eyes, scarcely aware of this trifle.

No lengthy explanation is needed for the reader to understand that after the Champmathieu affair Jean Valjean had been able, during his brief escape, to come to Paris and withdraw from the Lafitte bank the money he had accumulated as Monsieur Madeleine. Fearing recapture, he had buried it in the clearing in the Montfermeil wood. The sum of 630,000 francs in banknotes was not bulky and could be put in a box. In this he had also put the bishop's candlesticks which he had taken from Montreuil-sur-mer. When Valjean needed money he had returned to the clearing and when he knew Marius to be convalescent, foreseeing that the entire sum would come in useful, he had gone to retrieve it. He had put the silver candlesticks on the mantelpiece, where they glittered to the great admiration of Toussaint.

Preparations for the wedding were put in hand. Jean Valjean arranged everything and made everything easy. Having been a mayor, he knew how to solve an awkward problem, that of Cosette's civic status. To reveal the truth about her origin might, who knows, have prevented the marriage. He endowed her with a dead family, which meant that no one could make demands on her.

Jean Valjean, under the name of Fauchelevent, became her guardian and Monsieur Gillenormand her deputy-guardian.

Cosette had to learn that she was not the daughter of the old man whom for so long she had addressed as father, and that another Fauchelevent was her real parent. At any other time she would have been greatly distressed, but in her present state of happiness this scarcely troubled her. In any case she continued to call Jean Valjean 'father'.

It was arranged that the couple should live with Marius's grandfather. Since Valjean no longer needed Toussaint he had passed her on to Cosette who had promoted her to the rank of lady's maid. As for Valjean himself, a handsome room in Monsieur Gillenormand's house had been expressly furnished for him, and Cosette had said so bewitchingly, 'Father, I beseech you!', that he had almost promised to live in it.

While the wedding preparations were going forward, Marius subjected himself to scrupulous self-examination. He owed debts of gratitude both on his father's account and on his own. There was Thenardier, and there was the stranger who had brought him to Monsieur Gillenormand's house. He was resolved to find these two men.

That Thenardier was a villain did not alter the fact that he had saved the life of Colonel Pontmercy. Marius, not knowing what had really happened at Waterloo, was ignorant of the fact that, although his father owed Thenardier his life, he owed him no gratitude. The agents employed by Marius could find no trace of Thenardier. The woman had died in prison during the trial, and the man and his daughter Azelma had vanished into obscurity. Thenardier had been condemned to death in his absence.

As for that other man, the one who had saved Marius, his inquiries had come to a dead end. Only the porter with his candle had noticed the man, and all he could say was:

'He was a terrible sight.'

In the hope that they might provide him with some clue, Marius had kept the blood-stained garments in which he had been rescued. He made a queer discovery when he examined the jacket. A small piece was missing.

The night of 16 February was a blessed one, with a clear sky shading into darkness. It was the night of Marius and Cosette's wedding day.

This, as it happened, was *Mardi gras*, but a few days before the wedding Jean Valjean had an accident, injuring his right thumb. It was a trifling matter, but it obliged him to keep his arm in a sling, which meant that he could not sign any documents. Monsieur Gillenormand, as deputy-guardian, had done so in his place.

One of the wedding guests remarked that, being *Mardi gras*, there would be a great deal of traffic because of the masks.

'Splendid!' said Monsieur Gillenormand. 'These young folk are entering upon the serious business of life. It will do them good to start with a masquerade.'

Upon leaving the Rue des Filles-du-Calvaire they found themselves in a procession of vehicles stretching from the Madeleine to the Bastille and back. There were masks in abundance.

The wedding party was brought to a stop at the entrance of the Rue du Pont-aux-Choux, and the line going in the opposite direction stopped at almost the same moment. There was a carriage of masks in that line.

Two members of the company, one a Spaniard with an exaggerated nose and enormous black moustache, and the other a skinny young girl in a wolf-mask, had noticed the wedding party and were talking together amid the hubbub. Their dialogue was as follows, the man speaking first:

'See that old man?'
'Which?'
'The one in the first wedding coach, on our side.'
'The one with his arm in a sling?'
'I'm sure I know him. Can you see the bride if you stretch?'

'No.'

'Well get off the cart and follow them.'

'What for?'

'I'm interested in that fellow.'

'Sounds easy, doesn't it? A wedding party going somewhere or other on *Mardi gras*. Like looking for a needle in a haystack!'

'All the same, you've got to try, Azelma, do you hear?'

Then the two lines resumed their progress in opposite directions, and the wagon of masks lost sight of the wedding party.

When at length all the ceremonies were completed, at the *mairie* and at the church, when all the documents were signed, rings exchanged, they returned home, Marius and Cosette, seated side by side and Cosette, leaning towards Marius, whispered angelically:

'My name is now the same as yours, I'm Madame You.'

A banquet had been spread in the dining-room. In the antechamber three violins and a flute were playing Haydn quartets.

Jean Valjean was seated in a corner of the room by the open door. Just before they took their places at the table Cosette came over to him and, making a slow curtsey, asked with a half-teasing tenderness:

'Dear Father, are you happy?'

'Yes,' he said, 'I'm happy.'

'Then why aren't you smiling?'

Valjean obediently smiled, and a moment later Basque announced that dinner was served.

The company proceeded into the dining-room, led by Monsieur Gillenormand with Cosette on his arm, and seated themselves in their places. There were armchairs on either side of the bride, one for the old gentleman and the other for Jean Valjean.

But when they looked round for 'Monsieur Fauchelevent' they found that he was not there. Monsieur Gillenormand asked Basque if he knew what had become of him.

'Monsieur Fauchelevent requested me to say, monsieur, that his hand was paining him. He has gone out, but will be back tomorrow morning.'

This cast something of a chill upon the gathering, but fortunately Monsieur Gillenormand had high spirits enough for two.

It was a gay, delightful evening, the tone being set by their host, who was so nearly a hundred years old. There was a little dancing and a great deal of laughter and happy commotion. But suddenly a silence fell. The newly married pair had disappeared. Shortly after midnight Monsieur Gillenormand's house became a temple.

And here we must pause. At the door of every bridal bedchamber an angel stands, smiling, with a finger to his lips.

What had become of Jean Valjean?

After he had smiled at Cosette's gentle request, he returned to the Rue de l'Homme-Arme. The apartment was empty and the sound of his footsteps was louder than usual. He went back to his own bedroom and put his candle on the table. He had taken his arm out of its sling and was using it as though it caused him no discomfort.

He went towards his bed, and as he did so his eye rested on the little black box that Cosette had called his 'insepar-able'. He got a key out of his pocket and opened it.

Slowly he took out the clothes in which Cosette had left Montfermeil. Everything was black. He laid the garments on the bed, recalling the occasion. It had been a very cold December, and she had been shivering in rags, her small feet red from the clogs she wore. He spread the garments on the bed and stood looking at them. She had been so little, carrying that big doll. She had laughed as they walked hand-in-hand, and he had become all the world to her.

Then the stoical heart gave way. Anyone passing on the stairs at that moment would have heard the sound of dreadful sobbing.

The fearful struggle had begun again. How often had

Jean Valjean been darkly joined in mortal conflict with his own conscience! But this night Valjean knew that the struggle had reached its climax. An agonizing question presented itself. The question was this: how was he, Jean Valjean, to ensure the continued happiness of Cosette and Marius? It was he who had forged it. But what was he now to do with it, this happiness he had brought about? Should he take advantage of it, treat it as though it belonged to him? Cosette was another man's, but he still retained as much of her as he could ever possess. Could he not continue to be almost her father, respected as he had always been, able when he chose to enter her house? And could he, without saying a word, bring his past into that future? Could he greet them smiling and cross that innocent threshold, casting behind him the infamous shadow of the law? Could he still keep silent?

The day after a wedding is one of solitude. We respect the privacy of the newly-weds and perhaps their late arising. It was a little after midday when Basque, busily 'doing the antechamber', heard a tap on the door. He opened it and found Monsieur Fauchelevent. He showed him into the salon, which was still in a state of disorder.

'We're up late this morning, monsieur,' said Basque.

'Is your master up?' asked Jean Valjean.

'Which master, the old or the new?'

'Monsieur Pontmercy.'

'I'll go and see,' said Basque. 'I'll tell him you're here.'

'No. Don't tell him that it's me. I want to surprise him.'

Basque went out leaving Valjean alone.

Some minutes elapsed during which Jean Valjean remained motionless where Basque had left him. He stood looking down at the glow of light cast by the sunshine on the floor.

The sound of the door opening caused him to look up. Marius entered, head up and face aglow with happiness.

'Why, it's you, father!' he exclaimed. 'That silly fellow Basque chose to make a mystery of it. I'm so delighted to see you. Is your hand better?' He did not wait for a reply.

'You haven't forgotten, I hope, that you have a room here? We're absolutely determined to be very happy, and you're part of it, father, do you understand? Talking of which, you'll be lunching with us today?'

'Monsieur,' said Jean Valjean, 'I have something to tell you. I am an ex-convict.'

There are sounds that the mind cannot absorb although they are recognized by the ear. Those words 'I am an ex-convict', emerging from the lips of Monsieur Fauchelevent and entering the ear of Marius, went beyond the limit. He knew that something had been said, but he could not grasp what it was. He stood open-mouthed.

Valjean took his arm out of the sling and held his hand out to Marius.

'There's nothing wrong with my thumb,' he said. 'There never has been.' He went on: 'I invented this injury in order to avoid signing the marriage deeds, which might have nullified them.'

Marius stammered: 'But what does it mean?'

'It means,' said Valjean, 'that I have been in the galleys. I was imprisoned for nineteen years, first for theft and later as a recidivist. I am at present breaking parole.'

Marius might recoil in horror, might refuse to believe, but in the end he was forced to accept it. Indeed, as commonly happens, he went further. He shuddered as an appalling thought occurred to him.

'You are really Cosette's father!'

Jean Valjean raised his head with a gesture of such dignity that he seemed to grow in stature.

'I swear to you before God, Monsieur Pontmercy, that I am not Cosette's father or in any way related to her. My name is not Fauchelevent but Jean Valjean. You may be sure of that.'

'But what proof –?' stammered Marius.

'My word is my proof.'

Marius looked at him. He was melancholy but calm, with a kind of stony sincerity from which no lie could emerge.

'I believe you,' said Marius.

Jean Valjean bowed his head in acknowledgement.

'So what am I to Cosette?' he went on. 'Someone who came upon her quite by chance. Ten years ago I did not know that she existed. I love her certainly, as who would not? When one is growing old one has a fatherly feeling for all small children. She was an orphan and she needed me. That is how I came to love her. As for the six hundred thousand francs, I will anticipate your question. It was a sum held for her in trust. As to how it came into my hands, that is quite unimportant. I have fulfilled my trust, and nothing more can be required of me. And I have concluded the matter by telling you my name. I have done so for my own sake, because I wanted you to know who I am.'

Jean Valjean looked steadily at Marius.

Marius was so stupefied that he talked as though Valjean had done him a deliberate injury.

'Why have you told me all this? Nobody forced you to. There must be some reason – something you haven't told me.'

'My reason . . . well, it's a strange reason – a matter of honesty. There is a bond in my heart that cannot be broken, and such bonds become stronger as one grows older. I might have lied and deceived you all by continuing to be "Monsieur Fauchelevent". I did it where she was concerned; but now it is a matter of my own conscience and I can do it no longer.'

He sighed and added a last word, 'Once I stole a loaf of bread to stay alive, but now I cannot steal a name in order to go on living.'

He began to pace the room. Then, seeing Marius's eyes upon him, he said:

'I drag my leg a little as I walk. Now you know why . . . I ask you to consider this, monsieur. Let us suppose that I had said nothing but come to live with you as Monsieur Fauchelevent, to be accepted as one of yourselves, and then one day, when we are talking and laughing together, a voice cries "Jean Valjean!" and the terrible hand of the police

descends on my shoulder and strips the mask away! . . .
What do you think of that?'

Marius had nothing to say.

'Now you know why I could not keep silent. But no
matter. Be happy, be Cosette's guardian angel, live in the
sun and do not worry about how an outcast goes about his
duty.'

'Poor Cosette,' Marius murmured, 'when she hears . . .'

At these words Jean Valjean gazed frantically at Marius:

'Monsieur, I beseech you to promise me not to tell her.
Surely if you yourself know, that is enough.'

He sank into an armchair and buried his face in his hands.
He made no sound, but the heaving of his shoulders showed
that he was weeping.

'Don't worry,' said Marius. 'I'll keep your secret.'

'I thank you, monsieur,' Valjean said gently. He sat thinking. 'Nearly everything is settled, except for one last thing.'

'What is that?'

Making a supreme effort, Valjean said in a scarcely audible
voice:

'You are the master. Do you think, now you know everything, that I should not see Cosette again?'

'I think it would be better,' Marius said coldly.

'Then I will now do so,' said Valjean and, getting up, he
went to the door.

But with the door half opened he stood for a moment
motionless, then closed it again and came back to Marius.

'Monsieur,' he said, 'if you will permit me I would like
to come and see her. She was like my own child. To go
away and never see or speak to her again – to have nothing
left to live for – that would be very hard. I wouldn't come
often or stay for long. We could meet in that little room on
the ground floor. And there is another thing. If I never came
at all, that too would give rise to talk. It occurs to me that
I might come in the evening, when it's beginning to grow
dark.'

'You shall come every evening,' said Marius.

'Monsieur, you are very kind,' said Jean Valjean.

They shook hands. Happiness escorted despair to the door, and they parted.

At nightfall on the following day Jean Valjean knocked at the door of Monsieur Gillenormand's house and was received by Basque who, treating the visitor with every sign of respect, showed him into the downstairs room. 'I will inform madame,' he said.

Jean Valjean sank into one of the armchairs. But suddenly he started to his feet, knowing that Cosette was standing behind him. He turned and looked at her. She was enchantingly pretty.

'Well, of all things!' Cosette exclaimed. 'Father, I knew that you were a strange person, but I never expected this! Marius tells me that it is at your request that we're meeting down here.'

'That's quite true.'

'But why? This place is horrible.'

'*Tu sais . . .*' But then, having addressed her with the familiar *tu*, Valjean corrected himself. '*Vous savez*, madame, that I'm peculiar. I have my whims.'

Cosette clapped her hands together.

' "Madame" and "vous"! Is this another whim? What in the world does it mean?'

Valjean bestowed on her a heartrending smile.

'You wanted to be "madame" and now you are.'

'But not to you, father.'

'You mustn't call me "father" any more.'

'You must call me Monsieur Jean, or plain Jean, if you'd rather.'

'You're upsetting me very much. It's all very well to have whims, but they mustn't hurt other people. You've no right to be cruel when you're really so kind.'

He made no reply. She seized his two hands and pressed them to her throat beneath her chin in a gesture of profound tenderness.

'Please, please be kind! Come and live with us, be my father.'

Then suddenly she looked hard at him and asked: 'Are you cross with me because I'm happy?'

Unwitting innocence is sometimes more penetrating than cunning. Thinking to administer a pinprick, she plucked at his heart. He murmured to himself:

'Her happiness was the sole object of my life. God can now give me leave of absence . . . Cosette, you are happy, and so my work is done.'

'You called me *tu*!' cried Cosette, and flung her arms round his neck.

He clasped her despairingly to his breast, and it was almost as though he had got her back again. The temptation was too great. Gently loosening her arms, he picked up his hat.

'Well?' said Cosette.

'I am leaving you, madame. You are wanted elsewhere.' And from the doorway he said: 'I addressed you as *tu*. Please accept my apologies and assure your husband that it will not occur again.'

He went out, leaving her stupefied.

Valjean called every evening at the same time. He came every day, lacking the strength to take Marius's words otherwise than literally, and Marius arranged to be out when he came. The household accustomed itself to these novel proceedings on the part of Monsieur Fauchelevent, being encouraged to do so by Toussaint, who said, 'Monsieur has always been like this.'

One evening he stayed even later than usual, and the next day he found that there was no fire burning in the hearth. 'Well, after all,' he thought, 'it's April and the weather is no longer cold.'

'Heavens, how cold it is in here!' Cosette exclaimed when she entered.

'Not at all,' said Valjean.

'Was it you who told Basque not to light the fire?'

'Yes. It will soon be May.'

'But we keep fires going until June, and in this cellar one wants one all the year round.'

'I didn't think a fire was necessary.'

'Another of your absurd ideas,' said Cosette.

The next evening he stayed even longer than usual. When at length he rose to leave Cosette said:

'My husband said a queer thing to me yesterday.'

'What was that?'

'He said, "Cosette, we have an income of thirty thousand livres, twenty-seven thousand of yours and the three thousand my grandfather allows me. Would you be brave enough to live on the three thousand?" I said I was ready to live on nothing at all provided I was with him; and then I asked, "Why do you say that?" . . . "I just wanted to know," he said.'

Jean Valjean found nothing to say. It was evident that Marius had his doubts about the origin of those six hundred thousand francs and perhaps feared that they had come from some discreditable source – perhaps he had discovered that they had come from Valjean himself – and that he would sooner be poor with Cosette than live on tainted money.

Valjean had a vague sense that he was being rebuffed, and on the following evening this was brought forcibly home to him. The two armchairs had vanished. There was not a chair in the room.

'Why, what has happened?' Cosette exclaimed when she came in. 'Where have they got to?'

'I told Basque he could take them away,' Valjean replied, stammering slightly as he spoke.

'I shall only be staying a few minutes this evening.'

'Even so, there's no reason why we should stand up.'

'I think Basque needed the chairs for the salon. You're expecting company, I suppose.'

'Nobody's coming.'

Valjean could think of nothing else to say. Cosette shrugged her shoulders.

'You told Basque to take the chairs away. And you

told him not to light the fire. You really are very peculiar.'

'Goodbye,' said Valjean. He did not say, 'Goodbye Cosette', but he had not the strength to say, 'Goodbye Madame.'

He went off in despair, having now understood exactly what was happening, and the next evening he did not come at all.

Cosette was unperturbed and scarcely gave the matter a thought until the next morning. But then she sent Nicolette round to the Rue de l'Homme-Arme to inquire if 'Monsieur Jean' was well. Nicolette returned with the message that Monsieur Jean was quite well but was busy with his affairs. Madame would remember that he had sometimes had to go away for a few days. He would be doing so shortly, and would come to see her as soon as possible after he got back. In the meantime there was nothing to worry about.

To be happy is a terrible thing. How complacent we are, how self-sufficing.

Yet it would be wrong to blame Marius. Before his marriage Marius asked no questions of Monsieur Fauchelevent, and since then he had been afraid to question Jean Valjean. He had regretted the promise which he had been induced to make and had said to himself more than once that he should not have made that concession to despair. And so he had by degrees excluded Valjean from his house and effaced him as far as possible from the thoughts of Cosette.

At the same time he believed that he had a serious duty to perform, namely, the restitution of six hundred thousand francs to some person whose identity he was seeking to discover as discreetly as possible.

One day Jean Valjean walked downstairs and a few paces along the street, then seated himself on a kerbstone, the same one on which Gavroche had found him on the night of 5 June. He stayed there a few minutes, then went upstairs again. The next day he did not leave his room, and on the following day he did not leave his bed.

During the week that followed Valjean did not get out of bed. The concierge said to her husband: 'He doesn't get up and he doesn't eat anything. He isn't going to last long. He's very unhappy about something. I can't help feeling that his daughter has made a bad marriage.'

One evening Jean Valjean had difficulty in raising himself on his elbow. He realized that he was weaker than he had ever been. And so, because he was impelled to do so by some overriding consideration, he sat up with a great effort and got dressed. He put on his old workman's clothes. He opened the valise and, getting out Cosette's trousseau of small garments, spread them on the bed. The bishop's candlesticks were in their usual place on the mantelpiece; he got two wax candles out of a drawer and, putting them in the candlesticks, lighted them, although it was broad daylight.

With great labour he dragged a table and chair close to the mantelpiece, and arranged writing materials on the table. Now and then he wiped his forehead. His hand was shaking. Slowly he wrote the following lines:

Cosette, I bless you. There is something I must explain. Your husband was right to make me understand that I must go away. What he supposed was not altogether correct, but still he was right. He is a good man. Cosette, you will find figures on this paper if I have the strength to recall them. That is why I am writing to you, to assure you that the money is really yours. This is how it is. Black jade comes from England, and black glass from Germany. Jade is lighter, more rare and more expensive. Imitations can be made in France as they can in Germany. I hit upon the idea of making it of lacquer and turpentine. It costs no more than thirty sous and it is much better . . .

And here the pen slipped from his fingers and he sank down, sobbing from the depths of his heart, with his head clasped in his hands.

'Alas, alas,' he cried within himself, 'it's all over. I shall not see her again. It was a smile that came into my life and departed. To die is nothing, but it is terrible to die without seeing her.'

At this moment there was a knock on the door.

That same day, or, more exactly, that same evening, Marius had withdrawn to his study after dinner. Basque brought him a letter, saying, 'The writer is waiting in the hall.' Cosette at the time was strolling with her grandfather-in-law in the garden.

A letter, like a person, can have a displeasing appearance. This was such a letter. It smelt of tobacco. Nothing is more evocative than a smell. Marius remembered that tobacco and in a sudden flash of divination this brought a picture to his mind, that of the Jondrette attic . . . By the strangest of chances, one of the two men for whom he had searched so diligently had of his own accord come his way!

Eagerly unsealing the letter, he read:

Monsieur le baron,

Any kindness which you may do me will be reciprocated. I am in possession of a secret concerning a certain person. This person concerns you. I am keeping the secret for your ears alone. I can provide you with the means of driving this person out of your house where he has no right to be, Madame la baronne being a lady of noble birth. Virtue and crime cannot be allowed to go on living together any longer.

I await Monsieur le baron's instructions.

The letter was signed THENARD.

The signature was not wholly false, being merely a little abbreviated. But there could be no doubt whatever as to the writer's identity.

Marius's agitation was extreme. He went to his desk, got some banknotes out of a drawer, put them in his pocket and rang the bell. Basque appeared.

'Show the gentleman in,' said Marius.

'Monsieur Thenard,' Basque announced.

And now Marius had another surprise. The man who

entered was completely unknown to him. He was an elderly man with green-tinted spectacles and grey hair smoothed and plastered down over his forehead like the wigs of coachmen to the English nobility. Marius looked at him with a searching scrutiny that not even an examining magistrate could have bettered.

'What do you want?' Marius asked sharply.

The visitor responded with a grimace which may be likened to the smile of a crocodile. 'Monsieur le baron, I have a secret to sell you.'

'A secret which concerns me?'

'To some extent.'

'Well, what is it?'

'I will tell you the first part for nothing. Monsieur le baron, you have living with you a thief and an assassin.'

'Not living with me,' Marius said.

'A man has insinuated himself into your confidence, almost into your family, under a false name. I will tell you his real name and I will tell you for nothing.'

'I'm listening.'

'His name is Jean Valjean.'

'I know that.'

'I will also tell you, for nothing, what he is.'

'Please do.'

'He is an ex-convict.'

'I know that too.'

'You know it now that I have told you.'

'No. I knew it already.'

Marius's cool tone of voice and his apparent indifference to the information had their effect upon the visitor. He gave Marius a sidelong glance of fury which was rapidly extinguished.

The visitor smiled.

'I would not venture to contradict Monsieur le baron. In any case you will see that I am well-informed. And what I now have to tell you is known to no one except myself. It concerns the fortune of Madame la baronne. It is a remarkable secret and it is for sale.'

'I know this secret already, just as I knew the name of Jean Valjean and know your name.'

'Well, that's not difficult, seeing that I wrote it in my letter. It's Thenard.'

'You've left out the rest of it.'

'What's that?'

'Thenard*ier*.'

'Who might he be?'

'You are also the workman Jondrette,' Marius went on. 'At one time you kept a tavern at Montfermeil, and your real name is Thenardier.'

'I deny it.'

'And you're a thorough rogue. Here, take this.'

Marius got a banknote out of his pocket and tossed it in his face.

The man bowed while he examined the note. 'Five hundred francs!' He murmured in an undertone, 'That's real money!' Then he said briskly: 'We might as well be at our ease.'

And with remarkable adroitness he removed his disguise. 'Monsieur le baron is infallible,' he said. 'I am Thenardier.'

Thenardier was considerably taken aback and might even have been put out of countenance had this been possible for him. He was seeing this Baron Pontmercy for the first time in his life; nevertheless the baron had recognized him in spite of his disguise and seemed to know all about him. It must be borne in mind that, although at one time Thenardier had been Marius's neighbour, he had never set eyes on him. He had written the letter we have just seen without having the least idea who he was. Nor did the name of Pontmercy mean anything to him because of the episode on the field of Waterloo, when he had heard only the two last syllables.

For the rest, thanks to his daughter Azelma, and thanks also to his own researches, he had picked up a good many scraps of information. He had discovered, or perhaps guessed, who the man was whom he had encountered in the sewer, and from this it was a short step to finding out his name.,

To Thenardier's way of thinking his conversation with Marius had not yet really begun. He rapidly surveyed his resources, and having admitted that he was Thenardier he waited.

Marius broke the silence.

'Thenardier, I have told you your name. Do you want me also to tell you the secret you were proposing to sell me? I, too, have sources of information, and you may find that I know rather more than you do. Jean Valjean, as you say, is a murderer and a thief. He is a thief because he robbed a wealthy manufacturer, Monsieur Madeleine, whom he ruined. And he murdered the policeman, Javert.'

'Monsieur le baron, I think you are mistaken. Jean Valjean did not rob Monsieur Madeleine because he himself is, or was, Monsieur Madeleine.'

'What in the world . . . ?'

'And secondly he did not kill Javert because Javert killed himself.'

'What!' cried Marius, beside himself with amazement. 'But what proof have you of this?'

Thenardier fished in an inside pocket and got copies of two newspapers out of an envelope, both faded and creased, but one of which seemed very much older than the other.

The older of the two was the issue of the *Drapeau Blanc* dated 25 July 1823 in which Monsieur Madeleine and Jean Valjean were shown to be the same person. The more recent, the *Moniteur* of 15 June 1832, reported the suicide of Javert, adding that it followed Javert's verbal report to the Prefect of Police that, having been taken prisoner by the insurgents in the Rue de la Chanvrerie, he owed his life to the magnanimity of one of them, who had fired his pistol into the air.

Marius uttered a cry of joy.

'Why. The fortune was really his! He's Madeleine, the benefactor of an entire region, and Jean Valjean, the saviour of Javert. He's a hero! He's a saint!'

'He's neither one nor the other,' said Thenardier. 'Valjean did not rob Madeleine, but he is none the less a thief, and although he did not kill Javert he is none the less a murderer.

'On the sixth of June last year, Monsieur le baron – that is to say, on the day of the uprising – a man was hiding in the Paris main sewer. This man, who had a key to the sewer, had been obliged to go into hiding for reasons unconnected with politics. Hearing the sound of approaching footsteps, the man took cover. Another man was in the sewer. This happened not far from the entrance, and there was sufficient light for the first man to recognize the second, who was walking with a heavy burden on his back. The man was an ex-convict and his burden was a dead body. No need to tell you, Monsieur le baron, that a sewer is not as wide as the Champs-Elysees. Two men occupying the same part of it are bound to meet. That is precisely what happened, and this second man said to the first: "I've got to get out of here. You have a key. Hand it over." It was useless to refuse. Nevertheless the first man bargained, simply to gain time. While they were talking the first contrived to rip off a small piece of the murdered man's coat. As evidence you understand. He then opened the sewer gate and let the man out with his burden on his back. And now I think you will understand. The man carrying the corpse was Jean Valjean, and the man with the key was the person addressing you. As for the scrap of cloth –'

Thenardier concluded the sentence by pulling a muddy fragment from his pocket and held it out.

Marius had risen to his feet, pale and scarcely able to breathe. He was staring at the scrap of cloth, and without taking his eyes off it he backed towards the wall and fumbled for the door of a wardrobe. He opened the wardrobe and thrust in his arm.

'I have every reason to believe, Monsieur le baron,' said Thenardier, 'that the murdered man was a wealthy foreigner who had fallen into a trap set by Valjean.'

'I was the man,' cried Marius, 'and here is the coat I was wearing!'

Then, snatching the fragment of cloth from Thenardier, he found the place from which it had been torn. It fitted exactly. Thenardier stood petrified, thinking, 'I'm done for!'

Marius put a hand in his pocket and going furiously to Thenardier thrust a fist into his face, clutching a bundle of five-hundred and thousand-franc notes.

'You are an abominable liar and a scoundrel! You came here to accuse this man and you have cleared him, It's you who are the thief and the murderer! I saw you, Thenardier-Jondrette, in that foul garret in the Boulevard de l'Hopital. I know enough about you to have you sent to gaol and further, if I wanted to. Here's a thousand-francs for you, villain that you are!' He threw a thousand-franc note at him. 'And here's another five hundred, and now get out of here! What happened at Waterloo protects you.'

'Waterloo?' grunted Thenardier, pocketing the notes.

'Yes, you devil. You saved a colonel's life.'

'He was a general,' said Thenardier, looking up.

'He was a colonel. And now thank your lucky stars that I want to see no more of you.'

'Monsieur le baron,' said Thenardier, bowing to the ground, 'I am eternally grateful.'

And he left, having understood nothing, amazed by this manna from Heaven.

Directly he had left the house Marius ran into the garden, where Cosette was still strolling.

'Cosette!' he cried. 'Hurry! We must go at once. Basque, fetch a fiacre! Oh God, he was the man who saved my life! We mustn't waste a minute. Put on your shawl.'

Cosette thought he had gone mad, and obeyed.

Marius was beside himself, seeing in Jean Valjean a figure of indescribable stature, supremely great and gently humble in his immensity, the convict transformed into Christ.

The fiacre arrived. He followed Cosette into it and ordered the driver to go to No. 7, Rue de l'Homme-Arme.

'Oh, what happiness!' cried Cosette. 'I have been afraid

to speak to you of the Rue de l'Homme-Armé. We're going to see Monsieur Jean.'

'Your father, Cosette. More than ever your father. Cosette, I have guessed something. You told me that you never received the letter I sent by Gavroche. I know what happened. It was delivered to him, your father, and he came to the barricade to save me. He rescued me from that inferno and carried me on his back through the sewers, to bring me to you. I was unconscious, you see, and I didn't know what was happening. We're going to take him back with us, whether he likes it or not, and we'll never let him go again.'

Jean Valjean looked round on hearing the knock on his door and feebly called, 'Come in!'

The door opened and Cosette and Marius appeared. Cosette rushed into the room while Marius stood in the doorway.

'Cosette!' said Jean Valjean and sat upright in his chair, his face white and haggard, his arms extended and a glow of immense happiness in his eyes. Cosette fell into his arms. 'Father!' she cried.

Valjean was stammering broken words of welcome. Then he said, 'So you have forgiven me?' and, turning to Marius, he said: 'And you too, you forgive me?'

Marius could not speak. 'Thank you,' said Valjean.

Cosette tossed her hat and shawl on to the bed and, seating herself on the old man's knees, she tenderly parted the locks of hair and kissed him on the forehead. Valjean was in a state of great bewilderment. Cosette, who had only a confused notion of what it was all about, embraced him again. Valjean stammered:

'One can be so stupid! I thought I should never see you again.'

For a moment he was unable to speak, but then he went on:

'I really did need to see Cosette for a little while every now and then. The heart must have something to live on. But I felt that I was not wanted, and I said to myself, "They don't need you, so stay in your own place." And now I'm seeing her again!'

'Such a cruel father!' said Cosette. 'Why were you away so long? I sent Nicolette, but they always told her you were away. Do you know, you've changed a great deal. You've been ill and you never told us. Marius, take his hand and feel how cold it is.'

'Monsieur Pontmercy,' said Jean Valjean, 'have you really forgiven me?'

At the repetition of the words Marius broke down.

'Cosette, did you hear what he said? He asked me to forgive him! And do you know what he did? He saved my life and, even more, he gave me you! And then he sacrificed himself by withdrawing from our lives. He ran hideous risks for us and now he asks me to forgive him, graceless, pitiless clod that I have been! His courage, his saintliness are beyond all bounds.'

'You have no need to say all this,' murmured Jean Valjean.

'Why didn't you say it yourself?' demanded Marius, in a voice in which reproach was mingled with veneration. 'Why didn't you tell me that you were Monsieur Madeleine and that you had spared Javert? Why didn't you tell me that I owed you my life? Good God, when I think that I only learnt all this by pure chance! You're coming with us. You're part of us. You're Cosette's father and mine. I won't allow you to spend another day in this horrible place.'

'This time it's final,' said Cosette. 'We have a cab down below. I'm kidnapping you – if necessary, by force.'

'It is true,' said Jean Valjean, 'that it would be delightful for us all to live together. I would stroll with Cosette. Yes, it would be delightful, only –' he broke off and said softly, 'Well, it's a shame.'

Cosette took his two hands in hers.

'Your hands are so cold,' she said. 'Are you ill? Are you in pain?'

'No,' said Valjean. 'I'm not in pain. Only –' he broke off again.

'Only what?'

'I'm going to die in a little while.'

'To die!' exclaimed Marius.

Cosette uttered a piercing cry.

'Father! Father! Are we to lose you so soon.'

'To die is nothing; but it is terrible not to live. I will tell you what has grieved me. What has grieved me, Monsieur Pontmercy, is that you have made no use of the money. My life will have been wasted if you do not make use of the money that is truly Cosette's.'

When a person dear to us is about to die we fix him with an intent gaze that seeks to hold him back. They stood beside him in silent anguish, having no words to speak.

Jean Valjean was visibly declining, sinking down towards that dark horizon. But as the weakness of his body increased so his spirit grew in splendour, and the light of the unknown world was already visible in his eyes. He signed to Cosette to come closer to him, then signed to Marius. It was the last moment of the last hour.

'Come close to me, both of you. I love you dearly. How sweet it is to die like this. And you love me too, dear Cosette. You'll weep for me a little, but not too much, I want you to have no great sorrows. I am leaving the two candlesticks on the mantelpiece to Cosette. They are made of silver, but to me they are pure gold. You must not forget, my children, that I am one of the poor. You must bury me in any plot of ground that comes handy and put a stone to mark the spot. That is my wish. No name on the stone. If Cosette cares to visit it sometimes I shall be glad. And you too, Monsieur Pontmercy. I must confess that I have not always liked you, and I ask your forgiveness. Cosette, do you see your little dress there on the bed? Do you remember it? That was ten years ago. Do you remember Montfermeil, Cosette? You were in the woods, and you were frightened. I helped you carry the bucket, do you remember? That was the first time I touched your poor hand. It was so cold! All those things are in the past – the woods we walked through, the convent where we took refuge, your child's eyes and laughter, all shadows now. I believed that it all belonged to me, and that is where I was foolish. Cosette, the time has come for me to tell you your mother's name. It was Fantine. You must bow your head whenever you speak it. She loved you greatly and she suffered greatly. She was as rich in sorrow as you are in happiness. That is how God evens things out. And now I must leave you, my children. You will think sometimes of the old man who died in this place. Dearest Cosette, it was not my fault if lately I have not come to see you. It wrung my heart. I had more to say, but no matter. I can see a light. Come closer. I die happy. Bow your dear heads so that I may lay my hands on them.'

Cosette and Marius fell on their knees on either side of him, stifling their tears. His hands rested on their heads, and did not move again. He lay back with his head turned up to the sky, and the light from the two candlesticks fell upon his face.

In the cemetery of Père Lachaise, not far from the communal grave and remote from the elegant quarter of that city of sepulchres, is a deserted corner near an old wall, and here, beneath a big yew tree, surrounded by mosses and dandelions, there is a stone. It is quite unadorned. It was carved strictly to serve its purpose, long enough and wide enough to cover a man. It bears no name.

But many years ago someone chalked four lines of verse on it which became gradually illegible under the influence of wind and weather and have now, no doubt, vanished entirely.

> He sleeps. Although so much he was denied,
> He lived; and when his dear love left him, died.
> It happened of itself, in the calm way
> That in the evening night-time follows day.

PENGUIN POPULAR CLASSICS

PENGUIN POPULAR CLASSICS

Published or forthcoming

PENGUIN POPULAR CLASSICS

PENGUIN POPULAR CLASSICS

PENGUIN POPULAR CLASSICS

PENGUIN POPULAR POETRY

Published or forthcoming

The Selected Poems *of:*

Matthew Arnold
William Blake
Robert Browning
Robert Burns
Lord Byron
John Donne
Thomas Hardy
John Keats
Rudyard Kipling
Alexander Pope
Alfred Tennyson
William Wordsworth
William Yeats

and collections of:

Seventeenth-Century Poetry
Eighteenth-Century Poetry
Poetry of the Romantics
Victorian Poetry
Twentieth-Century Poetry
Scottish Folk and Fairy Tales